ARTIFACT

SATURN'S LEGACY BOOK 1

JOSHUA JAMES

GET FREE BOOKS!

Building a relationship with readers is my favorite thing about writing.

My regular newsletter, *The Reader Crew,* is the best way to stay up-to-date on new releases, special offers, and all kinds of cool stuff about science fiction past and present.

Just for joining the fun, I'll send you 3 free books.

Join The Reader Crew (it's free) today!

—Joshua James

SATURN'S LEGACY SERIES

All books available in Kindle Unlimited

Artifact

Cascade

Lineage

Awakened

PROLOGUE

2219 BCE
Ur-An, Mesopotamia

———

"THE SKY PEOPLE HAVE RETURNED," said Naram-Sin, King of the Heavens, the Four Corners, and the Universe.

He was afraid.

His grandfather had founded the largest empire on Earth, and Naram-Sin considered himself to be a living god—but even in the oldest stories, gods knew fear, and Naram-Sin was no exception.

"But why have we come here?" asked Enli, following close on his master's heels. "Heathens have toppled the walls of Akkad, my lord. Your son stands at the gates leading an army that is not his to command. What could possibly take precedence, when the rivers of the sacred city run bitter with the blood of your subjects?"

"The sky people have *returned*," repeated Naram-Sin. He clutched the sacred object to his chest. It was not the greatest prize

—that was hidden in the Temple of Anu—but the gods had entrusted him with its safekeeping. Now that the great city had fallen, he was tasked with hiding it from their enemies. It was by this right that Naram-Sin considered himself divine. After all, had he not ascended to the heavens, to break bread with creatures who were not men?

"Why do you not simply ask the gods for help?" asked Enli. He flinched when he realized his mistake. "The other gods, of course, my liege."

"I have tried to speak to the other gods," the king explained. "They do not listen. I fear that they cannot hear me."

The King of the Universe clutched his treasure to his embroidered tunic and hurried through the streets of Ur-An. A low droning noise from the sky made him look up. "They are here," he said quietly.

Enli recoiled. "Are they? How can you tell?"

From the sound of their sky-chariots, the great king thought, but he knew that his envoy would not understand. Instead of trying to explain, he shoved the relic into Enli's hands.

"You must do as I say," the king commanded. "You must take this, and you must go into the heart of the city. You must find a well, or a refuse heap, someplace the sky people will not think to look, and you must do whatever it takes to make sure that it will not be found. Afterwards you may flee, or do whatever you think best, but you must swear on the name of every god that you will not speak of where it is hidden. Do you swear it?"

"I swear it," said Enli, then lifted his eyes to the shadowed heavens. "As you say, your highness."

"Goodbye, Enli," said the King of the Universe. Then he turned to face his enemies.

The sky people and the gods were not the same, although they dwelt in the same dark, expansive firmament. The gods had tried to explain that they moved freely throughout the cosmos, making their homes among the stars themselves. Naram-Sin could not truly understand, although he had tried. The means by which they came and went were still as mysterious to him as magic, although he had learned to recognize the sound of the mighty fires that kept their sky-chariots aloft.

Other things, he had understood better. When Enli was safely out of sight, Naram-Sin stood his ground, prepared to buy his servant whatever time he had left. Reaching into the folds of his tunic, he produced one of the two weapons given to him by the gods. He unslung the bow from about his shoulders, nocked one of their arrows, and waited.

The first of the sky people's vessels appeared over the low clay roofs, familiar silver behemoths ringed with blinking lights. As they passed above the houses, the fires that powered them blasted holes through the wood-and-daub roofs. Naram-Sin heard his people crying out for help within.

Naram-Sin took aim, his bare arms glinting bronze in the afternoon sun. Planting his feet firmly, he raised the first arrow; there were only five. He would have to make every shot count.

A second before he released the arrow, a ring of blue light crackled around the hooked tip. As the bowstring snapped back, the arrow flew true, striking along a seam where the segments of the sky-chariot met. A moment later, a bolt of what looked like lightning split the vessel in two. The resulting explosion forced Naram-Sin to duck between two nearby houses as what remained of the vessel crashed to earth.

Four arrows left.

He flung the bow over his shoulder and hauled himself up the side of the nearest structure, then ran from roof to roof, leaping over the gaps in between houses.

You led your armies against the Lulubi, and they fell, he told himself, vaulting across the streets. *You will fight until your last breath.* As a second vessel approached, he straightened, his braided black hair blowing about his face under the force of the fire wings that the gods called "thrusters." This time he aimed for them. The resulting blast sent him flying off the roof, landing heavily on the ground below. When he rolled to his feet, he found himself face-to-face with a pair of sandals.

"It's the king," called a man's voice. Naram-Sin pulled himself to his feet, still gasping for air following the force of the blast.

"What has happened, Lord?" asked one of the men.

"Akkad has fallen," he told them. "The gods have cursed us." It was easier to speak this way—they would understand his explanation, even if it was only half-true. He pointed to the sky, where the vessels now hovered above them. There were nearly two handfuls of them. Naram-Sin sighed. He had secretly hoped that the people of Ur-An might be spared. There was little chance of that now.

"Shall we fight them?" asked one of the men, eyeing Naram-Sin's bow.

The king shook his head. "Take your families and flee the city. You are no match for them. I will do what must be done."

He didn't know what they saw when they looked at him, but they seemed to believe him. Whether they thought he stood a chance, or were simply hoping for an opportunity to escape, the king did not know. What he did know was that the ships were still coming.

Time. That was all that was needed of him.

He was not as young as he had been; his son would have been better suited for this task. *I do not think his reign will be a long one,* thought Naram-Sin sadly. Such was the way of gods. They came and went so easily.

He ran through the streets, ducking between the walls as people fled past, crying out in terror, dragging their loved ones and carrying what little they'd had time to collect on their backs. When he looked up to find himself centered beneath a vessel, he fired his third arrow; the damaged sky-chariot careened into the side of a temple, scattering the heavy stones across the sand.

Seconds later, two fiery blasts arced above him, collapsing one of the gates leading out of the city. Naram-Sin heard the screams, but when he looked toward the blast, he was only half-aware of the people digging through the rubble to rescue those who were buried.

The wall. He should go to the wall.

It wasn't easy to think quickly during a fight against demons, but the King of the Four Corners had faced greater challenges. He ran for the ladder, cursing mightily when a beam of green light from one of the vessels scorched his arm. When he reached the top of the wall, he fired on the vessel that had brought down the gate. As his arrow struck, he saw the look of surprise in his opponents' eyes. Their features were inhuman, but the expression of a creature who saw its death coming was familiar enough. The sky-chariot careened into the sand before it burst apart.

One arrow left. Ordinary arrows would have no effect at all; he had seen what happened when the people of Akkad fired on the sky ships. Once this last shot was spent, the king would have no recourse but to use the second and more deadly of the gifts he had been given. He drew a deep breath, calling on all the old divinities to stand beside him, although he knew it was futile. Like the great city where he had reigned for so long, his time was coming to an end.

At least he was determined that he would not die alone. These whoresons and their vessels would follow him into the underworld.

There was a whistling sound behind him, and the king turned, bow drawn, to face his enemy. The sky-chariot was already upon him, and the charged arrow burst across its hull; this time, when the airship blew apart, Naram-Sin fell as well.

He hit the earth with a tremendous *crack* and felt his bones give way. When he tried to move, his limbs would not obey him. He could barely turn his head. He could feel the weight of the pouch at his waist, but he could not reach for it.

No, he thought, *I need more time. Just a little more time. I will sacrifice all I have built, Inanna, if you will only grant me this one final mercy.*

"My Lord?" asked a familiar voice. "Do you hear me?"

"Enli?" asked Naram-Sin. His voice was weak; it hurt to speak. "I told you to flee."

"You told me to take the secret with me," said Enli reasonably, kneeling beside the king. "Dead men cannot speak. Tell me, my lord, what more do you ask of me?"

"In the pouch... at my hip..." the king breathed. He could already feel the life leaving him. "There is a weapon..."

Enli's hands fumbled at the pouch. There were so many ships in the sky now that they blotted out the sun.

"This, my liege?" he asked, holding up the small box.

"Open it."

Enli nodded, undoing the latch.

"Enli?" asked the king. "Is the relic hidden?"

"I did the best I could, Lord," said Enli. "I found a place beneath the city, and cast it into a well, in a place belowground where the sky people will never think to look. And I prayed to the gods that the tablet would not be found in a hundred lifetimes."

Naram-Sin smiled; maybe Inanna would answer Enli's prayers, since he still believed in her. "Open it."

When the other gods had shown Naram-Sin the stars in their sleek silver airships that danced along the edges of the night, they had tried to explain the box's purpose. Naram-Sin did not understand the mechanics of it; only that it harnessed the energy like that of the day star. He did not know everything, but he understood that there was more at stake than his life, than his dynasty, even his kingdom. He must protect what had been entrusted to him, no matter the cost.

Enli opened the box, activating the palm-sized device within. For a moment, there was silence as sound was ripped away into the vacuum. Then there was a burst of light, and every vessel around them blew apart, leaving Enli and his king at the center of a maelstrom that vaporized the flesh right off their bones, turning them instantly to ash.

Within moments, the sky was empty, and Ur-An had been stricken from the face of the earth.

ARTIFACT

July 20, 2061

Scientists Go Ga-Ga Over Underwater Discovery

ENCELADUS: *Xenoanthropologists were presented with a rare treat this week when an unmanned submersible on Saturn's moon Enceladus discovered complex amino acid chains that scientists say could be the dormant descendants of alien life that once existed on the tiny moon.*

"It's going to change a lot of assumptions," said MIT researcher Daisy Driskel, who was not associated with the finding. "If this holds up, it will be the first time we've found fully viable organic compounds anywhere outside of Earth."

Enceladus is an active moon that hides a global ocean of liquid saltwater beneath its icy surface, and has long been considered a potential environment for extraterrestrial life. The moon's most distinctive features are its plumes— geysers of ocean water that extend hundreds of miles into space to form Saturn's vast and spectacular outermost ring.

"If Saturn is the solar system's showpiece," Driskel said, "Enceladus is the engine that makes it go."

This week's announcement follows the recent discovery of an unusual ore deposit on the moon's ocean floor. Researchers aren't sure if the two findings are related.

1

Dec. 8, 2061
Near Base 4 Settlement, Mars

———————

WHEN CARPENTER LOWELL had applied to the United States Space Corps, he hadn't pictured himself babysitting scientists at an archaeological dig. What was the point of scraping up the Martian surface, anyway? It was nothing but dust and rocks out here. One of Mars' largest settlements stood only a few hundred kilometers away. If he'd been stationed *there*, Lowell would have understood.

Two Chinese Space Corps hovercraft had been spotted scoping out the surface only a few days before. A lot of funding had gone into establishing a major colony out here, and heads would roll if they let a foreign military interfere with that investment. That should have taken precedence.

And yet, here he stood, kitted out in his Corps suit, a low-grav rifle slung over his shoulder, watching a dozen archaeologists putter around a roped-off square of red soil on a remote section of the planet's surface.

"What are they looking for?" he asked his commanding officer.

Lieutenant Larry Munroe shrugged. "Does it matter?" His voice echoed crisply through the speaker in his helmet.

He wasn't wrong.

Lowell's unit had only been established about eight months ago. Most of them had been hand-picked from other branches of the military, chosen because they had some outstanding quality that made the higher-ups take note. A lot of them were sharpshooters, and like Lowell himself, they were all lifers.

Which begged the question: why would an elite squad of soldiers be sent all the way out here? Lowell's last assignment had been in the Middle East; before that, he'd been stationed near a refugee camp in Jordan, charged with protecting the med-student volunteers. Now he was working with a unit of twelve men who took rotating shifts to oversee the dig.

"So we get to stand around and watch a bunch of eggheads at play," said Collins dismissively. He struck Lowell as the kind of man who would have spat a lot, if it weren't for their helmets.

Sometimes he was glad that he couldn't see the other men's faces. The helmets lent everyone a bit of anonymity.

Lowell hadn't exactly loved his old assignments, but he'd liked knowing that he was one of the good guys, and that the other Marines had his back. Sure, there had been guys who'd spike your coffee with laxatives, given half a chance, but they'd also cover you in a firefight, no questions asked.

But things had felt odd since he'd joined Munroe's team. Some of the guys could be real assholes, and Munroe almost never bothered to call them out on it.

Vasko sighed. "I hate this. It's a waste of time. They should have us out there taking pot-shots at the Chinese." He jerked his thumb toward the sky. "I wouldn't mind taking out a couple of their ships. That would teach 'em a lesson, wouldn't it?"

"They're our allies," said Lowell evenly. "We might not like them hanging around, but if we fire the first shot, there'll be hell to pay."

"So bait *their* fire," said Vasko, shrugging. "You know what I mean? Taunt them until they slip up, then call it self-defense."

"Unless that's what they're doing to us," added Collins. "I hear they've got a cloaking device in the works. If they wanted to sneak around, they could. The fact that we saw them tells me that they *want* to be seen."

"Damn," muttered Vasko, "I hadn't thought of that..."

"We're not in a war zone," Lowell pointed out. "Nobody has anything to gain by firing shots out here."

"Christ, Lowell, you probably want to work with them," spat Vasko.

"Maybe I just don't feel like I need to discharge my rifle to prove something," Lowell muttered.

If they'd been standing fifty feet apart in the desert, his words would have been lost in the wind, but he sometimes forgot that the radio link meant that his squad could hear his every word, no matter how low he kept his voice.

"You wanna go, Lowell?" asked Vasko, whipping his head around. "I'll throw down. Come say that to my face."

"Kinda proving his point, aren't you?" Collins said amiably. He sounded like he was chewing gum, and Lowell had yet to figure out if he'd somehow found a way to keep a stash in his helmet with him, or if he just chewed the same piece all eight hours of their watch. "Besides, if the Chinese are scoping anything out, it's the settlement. They don't give a rat's ass about these dorks."

Munroe was silent. It was times like this that Lowell wished he could see the lieutenant's face to read his expression. Lowell would have bet all of his back pay that Munroe knew more about the mission than he'd passed on, and that there was more to it than met the eye.

Vasko had started ranting again, but Lowell tuned him out. Something was happening at the dig site: one of the figures had raised their arm, waving frantically as they pointed to something in the dirt. Lowell couldn't see what it was, but the person was obviously excited.

Their squad didn't have much interaction with the scientists, and the fact that they all looked the same in their suits made it impossible to keep track of which one was which. Only the dig lead, Samuel, stood out. He was tall with a bright blue helmet to make him easier for the team to identify. Samuel had chatted with the team a few times, and Lowell got the impression he was a nice enough guy, if a bit high-strung.

Within moments, everyone onsite had gathered around, and Samuel stood above the rest. He appeared to be talking, waving his hands for emphasis.

Lowell's squad communicated on an encrypted frequency, and the dig team had their own, but they had a less restricted channel they shared with Samuel. The doctor looked up from the find and waved Munroe over, hailing them on the main channel.

"I think we've found it, gentlemen," he said. "Care to come take a look?"

Munroe gestured for the men to hold their positions, and then jogged across the Martian surface, kicking up red dust as he went. He was able to cover the distance in only a few long strides—one of the advantages of Mars' low gravity.

So he does *know what we're looking for,* thought Lowell. He had the sense to keep the observation to himself—this time, at least.

He was used to only having the partial story on an assignment, but if that was the case, then whatever they were after was probably considered a state secret.

Which meant that maybe Vasko had a point about not trusting their allies.

Munroe bent over the dig site, peering down at whatever was there. "Well, I'll be damned," he said. "It *is* here. Good work, Doctor."

"What the hell is it?" asked Vasko over the private channel.

"Not our place to know," said Collins. "Mind your own business."

They were still turned toward the dig site, but the hair at the back of Lowell's neck had started to prickle. In his early days, he'd been stationed in the jungles of the Philippines. It had taken him a while to get used to the sounds of all the animals out there, especially at night; but he'd learned that whenever they got quiet, something big was coming.

There were no animals to alert Lowell in that moment, but there was something else, something neither seen nor heard, but *felt*, like the rumble of an engine reverberating through his bones. He looked back over his shoulder and saw a faint shimmer move across the sky.

I hear they've got a cloaking device in the works.

"Incoming!" cried Lowell.

Less than a second later, the vessel opened fire.

"What did I tell you!?" shrieked Vasko as he dropped onto his belly.

Lowell still couldn't see the ship, but he could see the place where it had passed. He fired two quick shots into the center of its mass, and he saw two accompanying bursts of sparks where the shots landed.

The vessel was still firing on the dig, and the archaeologists scattered. If he'd been on the dig channel, Lowell was sure he would have heard them screaming.

"Looks like you get to take your potshots, Vasko," Lowell grunted. "Cover me."

The Martian landscape didn't provide a lot of opportunity for cover, so Lowell didn't bother trying to hide. Instead, he bolted toward their transport, running in zig-zags to avoid any intentional fire from above. The ship was still strafing the dig site, its gunner more interested in whatever was there than in targeting the soldiers.

Bet they're not alone, he thought. *The report said there were two.*

Even as he thought it, another burst of gunfire kicked up plumes of red dust right on Lowell's heels. He rolled under the armored transport just in time and felt the vehicle rock as it was pelted with artillery.

One of the most frustrating things about space was how it robbed Lowell of his senses. In ordinary combat, he'd have listened for a break in the gunfire, or used the sound of engines to pinpoint his enemy's location. Now, he had to rely on sight and feel alone— and only what he could feel through the suit, like the percussive blasts of gunfire striking the vehicle above.

Screw it, he thought, rolling sideways until he emerged on the far side of the transport, and yanked the hatch open. If his senses were going to be limited, he'd have to rely on his instincts. He hauled himself up the ladder toward the top of the vehicle, where a glass dome enclosed the controls for the transport's turret.

Lowell's grasp of physics had never gotten beyond a high school understanding; he'd shipped out with the Marines right after senior year, and never looked back. In the two months of debriefing he'd gone through before taking this assignment, he'd sat through an excruciating presentation about how munitions worked in Mars' low gravity, and why carrying anything other than the approved guns could result in... well, all right, Lowell had zoned out for that part. Something to do with blowback, and how shrapnel traveled farther in the low grav.

That didn't mean that they were sent out unarmed. With an ordinary gun, the recoil presented a problem. The soundwave cannon on the turret could do a bit more damage; if he fired it directly at a person, it could vibrate the water in their bodies to the point that it would induce tissue shearing. The hull of the ship might protect the soldiers aboard enough to keep them from dying.

Maybe. At this point, Lowell didn't care either way. They'd fired on him first, and they were fair game now.

"What's the plan?" asked Vasko.

"I'm going to see if I can knock out their cloaking devices," said Lowell. "Can you get a bead on either of the vessels?"

"You mean there's more than one?" asked Collins. "Oh, hell yeah. Let's take 'em *down*."

"One at a time," said Lowell.

"Yeah," said Vasko, "I got an idea."

While Lowell fired up the cannon, he saw Vasko stand up from the rubble of the dig site. He lifted one arm high over his head and hauled back, then lobbed something into the sky, close to where the last of the shots had been fired.

Paint grenade, thought Lowell. *Smart.*

It arced through the air until it hit something mid-flight, then burst apart, splattering across the side of the ship. Lowell grinned. They'd been using the devices in training, along with paintball guns, to get used to combat in Mars' lower gravity. All the grenade did was burst open, leaving a splatter of blue paint across the ship's hull.

It also gave Lowell an easy target.

"Gotcha," Lowell muttered, and locked the cannon's sights on the paint splatter.

He felt the whole transport rumble beneath him as he fired. He could *see* when the shot hit, rippling off the surface of the other vessel and making the fresh splatter of paint across the side bubble and pop. The ship came into view as the sonic wave shut down parts of its engine function. Through the windshield, Lowell could see the pilot's wide, bloodshot eyes just before the ship banked to the side, crashing into the ground. Lowell saw a gout of fire erupt within. The fire died within seconds as the hull was breached and Mars' atmosphere smothered the flame.

Collins whooped so loudly that the speakers crackled. "Yeah! That's what I'm talkin' about!"

"One down," said Lowell, rotating the turret. "One to go."

All of the archaeologists had taken cover by now, and the crew of the second ship must have realized how they'd targeted the first. They had the good sense to hold their fire.

Maybe the other vessel had left when it had the chance, but Lowell doubted it. The CSC wouldn't let one of their experimental ships fall into the hands of a US force without a fight.

Common sense said that the two vessels were probably the same model, especially if this cloaking device was still in the experimental phases. The downed ship was small, probably a three-man crew at most. The smoking wreckage was covered with a thin, silvery material that had peeled back in places. If that, as Lowell suspected, was part of the cloaking device, then the other ship had three-hundred-and-sixty-degree coverage. It was small enough that firing randomly would be a waste of time and power.

"I don't see the other one," said Collins. Lowell wasn't sure where the man had holed up, but he wasn't visible from the turret.

Vasko, on the other hand, was still standing up, spinning around and around as he looked into the sky. "Me neither."

"Take cover, you idiot," Lowell barked. "You're making yourself a target."

The figure fell to the ground immediately, and he heard Vasko's grunt through the channel. "Aw, Lowell," he said, "I didn't know you cared."

Lowell felt that prickle on his neck again, and he caught a slight movement out of the corner of his eye. It might have been nothing more than a reflection in the polished dome of the turret, but all he had was his gut to go on. He didn't hesitate; he swung the turret to the left and slammed his palm down on the controls.

The CSC ship came into view just as it closed in on him, opening fire as it did so. His aim had been good and the ship bucked pleasingly from the impact, but then it banked sharply lower than he'd expected. Instead of passing over him as he'd hoped, the ship was now careening toward the rocky ground just in front of him.

"Jesus Christ, Lowell, get out of there!" screamed Collins.

There was no time to make a clean exit. Instead, Lowell lifted his gun and fired a shot into the side of the clear dome, blowing a hole through it. Then he launched himself out only a second before the ship smashed into the side of the transport.

He flattened himself as close to the ground as possible as the ship tore through the vehicle. He felt the impact echoing up through his chest, and flinched as bits of the wreckage collapsed around him. There was less danger of being crushed by debris than there would have been in a collision on Earth, partly because of the lower gravity and partly because of the protection offered by his suit. Still, if any of the metal shards did manage to puncture the suit or crack his helmet, he'd be dead inside a minute.

He lay there, breathing hard, for a long moment. But the oxygen didn't run out, and he didn't die.

"Lowell?" asked Vasko urgently. "Lowell, you okay?"

"I think so," he grunted.

"You crazy bastard," cackled Collins. "How did you even see that guy coming?"

"Lucky, I guess," he said, which was probably at least half-true. The rest was pure instinct.

He tried to sit up, but a panel of the transport lay on top of him. It was hard to lift himself up enough to get any leverage. He didn't have to struggle for long, however, before the panel was lifted off of him, and Vasko and Collins hauled him to his feet.

"Damn," said Vasko, "I take it back. You might be worth two shits after all."

"Likewise," Lowell said. "Paint grenade was smart."

Collins nodded his agreement. "Yeah, Vasko, you're not as dumb as you look."

Vasko gave him the finger.

Lowell turned to look at the wreckage of the two small vessels. "So much for the new cloaking devices."

"Let's make sure they're down," said Collins, patting Lowell on the back of his suit. "Nice work."

Collins and Vasko each ran off toward a different CSC ship to check for survivors. Lowell stood there for a moment, just breathing. He was punchy with adrenaline, which was why it took him so long to remember the dig.

The scientists hadn't hailed them. Nor had Munroe.

That was odd. Lowell turned back toward the dig and switched over to the shared frequency. "Everything all right over there?"

No one answered. "Lieutenant?"

Still nothing. He jogged over. The ground was pockmarked from when the other vessel had strafed over the site, but he saw no sign of the scientists or Munroe. There was a little rise in front of him, and then a dip in the ground just beyond; he made for that, wondering if they'd managed to hide there.

"Hello?" he asked.

The channel was dead. He was just wondering whether he had gotten the frequency wrong when he tripped over a rock.

Except it wasn't a rock. It was a helmet.

A sour taste rose in Lowell's throat. Whoever the helmet had belonged to was dead; there were no two ways about it. He took another nervous, shuffling step forward.

"Good work, Lowell," said Munroe suddenly, and Lowell jumped. He looked up to see the other man's figure cresting the rise. "Nice shooting. I'm impressed—but that's why we hand-picked you, of course."

"Sir?" asked Lowell. "Where's the science team?"

Munroe shook his head, and his voice sounded sorrowful. "The enemy vessels opened fire right on the site. There was no chance for them to get away."

"But we saw them running for cover," said Lowell. "Surely some of them must—"

"Those who didn't die from their wounds were killed by exposure," said Munroe. "Punctured suits. They're gone, Lowell. All of them."

Lowell opened his mouth, then closed it again. He looked down at the helmet resting by his foot. Despite the film of red dust that clung to it, the paint underneath was recognizably blue. As much as he didn't want to see a severed head along with the helmet, *not* seeing one was a bigger problem. It meant the helmet had come off at some point on its own. He could see the clasp on the back—it was intact and undamaged, yet partially removed from its housing. No Chinese strafing fire had done that.

That helmet wasn't blown off. It was taken off.

"We'll have to bring a team out here to clean up," Munroe

continued. "Maybe we can recover the artifact, but the loss of civilian life is our primary concern, of course. We'll get the rest of the squad out here to help see what we can save."

"Of course," Lowell echoed.

Artifact. That must be the thing that Samuel had told Munroe about. He knew enough to bite his tongue this time to make sure that his thoughts weren't accidentally broadcast to the lieutenant and his companions. But he'd been standing and staring too long not to catch Munroe's attention.

"Problem, Lowell?"

Hell, yeah, there's a problem, sir. Somebody used this attack as cover to kill at least one of these guys—probably more—and take whatever they found. And I'm starting to think it was you. Sir.

"No problem," Lowell said. "Just a shame."

He made a mental note of the location of the helmet and the approximate position of the other bodies. Lowell wasn't naïve. Targeted killing was part of the business, so it was possible that Munroe's actions were sanctioned. But this wasn't a designated mission, and the lieutenant was clearly trying to cover his tracks. At the very least, Lowell had to report this.

He felt Munroe studying him. He wished he could read his superior's expression through the helmet as he held his gaze for a long second. Then two. Then three.

At last, Munroe nodded in Lowell's direction. "A damn shame."

He turned. "Do us both a favor and don't try and grow a brain, Lowell," he said over his shoulder as he strode away. "It's bad for your career."

2

FOUR YEARS LATER
Ur-An, Iraq

———

IN THE THREE months since he'd arrived at the dig site in Southern Iraq, Peter Chang had visited every part of the ancient settlement.

He'd spent his undergrad days dreaming of Çatalhöyük and Chichen Itza, signing up for every study-abroad opportunity that the university offered. He'd spent three weeks digging at a Roman port on the northern coast of Minorca; a weekend in Sbetlia in western Tunisia; a month in Athens mapping ancient grave sites beneath the modern-day Monastiraki Market; and one perfect, scorching summer in the Valley of the Kings, praying to stumble upon a hidden chamber that would put the discoveries of Howard Carter to shame. He had all but harassed the head of the dig at Ur-An to add him to the permit.

And what had he found in those last three months?

Pottery.

Miles upon miles upon *miles* of pottery.

"This is Nile clay!" said Jana, bouncing with glee as she held up three large sherds of a clay bowl.

"Are you serious?" asked Amira, scooting closer to examine it. "Oh my gosh, do you know what this means?"

"Of course we do," sighed Connor, rolling his eyes. "We all have the same degree, you know."

Amira smacked his arm. "Then why aren't you excited? This could revolutionize our assumptions about trans-Mediterranean trade from the era. Professor Keating might let us help with the research! Can you imagine what it would do for us to have our names associated with a groundbreaking paper on the trade? Peter, have you *seen* this?"

"He doesn't care," smirked Connor. "He's over there sulking because he doesn't get to play Indiana Jones."

"I'm not sulking," lied Peter. "May I see it, Jana?" He held out a gloved hand, and Jana gently placed the fragile sherd on his palm. Jana had a magnificent eye for pottery, and Peter was sure that a more complete examination of the piece would prove her right. That would be big news in their circles. Professor Keating would be thrilled with her find.

The trouble was, Peter simply didn't *care*. Connor might be a jerk, but he was right about one thing: Peter had gone into this field for all the wrong reasons, and there was no pottery sherd thrilling enough to hold his attention for long. A seal, a tablet, even an anachronistic ripple-flaked knife would have gotten his blood pumping, but he seemed to have found himself in the one Sumerian site where there wasn't a single exciting item waiting to be discovered.

Perhaps Keating had heard their commotion, because a

moment later he strode out from their dig building. He loped over to them, wearing a long-sleeved button-down despite the heat, just as he always did. The man was hardcore, and he had a list of accolades a mile long. Someday, Peter hoped to achieve that level of badass-professor aura. Peter had worked as a TA last semester, and he doubted that Professor Keating put up with the same types of sloppy nonsense that so plagued the classrooms of the other profs.

"Did you find something?" asked Keating, adjusting his glasses. The girls swooned as his arms flexed beneath his sleeves. The man was *built*.

That's because his dissertation is miles behind him, thought Peter, who couldn't remember the last time he'd had the leisure to go to a gym. At home, his dissertation consumed his every waking thought. Out here in the desert, it was all he could do to keep up with his academic duties and drink enough water to stay alive.

Jana took the pottery back from Peter and held it up. "Nile clay," she said, fluttering her eyelashes. "What do you think, Professor? Good find?"

"*Excellent,* Jana," he told her, holding the sherd up to the light. "I'll take this inside right away. You can do the honors later, all right?"

Jana beamed.

As Keating strolled back to the dig house, Connor let out a world-weary sigh. "Oh, come *on,* how come he's never out here working with us?"

"I know," said Amira, pulling at the front of her shirt to fan herself. "I'd pay good money to have him out here."

"Oh, I think we'd overheat," chuckled Jana. "He's *smoking.*"

Connor turned to Peter and jerked his thumb toward the girls. "Dude, what is wrong with them?"

"I seem to recall you having the hots for Professor Gill," said Peter, wiping a trickle of sweat from his forehead. If *he'd* had to wear long sleeves in this weather, he'd have dropped dead from heat stroke. He wouldn't last half an hour.

"That's because she's a cougar," said Connor, growling. "She has a bangin' bod."

"Gross," said Amira, rolling her eyes.

"How come it's okay when you're a creep, but not when *I* do it?" Connor demanded.

Jana and Amira looked at each other, then slowly shook their heads.

"Whatever," said Connor, shaking his own head and getting back to work. "Oh, hey, look what I found. More pottery!"

"Let me give you some suggestions about where you can shove that crummy attitude of yours," said Jana, narrowing her eyes.

Peter turned back to the soil, digging his gloved hands into the sandy ground. They were only irritable because of the heat and the long, repetitive days. If they found something good, their moods would bounce back immediately. Peter had seen it happen on more than one occasion at other sites.

"That was a great find, Jana," he said, wiping another rivulet of sweat out of his eyes. The salt burned. "Beer's on me tonight."

"Yes!" cried Amira, pumping her arm in victory. "Maybe we'll get something other than Stella for once."

"I meant for Jana," Peter said. "But if either of you can one-up her, then sure, I'll buy enough for everyone."

Buoyed by the promise of free drinks, the four of them got back to work with renewed vigor. Peter was silently promising himself that he would try to be more excited about his colleagues' finds in the future, when his fingers struck something hard and cool beneath the sand.

More pottery, he thought, sifting the grey dust aside.

He was wrong. Lying in the sand, winking bright in the sun

despite the four millennia it had spent buried in the earth, was something that Peter had never seen before.

"What do you have there?" demanded Connor, peering over at his square.

"I don't know," said Peter, reaching for his brush so that he could excavate more carefully.

Peter would have been surprised to unearth a bit of iron, or even steel, within the ruins of Ur-An. Even a corroded copper ingot would have been an exciting find. Instead, the edges of the squared-off object glittered in the sun like freshly-burnished stainless steel or newly polished silver.

"What the heck...?" Amira asked.

"It looks modern," said Jana, frowning. "How did it get all the way down here?"

Peter had known from the moment he touched it that the thing beneath the sand would be a tablet of some kind. As he worked his way in from the edges, he gasped in delight. It was a long, flat sheet, into which tiny cuneiform writing had been etched. Most tablets were formed from impressions left in soft clay, dried in the sun for preservation. Sometimes the words were carved into stone. Peter had never seen one cut into metal before, and he'd never read about one, either. The material itself was strange. When Peter lifted it to shake the sand loose, he realized that the metal was nearly as lightweight as aluminum.

"What *is* that?" Jana demanded, poking her head over Amira's shoulder. "Is this one of your stupid pranks, Connor?"

"Me?" asked Connor, looking up from the tablet. "What, you think I buried this here as a practical joke or something?"

"Well, *I* didn't do it." Jana crossed her arms. "And I was talking with Amira last night."

"Which leaves Peter, too," Connor pointed out. "Why not blame him?"

"What if it's not a prank?" Peter asked. His eyes were still fixed on the tablet. The words were rendered with all the precision of a laser cutter.

"No," said Jana suddenly. "Peter, if you say it, I will slap you."

"Like that's going to stop him," Amira snorted.

"Let me guess: you think it's aliens?" asked Connor.

"But what if it *is*," said Peter, eliciting a groan from the whole group. "People have reported encounters with extraterrestrial life for millennia. There are *photographs*."

"Told you," said Amira smugly, looking down at Jana.

The other girl had buried her head in her hands. "Every time," she groaned. "Without fail. Why does it even surprise me anymore?"

"No idea," said Connor. "It's inevitable. He can't help himself. All right, Peter. Let's hear the next great Chang Conspiracy."

"Or better yet, let's not," said Jana, pinching the bridge of her nose between her fingers.

"Oh, let him tell us," said Amira, winking at Peter. "I think it's cute."

"Dude, we all know you guys hooked up at the start of the summer," Connor groaned. "Get him to tell you as part of his pillow talk or whatever. We don't need to see a *cute* side of Peter."

Peter scowled at him, brandishing the tablet. "You didn't accuse Jana of sneaking out in the night to plant Nile-clay pottery. Why won't any of you even consider that this could be the real deal, too?"

"Uh, because the ancient Egyptians existed," said Connor slowly, as though Peter was being willfully dense. "Ancient aliens did not. You see my point?"

"Prove it," said Peter. "Because I'm sitting here with evidence that they *might* exist, and you've already written it off."

"*I* haven't," said Amira. "I'm not saying that it proves anything either way, but I'm not dismissing you out of hand."

"Listen, there's plenty of proof—" Peter began.

Connor scoffed. "Let me guess. This conversation is going to drag on for three hours and include a lengthy description of ley lines, magnetic hotspots, ancient religions, little green men, and a bunch of other mumbo-jumbo. I swear, it's like listening to one of your old man's lectures. Can it, Chang. We've heard it all."

"Actually, I think greys are a lot more likely than LGMs," Peter said. "Not that it matters, I suppose, because so many people describe UFOs as having a green light that they might make green skin *look* grey..."

"None of it matters," Connor snapped. "Unless you want to talk about probing. I'm down to hear about a good probing."

Peter snapped his mouth shut, but Amira put a comforting hand on his shoulder. "Can you read it?"

"What, just free-reading?" asked Jana. She shielded her eyes with her hands; the reflection of the sunlight on the polished tablet was nearly blinding.

"He's really good at it," said Amira encouragingly. "He's a linguistics guru. Go on, Peter, what does it say?"

Peter sighed. "You're just humoring me."

"I'm not," Amira insisted. "It's impressive."

Bending over the tablet, Peter cleared his throat, only to be cut off by Connor. "*Dear Ea-Nasir, your copper ingots are of poor quality...*"

"Shut up," said Jana, elbowing him in the ribs. "Let him read it, at least."

"I'm already seeing problems," said Peter, doing his best to ignore Connor. "The lettering is cuneiform, but the language itself is odd."

"It's Sumerian," said Connor. "Of course it's odd."

"No, I mean..." Peter twirled one finger, searching for the right words. It didn't help that the blazing sun above had all but fried his brain. "I mean, you know how even people who know the Roman alphabet can't automatically read French? It's like that. I know the letters, but some of the words are really strange. I think... I think this bit here says something about the Star Key. Or Stellar Key? Something like that. And this line might refer to an ice river, or a frozen sea... on the moon?"

"Here it comes," said Connor, flopping back in the sand. "Proof positive of life beyond our solar system!"

"Can you really read that?" Jana asked, flipping her long dark braid over her shoulder.

Peter nodded. "More or less. Like I said, some of the words are iffy."

The trouble was that even what he *could* read didn't make sense. It almost sounded like the tablet was a map of some kind, but the directions that it gave were strange and difficult to follow. They also probably referred to ancient sites that didn't exist. What, for example, was '*the great plume*'? Or '*the giantess' sister*'?

"Maybe it's a ritual artifact," suggested Connor. "Like, some kind of religious thing."

Amira snorted. "Anything people don't understand gets categorized as 'a religious artifact.' How is that a better explanation than aliens?"

Peter stood up abruptly. "I'm going to go talk to Professor Keating, okay?"

"Aw, don't go!" called Amira. "They're just ragging on you."

"I know." Peter clutched the find to his chest. He knew that Connor was right—it didn't really bother him, either. He'd been teased about his obsession with aliens and government conspiracies since he was a kid, but he could take it. Even he didn't believe it half the time, not like his old man did; it was just *interesting*. Fun to think about, fascinating to read about, and a good conversation starter in the right crowd. Even so, deep in his heart, there was a little boy who still wanted to believe. He'd applied for SpaceX missions, and had even made it to the first round of interviews to join the most recent mission to Mars. When he'd stated that he wanted to serve as the team's leading xenoarchaeologist, the interview team had laughed him out of the room. He'd settled for an Iraqi dig site as the best alternative he was going to get.

Maybe he'd have the last laugh, if this object turned out to be as important as he thought. Peter trotted off down the sandy path toward the dig house, taking a deep breath before he knocked on Professor Keating's door. Hopefully the professor would be a bit more receptive to his ideas.

"Come in," the prof called, and Peter ducked inside. There was no AC, but at least there was a fan, and even the shade was a relief.

"How can I help you, Peter?" asked Keating, looking up from his computer.

"Oh, uh." Peter shifted from foot to foot. "Well, we found something." He held out the tablet.

Keating's reaction was instantaneous. He leapt up from his desk, blue eyes wide behind his glasses, and held out his hands. Peter surrendered the object, squashing a pang of reluctance to part with it. This was Keating's dig, after all. The object belonged either to the university, or to the Iraqi government. If Peter got lucky, his name might go on a museum plaque someday.

"Fascinating," breathed Keating. Peter couldn't help noticing that he brushed the Nile-mud pottery aside as he bent to examine it. "You found this at the site?"

"Yes, sir," said Peter. "What do you think?"

Unlike Jana, Keating didn't seem to think that its presence was a prank at all. Keating stared at the object and sucked his teeth. "I think you've found something very special, Peter. I can't wait to translate it."

"I hope you'll have more luck than I've had," said Peter sheepishly, scratching the back of his neck. "I can't make sense of it. I mean, what could it possibly mean by a 'stellar key'?"

Keating glanced up at him in surprise. "Pardon?"

"The first line." Peter pointed. "It says something about a stellar key, or a star key. The directions don't make sense either, but if I knew the area better, I might be able to sort it out."

Keating tilted his head. "You can read this," he said. It wasn't a question.

Peter had viewed Keating as an inspiration since the first time he'd shaken the man's hand. He'd read Keating's articles; the man had quite a reputation. Peter had always assumed that Keating would be older and greyer, the sort of man who preferred tweed coats with patches at the elbows and smoked a pipe just for the effect. To find that he was so young, relatively speaking, and trim and fit ... Well, these days whenever Peter fantasized about his future, he imagined himself in Keating's shoes.

And if Peter couldn't become him, the next best thing would be to join him.

"Yeah, I can translate it all right," he said casually. "I mean, not *perfectly,* but—"

"Show me," said Keating, shoving the tablet his way.

Peter bent over to examine it. "All right." He scooted around so that he and Keating stood side by side. "It'll be rough, mind you, but here goes." He pointed to the inscription, following along with his finger. "*The star key. At the,* ah, no, *on the floor at the heart,* or maybe the *core... of the ice sea...* Hold on, let me think about this one." He squeezed his eyes shut, trying to remember long nights spent poring through Perseus and Musgar, translating cuneiform into Greek into English, and then back again. "*Object* isn't right.

It's more like... *artifact. On the floor of the frozen sea lies the arti-fact.*" He turned to him. "Does that mean anything to you?"

Keating nodded slowly. "Very impressive."

Feeling pleased with himself, Peter smoothed down the front of his rumpled, dusty shirt. "Some would call it nerdy, sir."

"Well, I'm not one of them." Keating tapped his finger next to the tablet. "You possess a rare talent. It will serve you well, I think."

Peter knew exactly how Jana had felt when Keating praised her earlier. "Thank you."

"Tell the others that they can take the afternoon off," said Keating, already reaching for his laptop. "I'm going to notify my colleagues of this find."

The laptop was surprisingly advanced-looking. Most of the tech on the dig was leftover university scraps. As the 3D display came to life, it almost looked military, Peter thought.

Keating caught him watching. "I'm going to mention your name to the higher-ups, Peter. I think they'll want you working on this long-term."

3

US Research Station, Enceladus

———

WHEN THE US military wanted to get troublemakers out of their hair, they shipped them off to a no-name base in a third-world country. You had to *really* piss someone off to get demoted and stationed on one of Saturn's moons. Lowell looked at his reflection in his lukewarm coffee. *You just had to be an overachiever, buddy boy.*

Munroe had been right. Reporting up his chain of command that he strongly suspected his direct superior had orchestrated the murder of civilians was, in fact, bad for Lowell's career. He should have kept his mouth shut. Clearly, somebody with plenty of weight to throw around was protecting Munroe, and they didn't mind squashing one insignificant corporal—make that *private.*

After the dust had settled, Lowell found himself guarding one of the asteroid mines. But when the World Trade Organization started asking probing questions about the legality of outer space mineral rights, the Pentagon had quietly reshuffled the Space Corps. He'd landed at the new research station on Enceladus. He'd been told that the changes were temporary, but there'd been the Venus scandal, and the trade embargo with Korea, and soon everyone seemed to have forgotten about him.

Lowell decided he liked being forgotten.

There was a new video message waiting in his inbox from his sister Heather and her daughter Kylie. The higher-ups had been promising live-feed technology since what felt like the dawn of time, but Lowell wasn't holding his breath.

"*Rob says hi. Dad's...*" Heather grimace was familiar enough. Lowell hadn't seen his sister in person since just after the inquest, but the regular video messages were almost as good. She didn't edit out the rough parts; he appreciated that. As a man who was nothing *but* rough parts, he could get behind the honesty. "*Well, Dad's okay. But Kylie here's the one with the big news...*"

"*We got a puppy!*" Kylie exclaimed, turning the camera toward a leggy, awkward black Lab pup who sat up and wagged her tail at the sound of the girl's voice.

"*You want to tell him what you named her?*"

"*Gucci!*" Kylie exclaimed, then giggled.

"*Gucci hopes that she's going to meet her Uncle Carp one of these days,*" said Heather significantly. "*In the meantime, stay warm! We'll keep you posted. Sorry we don't have more news.*"

"*Say bye to Uncle Carp, Gucci!*" said Kylie. The puppy yawned.

Lowell took a deep swig of his instant coffee, smiling at the image frozen on the screen. Kylie was getting so big now. He hadn't seen her in person since she was three years old—look at her now, what, eleven? Pushing twelve? She probably didn't remember the last time they'd been on the same planet.

Lowell was pretty sure that his dad was happier that way, even if Heather wasn't. Mark Lowell was one of the many people who'd been disappointed with him, or at least with the stories that circulated about him.

So much for feeling like the good guy.

Lowell spun the laptop screen around, wondering what the heck he was going to say. Heather's weekly messages had been getting shorter lately, but it wasn't like Lowell had a lot to tell her, either. After all, aside from the folks at the research station and a low-level security detail, he was pretty much the only one out here. Just craters and plumes and the endless frozen sky, with Lowell hanging around to do maintenance on the equipment.

Fine by him. Lowell was good with silence.

———

OUT OF SATURN'S eighty-two moons, Enceladus was among the most hospitable—not that it was saying much. The power had glitched a couple of times since Lowell had arrived at the research station, which would have been bad enough if his only concern had been the availability of oxygen. The fact that he could freeze solid more or less instantly if he stepped outside without a protective suit sure didn't help.

On the other hand, there were perks to living off-world. When he'd been on assignment in Saudi Arabia back in the '50s, he'd started to put on his boot, only to discover that a massive and deadly fattail scorpion had taken up residence in the toe. He'd managed to avoid getting stung, but he'd been moderately paranoid about the experience for years afterward. Thankfully he hadn't had to worry about insects since arriving on Enceladus.

If only he could say the same of the military's other rejects. They all seemed to have something to prove, and throwing down with him seemed to be almost a hazing ritual at this point. He avoided them when he could.

Most of the other patrols went out in pairs, but Lowell preferred to do his rounds alone. He piloted his hoverpod across the ice in the old familiar loop around the station's perimeter. He was reaching the far point of his path, and the station lay on the horizon like some sort of ancient, frozen battlement. When they'd been kids, Heather had been obsessed with a movie about a girl with ice powers—to his chagrin, Lowell still knew the words to every song. Maybe he'd post a video from out here sometime, singing with the fortress in the background. Heather would get a kick out of that. It would at least be proof that he hadn't forgotten about their old life entirely.

He reached the data collection station and landed the hoverpod. The unit was comprised mainly of a service tower, a scanner, and a log machine. Honestly, Lowell had never seen the point of these things. They only recorded temperature and surface activity, as far as he could tell. Still, his job was to keep the machines in order, and that was what he did.

A film of ice had formed over the surface of the service tower. The whole structure was only about eight feet tall, which meant that he didn't really have to climb to scrape the sensors clear of ice. When he'd first arrived, they'd been using the old thirty-foot-high models, but after one of the lab techs fell trying to climb to the top without remembering to de-ice the rungs, they'd downsized significantly.

He had just finished scraping off the scanner and was about to sync the log records when he felt a tremor in the ice beneath his feet. Lowell turned to find another pod landing next to his own. There were two men inside: members of his platoon, supposedly, but Lowell had never felt like he belonged with the group. After what had happened on Mars, he hadn't *wanted* to belong. Trust was a little hard for him to scrape together these days.

"Hey, Lowell," said one of the guys, tuning into the local channel. Lowell sighed silently. It was Horne, which probably meant that the other figure was Wilcox.

"Hey, Lowell." It was indeed Wilcox, one of Lowell's least favorite people on-base. He'd been a brat ever since he'd arrived. "You know, a buddy of mine just got a job at the Pentagon, and he told me a funny story about you. Something about Mars, back in '61?"

Like the rest of the men onsite, Lowell mostly ignored Wilcox's baiting. Sometimes that was enough to deter the troublemakers, but Wilcox was like a chihuahua: he was a little pup who wanted to feel big, and running his mouth was the only way he knew how.

"Dunno what you're talking about," said Lowell. "Did you guys not see the route map today? I'm wrapping up here."

"Yeah, we saw the map," said Horne. "And you know damn well what he's talking about."

"And here I thought you were a brownnoser," said Wilcox. "Turns out, you're a *backstabber*." He leaned back against the side of the hoverpod and crossed his arms, watching Lowell.

"That's one interpretation," said Lowell, getting back to work. "Another is that I thought I was doing my job. Speaking of which, don't you two have somewhere to be?"

"I don't get the high-and-mighty act," said Horne. "We all know you're a washed-up has-been, and a traitor to boot. But it didn't work out for you, did it?"

"No," said Lowell quietly, finishing his work and packing up his kit. "Can't say it did."

Wilcox snorted. "You're like Teflon. Things just roll off of you. Is that what a court martial does to you? Just breaks your spirit?"

"I'm just following my route," said Lowell. *I'm going to get back in the hoverpod,* he told himself, *and move on to the next site. That's it. I'm not going to let them bait me.*

I'm not.

I'm not.

"Hey, I just had a thought," said Horne, slapping his gloved hand against the chest piece of Wilcox's suit. "Why don't you take his pod? Let the snitch hoof it back."

"You know what?" said Wilcox theatrically. "I think that's a great idea."

"I wouldn't try that," said Lowell in the same flat voice he always used with their type. He'd seen green recruits come and go. They seemed to get dumber every year—or possibly Lowell just got tired of their nonsense faster.

"What are you gonna do, grandpa?" asked Wilcox, striding over to Lowell's hoverpod and blocking his path back to the door. "You want to fight me?"

"Not particularly." Lowell could feel his nerves fraying. He preferred not to get into it with guys like Wilcox, but he sometimes wondered if he had magnets in his pockets that attracted them. They seemed to crop up everywhere he went.

"Then what's going to stop me from taking your pod?" asked Wilcox.

"Your better judgment," Lowell replied.

"I've had it with your attitude," snapped Wilcox, as though Lowell was the one causing trouble. "If you want your pod back, you're going to have to go through me."

Lowell sighed and bent down slowly to set his toolkit on the ground. "Have it your way," he said, and he lunged.

New recruits always walked carefully on the ice. The surface was several kilometers thick so there was little danger of it cracking unexpectedly, but it was still slippery. After a couple of falls, most people learned to watch their step. They tended to wear grips on the bottoms of their boots, too, just to make things easier.

Lowell, on the other hand, had ditched the traction cleats a long time ago, and took advantage of the moon's slick surface. He pushed off, then crouched as he skidded, lowering his center of gravity. His shoulder caught Wilcox in the waist, and the younger man went down. The back of his helmet cracked hard against the ice, and he swore.

"What's wrong with you?" demanded Horne, reaching for his toolkit.

Lowell leaned to one side, extending one leg so that his course adjusted to target Horne. He'd spent hours practicing his movements that first year, and he'd perfected his technique early on.

The other man braced for impact, but at the last second, Lowell dropped to his knees and held out his arm, catching Horne's legs as he slid by. Horne fell, too, and uttered a string of curses as he landed.

Lowell slid into the side of the pair's hoverpod, rolled, and kicked against the side of the machine, shoving himself back the way he'd come. He collided with Horne, who was still struggling to get to his feet. Lowell yanked the other man back down and put him in a headlock, pressing Horne's chest against the ice. The younger man scrabbled at the frozen surface, but found no purchase.

"What the hell, Lowell?" screeched Wilcox, pushing himself to his feet. "You cracked my friggin' tooth!"

"Go cry to the commander about it," Lowell grunted, leaning down on Horne.

"You'd better believe I'm going to," Wilcox snapped.

Lowell leaned down on the still-struggling Horne and grinned up at the younger man. "Snitch."

"Okay, okay, let me up," Horne whined.

"That depends. You gonna let me go back to my pod?"

Horne went limp. A moment later, his sulky voice echoed through the mic. "Yeah."

Lowell let him go and got to his feet. When he passed Wilcox, the young cadet slammed his shoulder into Lowell's.

"Crazy how they'll recruit middle schoolers these days," said Lowell, bending to retrieve his toolkit and opening the door of his pod. "Looks like they're scraping the bottom of the barrel when it comes to new blood." He slammed the pod door behind him and powered up the controls. Horne was still sliding around on the ice when he took off, and he could hear Wilcox muttering curses.

So much for the Space Corps being the cream of the crop, Lowell thought darkly. At least his old squadmates would have been able to put up a decent fight. Shaking his head, he set his course for the next stop on his route. A little scuffle like that was no reason to fall behind in his work.

If anything, it was just more proof that Lowell was better off working alone.

4

"TO PETER," said Jana, raising her bottle of Stella.

"To Peter!" Amira echoed.

"Oh, heck, I'll cheer him, too," said Connor grudgingly. "After all, he got us the afternoon off. Who could ask for more than that?"

"To Professor Keating," said Peter, lifting the bottle to his lips for a deep swig of the ice-cold beer. He wasn't a big drinker when he was on campus, but after a long day under the hot sun, nothing tasted sweeter. "And to Jana for her Nile-clay find!"

"To Jana," echoed Connor, happy for any excuse to imbibe.

Any ruffled feathers had been soothed by the application of light beer, and Peter found himself feeling sleepy and contented, like a lizard that had spent the afternoon basking on a hot stone. He stretched lazily as he leaned back, popping the joints in his neck.

"Gross," said Amira, but without real feeling. "Do you think Keating's going to ask you to help translate?"

"He said he was," said Peter, finishing his bottle and reaching for another. In the Mediterranean, he and his classmates had drunk wine by the liter, but in Muslim countries, stiff beverages were harder to come by. They took whatever they could get—not that any of them were complaining now.

"God, I would kill for a chance to work more closely with him," Connor groaned, letting his forehead thump down onto the table. "If you did plant that thing, it was brilliant of you."

"I didn't plant it," Peter assured him. "And if you ask nicely, once I get my professorship, maybe I'll hire you on as an assistant."

Connor swatted at him, then got up from the table, swaying woozily. It might have been the alcohol, but his unsteady legs might just as easily be the result of another long day under the blistering desert sun.

"Well, you kids have a lovely evening," he said, saluting them. "I'm off to bed."

"We should all get going," said Jana, although Peter couldn't help noticing that she took another bottle with her for the road. "See you at the ass-crack of dawn, children." She tottered off to the girls' tent, and Amira followed, blowing Peter a kiss. He could never tell if she actually liked him, or if she was just a terrible flirt with limited options on hand. People were so hard to read.

This is why you're still single, he thought, watching as she disappeared into the tent.

"Dude, you need to lock that down," said Connor, gathering the rest of the beer in his arms. "She's totally into you. I guess she likes all that alien talk."

"Maybe," said Peter. "Or maybe she's just bored."

Still, as he settled into his bunk that night, he thought about life after the dig. Maybe, if Amira still bothered to talk to him once they got back to California, he'd ask her out on a date. He could take her to the retro coffee shop that still had Blu-ray rentals. She would get a kick out of that.

———

PETER WAS DREAMING of having his name printed first when they published the tablet's translation—*It's alphabetical, Professor Keating,* he'd been saying, *I couldn't convince them to print your name first...*—when he woke to a sharp and unfamiliar noise. In the cot next to him, Connor sat up ramrod straight.

"What the hell...?" he asked.

A sudden high-pitched scream sounded from the direction of the girls' tent, and then a loud *pop* that echoed in Peter's ears.

"Oh my God, oh my God," said Amira's voice. Then another *pop.*

Gunfire.

Peter scrambled out of his cot, tripping over the sheets. He was wearing nothing but his boxers and an undershirt. They had no weapons. They'd been warned that Americans were sometimes targeted by locals, and Peter had heard hostage horror-stories in abundance. His mother had panicked when she found out he was headed to the Middle East for this dig. He'd told her he'd be fine.

He couldn't hear Amira anymore.

"Grab your shoes and your passport," Connor hissed. "We'll go out the back of the tent, come on..."

Peter grabbed for his bag, but before he could pull on his shoes, three black-clad figures bearing assault rifles burst in through the front flap of the tent. At least, Peter assumed they were assault rifles. His family had never been big on firearms.

"Which one of you is Peter Chang?" barked the nearest man. His accent was American. So much for the theory that they were being attacked by insurgents. Peter whimpered, stumbling back into the cold metal lip of the cot.

"Come on," the man said, jabbing the gun toward them, "speak up."

Peter and Connor exchanged a look. *He's going to rat me out*, said Peter. A hundred conspiracy theories were already spinning through his mind, and he was never going to get answers. Connor was going to point to him, and then he'd be dead.

But Connor only stared at him and didn't say a word.

The tent flap opened again, and Professor Keating stepped in.

"Professor!" Connor yelped. "Watch out!"

Keating sighed. "What's the holdup, men? That's Peter." He pointed directly at Peter's face, and the world seemed to tilt sideways. "The other one is dead weight."

"Profess—!" Peter gasped, but then two of the men fired at once. One shot hit Connor square in the chest; the other went right through his eye. He dropped without a sound, his blood spattered scarlet across the white wall of the dig tent. Peter stared. He had never watched anyone die, and he had certainly never seen anyone get shot before.

This is the dream, he thought. *This part is only something awful I've imagined.* He was still in denial when one of the nearest men yanked him forward, zip-tying his hands in front of him, and all but dragged him out of the tent. Peter's feet scraped across the rocky sand. The encampment, usually dark at night, was lit up with floodlights. Peter tried to block the light with one hand, but when the man in black yanked him, he lost his footing and fell onto the sand. It was only then that he saw Amira's body lying face-down, her fingers dug into the sand. The back of her head had been blown open.

We were just talking, he thought wildly. *We were only just talking. She can't be dead...*

The man hauled him back to his feet. A second man grabbed Peter's other arm, and they hauled him across the ground to a truck waiting nearby. They shoved him through the open door, then turned to Professor Keating, who was still following on their heels.

"What are we doing with the site, sir?"

Keating waved a dismissive hand. "Torch it. Make it look like a strike against the American government. Their families will have questions, so make it look good." Then he hauled himself into the truck as well. "Well, Peter, haven't we had an exciting night?"

Peter lay on the truck bed, painfully aware that he was practically naked. The sight of Amira's body reappeared each time he blinked, and he kept seeing Connor fall, over and over, like a video loop in his mind. Keating was acting like nothing had happened.

"Are you just going to lie there?" asked Keating, looking down at him in disgust. "Come on, sit up. This is a pretty pathetic display." He sat in one of the fold-down chairs along the side of the truck's wall.

"You told them that Connor was dead weight," said Peter numbly. He was aware on some level that Keating might shoot him if he talked back, but he felt very far away from his body, as if all of this was happening to someone else.

"He was." Keating shrugged. "He'd outlived his usefulness. We have the key, we have the map, and now we have our translator. So get up, translator. You got lucky this time."

Peter lifted himself into the seat across from Keating, swallowing hard. At first he'd thought that the men were here for him, but of course, this all made sense. There was only one explanation he could concoct that explained the whole situation.

Aliens were real.

The tablet he'd found today was, indeed, an alien artifact.

The men who'd killed Connor and Amira and probably Jana knew the truth, and didn't want anyone to know.

"Are you really a professor?" asked Peter quietly.

The man across from him snorted. "Hell, no. We made the real Samuel Keating disappear years ago on Mars."

"So who are you?" Peter asked, although he could already guess at least part of the answer.

"I'm Lieutenant Larry Munroe," said the man whom Peter had been calling Keating all summer. "Special ops."

"US military," said Peter dumbly.

Connor's going to flip his lid when he finds out, thought Peter, before remembering that Connor was dead.

Munroe had told Peter that he'd gotten lucky, which by some standards might be true. He was still alive.

Although who knew how long that would last?

———

AT FIRST, Peter tried to mark the days since his friends had been killed. That had been easy enough as he, Munroe, and the lieutenant's platoon travelled to the US military base outside of Baghdad. Then they'd taken a jet back to the States. When they'd shoved him out of the jet, he'd been hit by a blast of hot, humid air. Were they in Florida? Texas? He couldn't be sure.

Peter had spent his last four days in rooms that were either brightly lit and painfully nondescript, or else so dark that it was impossible to see clearly. The men who'd taken him prisoner didn't speak to him, didn't tell him what was happening or what to do. They only shoved him through the next door, out of a white-walled room and into the most recognizable place he'd seen since they left the dig site, one of the first spaces he'd been where there was open air.

A launch pad.

Peter staggered, spinning slowly on the spot as he took in the enormous area. Men and women in uniform walked past, none of them looking the least bit alarmed by the suited platoon of men marching across the concrete with Peter in their midst. They were headed toward a ship, not the smooth, rocket-shaped vessels he'd seen so many times in the launch videos live-streamed online. This ship was enormous and brilliant white, shaped like some sort of snub-nosed sea creature ringed with jets. Peter closed his eyes, remembering a hundred late nights spent on his laptop, poring over conspiracy theory boards and wondering just how crazy the guys posting this stuff were. Not so crazy, apparently—the government really *did* have top-secret spaceships in the works.

He wanted to get a better look, but he was carried forward by the press of men around him.

When they finally cut the zip ties around his wrists and told him to put on the suit, Peter stared at them.

"Is there a problem?" asked Munroe coldly.

Peter shook his head. He was familiar with the reflective, flexible space suits used in the old launch videos. The one Munroe's men handed him looked more like something out of those old Marvel Universe movies, sleek and metallic. He'd watched all the films, and he was pretty sure that whoever designed his suit had as well. As he pulled it on, watching the men around him in action, Peter's heart began to pound. He'd been able to grasp the reality of the situation already, although he was still coming to terms with it. But this... this was meant for *space*. Real, honest-to-God *space*. He stood in the brightly-lit, nondescript room, staring down at the helmet clutched in his shaking hands.

Impossible, he kept thinking. *Impossible.*

The worst part was that he was almost excited. He didn't deserve to be excited, not when Amira and Connor and Jana were dead, and their families were forced to swallow whatever lies the government fed them.

It wasn't until that moment, staring down at the helmet into his own reflection, that he realized that his own family thought that he was dead as well—they must have been told that his body was never recovered.

We made the real Peter Chang disappear, Munroe was going to say someday. He might be useful now, but the moment he outlived that usefulness, he'd become dead weight, and they'd drop him, too.

"Got your helmet?" asked Munroe, appearing at Peter's side.

Peter nodded, holding up the object in question.

"Good, good," said Munroe. He flashed the same smile that had made the girls swoon, and that was currently making Peter's blood run cold. "I'm glad to hear it. You won't need it yet, but you'll want it where we're going."

"And where is that?" asked Peter, as they climbed up a ramp that he realized with stunned silence led directly up under a waiting spacecraft.

"Just like you said in your translation: *The floor of the frozen sea.* We're following your map." Peter tore his eyes away from the spacecraft to look at Munroe, who winked at him like they were old friends sharing a secret. "We're on our way to Enceladus."

5

AFTER ANOTHER LONG, tedious shift spent patrolling the perimeter of the research station and scraping ice off the equipment, Lowell headed to the station's cantina.

Despite the issues he had with the other members of the Corps, the scientists were a surprisingly outgoing and jovial lot. He chalked it up to the fact that they came and went along with their research projects. For many of them, this was an exciting sabbatical rather than a punishment for nonconformity.

"Hey, Lowell!" called Dr. Hansen when she saw him collecting his evening rations. "Come sit with us!"

Why does she bother? he wondered as he dropped into a chair between the doctor and one of the other researchers. He was pretty sure that her name was Lily, but he wouldn't have bet money on it.

"Did you discover Atlantis today?" he asked, peeling back the wrapper of an MRE.

Hansen shook her head. "Not yet. But we *have* confirmed the presence of nucleotides in the sample Anjali took from the geyser."

She raised her eyebrows significantly, as though that might mean something to him.

The NASA-backed research station on Enceladus was ostensibly there to gather data about the frozen moon. From what Lowell had pieced together, the moon itself was geologically active, and there was some small possibility that amino acid chains found in the planet's frozen sea might eventually lead to the development of lifeforms a few billion years down the line. It had something to do with hydrothermal vents and atmospheric conditions. Hansen had tried to explain the theory in laymen's terms on more than one occasion, and Lowell had listened patiently.

He appreciated the effort, but honestly, it all sounded like some hypothetical mumbo-jumbo to him. Not that it mattered. There had been a time when Lowell had believed everything that he was told, but those days were long gone. He'd leave the research to the scientists and stick to his lane.

"You know," said the researcher, digging her spoon into a pouch of nonperishable cheese tortellini, "I've heard that we might be getting a new assignment. Any word on that, Doc?"

Hansen's eyes twinkled. "That's top secret, Lily," she said.

Lily. He'd gotten her name right. Maybe that was proof that he wasn't a total wash when it came to human interactions.

"Oh, come on, Lowell's not going to tell," Lily assured her. "Are you, Lowell? You seem like a guy who knows when to keep his mouth shut."

From someone else, her words might have felt like an insult, but Lowell didn't talk much about his fall from grace with the civilians. As far as they knew, he'd elected to come out here. That was what it looked like on paper, anyway.

"Yeah," Lowell grunted. "Learned that the hard way."

"Oh, all right." Hansen leaned closer. "I'm sure that you'll be briefed soon enough. Supposedly, we'll be getting a visit from a special ops team—I can't talk specifics, but I can tell you that the lieutenant has been in touch with me directly. He's a fascinating man." She winked at Lily. "Handsome, too."

"Weren't you special ops back in the day?" asked Lily, jabbing her spoon in Lowell's direction. "I didn't make that up, right?"

"It was a long time ago," Lowell said.

"Well, then maybe you know the guy I'm talking about." Dr. Hansen reached for her water bottle. "Does the name Munroe mean anything to you?"

Lowell set the MRE down abruptly. "*Larry* Munroe?"

"Yeah." Dr. Hansen took a long drink. "You know him?"

"Lieutenant *Larry Munroe*?" His jaw seemed to be clenched of its own accord. It felt like he had to fight to form words. "Is going to be *here*?" Lowell heard the strain in his voice and tried to check it, but he doubted there was anything to be done about the angry wave of red rising up his neck.

"Yeah." Hansen exchanged a look with Lily. They both leaned subtly away from Lowell. "Is something wrong?"

"You can't trust him." The words tumbled out of Lowell's mouth before he could stop them.

Hansen frowned. "Beg your pardon?"

"Keep your team away from him. You don't want to go near that guy."

Hansen and Lily exchanged a look before the latter leaned forward. "He just wants us to take *Moby Dick* out to scope the mineral deposit they found a few years back. It's no big deal."

The scientists all loved to name things. *Moby Dick* was the name of the biggest of the research submersibles on the planet. It had required a special spaceship to bring it over in pieces and assemble it below the ice. It was packed with scientific instruments, but its most impressive feature was that it could be operated by a skeleton crew while it did its work. The sub was responsible for much of the deep sonar mapping that took place on the station, although it was Lowell's understanding that they'd mapped less than ten percent of the crevice-filled ocean floor. Lowell had done maintenance on it a couple of times when the seals froze over after a crew kept it out too long, but like the leviathan it was named after, the sub could take just about anything the ocean threw its way.

It's no big deal, Lily had said.

That's probably what Samuel Keating thought back on Mars, before Munroe made him disappear. Lowell tapped his knuckles on the table in an unconscious rhythm.

"What exactly is the problem?" Hansen asked. There was serious concern etched on her features.

Well for starters, Dr. Hansen, I think Munroe offed a team of civilian scientists years ago on Mars—scientists just like you. What's that? Do I have proof? *No, of course not. All the evidence was destroyed long before any of my questions reached the ears of anyone who cared. And once it did land on the desk of somebody at Internal Investigation Command, everyone I knew instantly turned on me and IIC railroaded me within an inch of a dishonorable discharge.* What's that? Why would they do that? *Simple. Because I dared to look sideways at Munroe, who clearly has angels up the chain of command.*

Lowell didn't say any of that. There was no point. He'd been on that ride enough and he didn't like where it ended up. He wasn't getting back on it again.

"He's going to get people killed," was all he managed.

Lily and Hansen again exchanged a look, and Hansen spoke first. "It seems like you've had a run-in with this guy before, huh?"

"Something like that," Lowell said.

Hansen sat back and stared at Lowell as she mulled something over. Lowell genuinely liked her. This whole thing made him feel sick. What the hell was Munroe up to? Did he even know that Lowell was here? Did he care?

"How would you feel about being on our team?" Hansen asked.

The question caught him so off guard he took a double take. "Excuse me?"

Hansen leaned forward in her seat again. "Just while he's here. We'll be on the sub, and you can stay in the command center with him. Keep an eye on him. I think the commander would go for it if I asked nicely."

Lowell's knuckles kept beating a rapid-fire rhythm on the table. The idea of facing Munroe again made him want to put his fist through something. *And it's not like you were able to protect Keating and his team. Why would this be any different?*

Because he was smarter now. If Munroe tried anything, Lowell could take him out, no matter the cost. He wasn't above shooting a man who'd proven himself capable of murder.

"Sounds good," he said at last. "And seriously, Doc, watch your back. You don't know what this guy's capable of."

She smiled knowingly. "We always do with you military types."

"Besides, you'll keep us safe," said Lily, winking at him. "You're one of the good ones."

6

ENCELADUS WAS BREATHTAKING. As their station-to-surface shuttle left the main spacecraft, Peter was grateful for the protective coating on the inside of his helmet. The frozen tundra below them was so blindingly white that even with the barrier, he had to squint to see.

"How did we get here so fast?" he asked, peering out the shuttle window into the vast, icy landscape. "And how long has the military had a colony out here?"

According to the media, Enceladus only hosted a few unmanned drones, but the station they were approaching now stood out like a gleaming black fortress on the surface of the frozen world.

"We've made some advances," Munroe said noncommittally. "Like everyone, we don't publicize them if we don't have to."

Peter was beginning to understand how his media-informed view was woefully outdated.

"It's massive," he breathed. If his father could see this, he'd absolutely lose his mind.

It wasn't until they pulled closer to the research station that he realized how much of the outside was covered in solar panels. Of course, there wasn't likely to be much fuel out here, and waiting for shipments from Earth would be unsustainable, even with the much shorter transport time that Peter himself had just experienced.

The gates of the research station opened, allowing their shuttle inside. Even with the insulation and heating elements in his suit, Peter could feel the chill.

I guess that's what −198°C feels like, Peter thought, wondering if he could adjust the settings on his suit. A second later, he could feel the heating element power up automatically.

"Welcome, Lieutenant!" said a voice through the helmet's speakers. Peter was pretty sure that they were all on a shared frequency, allowing the team to speak to each other while still wearing their protective gear. The figure who approached to shake Munroe's hand looked quite androgynous beneath the suit, but judging by the voice still ringing in Peter's ears, she was an older woman. "A real pleasure, sir. I hear you have a special mission for us?"

"Yes," said Munroe, waving toward Peter. "This man is going to be helping us with something that my superiors have deemed to be of *particular* significance."

The woman turned her attention to Peter. "Is that so? And who might you be?"

"Peter Chang," he said, looking to Munroe for instructions. He wished that he could see the man's face. No one had told him the rules out here, and although he kept telling himself that it didn't matter, he still wanted to live long enough to at least figure out what the heck was happening.

"Nice to meet you, Dr. Chang," said the woman pleasantly. She held out a hand to him, just as she had to Munroe. "I'm Dr.

Fran Hansen. I look forward to having another specialist on staff. Have you read my articles on the Anomaly?"

Anomaly? Peter wondered as they shook.

"His specialties are complementary to yours, Doctor," Munroe cut in. "But you're correct that it will be our destination. Peter has some vital information that we've been waiting for."

"Is that so?" Hansen asked. She sounded genuinely excited.

Does she know what they did to bring me here? Or does she really think they recruited me?

"So what are our marching orders?" she asked Munroe casually. Something about the way she said it made Peter suspect that she was here for the advancement of science rather than a military advantage, genuinely unaware of the things going on behind the scenes. This made him think of Jana, and her sincere thrill of joy over an unexpected sherd of Egyptian pottery. He hoped that Dr. Hansen would be better off than Jana when all of this was over.

Munroe reached into one of the suit's exterior pockets and produced an orb. It was made of the same gleaming substance as the tablet. The object wasn't perfectly spherical; the surface was marked with what looked like sigils, and inlaid with bands of some bright element that Peter didn't recognize.

"A colleague of ours discovered this on Mars a few years back," he said, turning it over in his hands. "We have a sense of what to do with it, but we've been waiting for the instructions." He held up the tablet. "And here they are."

"Interesting," said Hansen, reaching for the orb.

Munroe subtly pulled back before she could touch it. "I believe that you have a submersible available?"

"Of course. We can be ready to launch within the hour."

"Perfect. I'll hand over the orb then. After that, it's all up to... *Doctor* Chang."

"Excellent," said Hansen. "We'll be going down in *Moby Dick,* but you'll have someone with you on the station to help you with anything you might need." She gestured over her shoulder to a tall, broad-shouldered figure standing at the back of the group. "Lieutenant, I believe you've met Private Lowell?"

"Lowell?" Munroe's tone shifted slightly, and a predatory note that had been absent from the conversation with the researchers suddenly returned. "What are the odds? As a matter of fact, we're old friends."

Even with a poor view of the other man's face, Peter could feel the hostility radiating off of him. In some odd way it was comforting, this naked show of contempt for Munroe, except for the fact that the man made no move to interfere. As the scientists shepherded them deeper into the research station, Lowell simply took up the rear guard.

Is he trapped under Munroe's thumb like I am? Peter looked over his shoulder, trying to get a better look at Lowell's face, but one of Munroe's men stepped into his line of sight and beckoned him forward.

After a dizzying array of turns through narrow passageways and tight hatches that connected the station's maze of modules, they arrived at the comm station of the lab. It was a fairly small compartment that was dominated by a bank of screens and communication equipment along one wall.

Munroe stepped out while one of his men sat Peter down at the main screen. He watched as a small team of scientists, several wearing diving gear, entered the docking platform. Munroe soon entered as well and handed the orb-shaped object to one of the scientists—Hansen, presumably—before he turned away and the others were lowered into the giant craft.

Peter felt sick. Munroe clearly knew more than he did. It all felt like a test Peter was set up to fail. He was thankful the group seemed to already know where they were going. While he was confident in his translation of the tablet, he wasn't sure he was ready to guide a team inside what was probably a multibillion-dollar piece of high-tech machinery as they navigated through a subterranean sea.

"Here we go," said Dr. Hansen as Munroe returned to the comm station. "Diving down to the Anomaly."

They were talking on a split-screen video chat, with one of the live feeds coming from inside her helmet. He'd been right: she was a pleasant-faced woman in her mid-forties, with coppery hair and clever eyes. Peter wished he could pick her brain without Munroe hovering over his shoulder. One of the other panels was a feed from the front of the vessel, so that they could witness the crew's slow progress through the water. The sea of Enceladus was murky, with limited visibility.

At last, Munroe handed over the tablet. Peter accepted it reverently. It gave him a little thrill to know that he was the only one here who could make heads or tails of the inscription. This might be a false sense of power, but he'd take whatever he could get.

Knowing that they were starting on Enceladus had given Peter a different take on some of the translation. The phrase that he'd thought meant *'the giantess's sister'* probably referred to the moon itself; the giantess in question must be Saturn. He tried to keep that in mind as he translated, despite the massive amount of cognitive dissonance it gave him to blend his love of the ancient world with the new reality slowly opening up before him.

"Bear with me," said Peter, looking down at the tablet. "What exactly is the Anomaly?"

Hansen winked. "You'll see soon enough."

Peter cleared his throat. "Right."

He thought about the tablet. He'd decided that the words related to the artifact in question must mean *metal* or *steel*—and it would be pretty easy, considering the amount of sonar mapping they'd already done here to spot purified ore. It would stand out like a sore thumb. That must be the Anomaly.

Guess I'll see soon enough, he thought with annoyance. It was a bit condescending, since as far as Hansen knew, he really was a doctor. *It sure didn't take you long to grow a thin skin about your fake title.* Then he remembered the pride with which Jana had shown off the fragment of Nile pottery. Maybe Dr. Hansen wasn't being condescending. Maybe she was just showing off. It was the kind of thing his dad pulled in lectures, the theatrical reveal of some new find.

Peter found himself trying to follow along with the tablet's directions, more out of pride than anything. He just wanted to be sure he'd gotten it right.

Something moving through the waters caught Peter's eye; it was only a dim shape, more shadow than identifiable mass. "What was that?" he asked, pointing at the screen.

"What was *what?*" asked Hansen.

"I saw something move out there." Peter squinted, but the shape was gone.

"Part of a plume before it breaches the surface," said Hansen. "We've found traces of amino acid chains in the water, but to call it even a proto-lifeform would be an exaggeration. We see shadows through the ice all the time, and plumes forming before they're fully pressurized."

Peter nodded. "Okay. Got it." If Munroe had told him that, Peter wouldn't have bought it for a second, but Dr. Hansen had no reason to lie to him. As far as she knew, they were colleagues. Still, Peter kept a wary eye on the front cameras, just in case.

The seabed was fairly uniform, as far as he could tell, although the ship stayed far above it. In some ways, it reminded Peter of the desert he'd crossed to reach Ur-An: apparently featureless, with secrets hidden beneath.

"There," said Hansen, and Peter's eye refocused on a pinprick of silver on the ocean floor. The ship dove, and the object grew clearer, glinting in their floodlights.

On the split screen, Peter could see Dr. Hansen watching his face with amusement. "Welcome to the Anomaly, Dr. Chang."

It was obvious to Peter that the object was made from the same material as the orb and the tablet. As they drew closer still, he could see that the entire site was lit with floodlights that were attached to the ocean floor.

In spite of himself, Peter's heart began to pound. The light illuminated the metal surface, a gleaming metal deposit on the seabed. Although its edges faded naturally into the ocean floor, a little hump in the middle was polished to a smooth sheen.

"Fascinating, isn't it?" asked Hansen proudly. "We've taken samples, but we haven't been able to identify the material, although it looks awfully similar to the material of the artifact you gentlemen handed over."

Lowell shifted at the periphery of Peter's vision. "What the hell are you playing at, Munroe?"

"Sorry," said Hansen, "that last transmission was staticky. What was that?"

"Nothing important," Munroe assured her. "Please, Doctor, carry on."

Peter was considering how to respond when his eye caught something on the silver ore.

"What am I looking at?" he asked Hansen. "There, on the surface of the Anomaly."

"Just irregularities in the surface," said Hansen. "I know they *look* like patterns, but it's just apophenia—you're familiar with the term?"

"Yeah," Peter muttered distractedly. "Seeing patterns where no pattern exists."

Hansen smiled. "Right. The marks *look* like patterns, but they're meaningless. After all, it's a raw ore deposit in deep space..."

She went on, but Peter had tuned her out entirely. Whatever logic told her, he wasn't experiencing apophenia. The Anomaly was covered in hundreds, if not thousands, of glyphs and sigils. Some of them, like the tablet, were a recognizable variation of cuneiform. The marks didn't have the sharp lines of the usual stylus impressions, but it was no different than reading English in another font. Other languages, too, freckled the bright surface: Egyptian hieroglyphs, Linear A, and archaic Chinese script were all present, but unfamiliar marks, too, belonging to languages that Peter didn't know.

Alien languages, he thought with a shiver. *This thing is the Rosetta Stone for ancient alien script.* He let out a high little whine of excitement.

If Munroe hadn't been hovering there, Peter would have explained his theory to Dr. Hansen—and any of the other scientists who cared to listen. Perhaps they'd already come to this conclusion. It occurred to him that the tablet—*his* tablet—was the key to understanding all of this.

He focused on the scripts he *did* know. The Chinese script predated anything he'd seen, and Linear A was still untranslated, but he knew the cuneiform well enough. If he could only get a clear view of the surface...

"We sent a picture to a colleague a while back," Hansen assured him. "Just to make sure. He tried to translate them, but it didn't mean anything."

Peter sighed and slumped back in the chair. "Oh."

Munroe leaned over his shoulder again, as if he was speaking directly into Peter's ear. "Focus, *Doctor Chang*. The tablet."

Lowell took a protective step forward, and Peter hurriedly turned back to the rectangular object in his lap.

"We're getting into position now," announced Hansen. "Dive teams should be in the water in two minutes."

"All right," Peter said, quickly scanning the writing that *did* have some meaning. He skimmed it in silence, moving his gloved finger across the surface to show Munroe that he was making an effort. *Bright metal. Sea floor. Key in the beginning...* Beginning?

Like a transmission.

"They're instructions," Peter murmured.

"Instructions?" repeated Hansen. "For what?"

"For what to do with the orb," he told her as he scanned further down the tablet. Before he said more, Munroe gripped his shoulder tight. Peter flinched.

"Let's skip the speculation, *Doctor*. You're going to have some divers down there that could use your help soon."

Peter nodded, and the pressure on his shoulder relaxed. Whatever the key did, it was pretty clear from the tablet that it was meant to interact with the Anomaly. But what could that actually mean? These were a couple of ancient artifacts separated by millions of years and half a solar system.

What could possibly happen?

7

LILY NGUYEN HAD GONE on her first snorkeling trip with her family when she was eleven years old. She'd been astonished by the variety of fish found in the reefs of Cozumel. In college, she'd gotten her scuba cert, and had vacationed in Roatan, Bonaire, Hawaii, and Raja Ampat.

Gearing up for a dive in Maui was a little different than diving on Enceladus. For one thing, she was able to use the same suit she wore on the moon's surface. All she really needed were fins, which she slid on over the boots she already wore.

She was working on a proposal to use the suit's technology in a marine study capacity back on Earth. Sometimes, Lily lay awake at night and fantasized about what it would be like to free-dive the Mariana Trench. The sea floor of Enceladus was even deeper, but it lacked the life of Earth's oceans. Just think what they could do with the knowledge they would gain from direct study of the thermal vents in the Challenger Deep...

"Are you ready?" Munroe asked over their mics.

"My dive team is heading out for the Anomaly now,"

answered Hansen, gesturing for Lily to come closer. "I'm passing over the orb as we speak." True to her word, she placed the bright metal ball into Lily's hands. Anjali was still pulling on her fins.

When her colleague was ready, the two of them stepped into *Moby Dick*'s lockout chamber, and Hansen closed the hatch behind them. Once the ship was sealed off, they opened the exit hatch above, and let the sea of Enceladus in.

"All right in there?" asked Hansen over the channel. "Your cameras are on. So far, so good, right?"

"Yes," said Anjali. "We're ready to go."

Lily swam up into the darkness. Once they were clear of the ship, she angled herself down toward the seabed. The water was pitch black, except for where the beams of the headlamps illuminated the strange artifact below them.

"How did this get down here?" asked Anjali, who was far less used to diving around the Anomaly than Lily. "This is crazy. It looks like something from a history vid."

"Do you have the key?" asked Dr. Chang, ignoring the question. "The orb, I mean."

"I do." Lily held the ball in both hands and moved only by kicking her feet. Due to the tech in her suit, she could have used her arms to swim without worrying about her air consumption rate, the way she would have with a tank. Still, old habits die hard.

The Anomaly lay before them, glinting silver in the artificial light. She was as transfixed by it as the first time she'd seen it. As alien in this landscape as any other—and just as baffling. Whatever its exact chemical composition, the metal hadn't oxidized in the salt sea of the frozen moon.

Dr. Chang's voice came through the speakers. "All right, looking at the instructions... There should be a bevel or a dip in the face, something about the size of the orb that Keating—uh, *Munroe* gave you."

Lily examined the top of the metal hump. It was close enough to touch now, and she ran her gloved hand over the inscriptions. "No, I don't see anything like that."

"Perhaps you've misread it, Dr. Chang," said Munroe. Lily shivered. There was something about these military guys that made her nervous. They always sounded like they would just as soon shoot you as look at you.

They're on our side, she reminded herself.

"No," Dr. Chang insisted; he sounded a little panicked. "It says *birim kunukki*, that's a seal impression, so there must be something..."

"Over here," said Anjali.

Lily looked across to where her colleague had let herself sink down the side of the polished mound. She was impressed. Far from being wide-eyed and overwhelmed, Anjali was focused and sharp. *Better than I was the first few times I was down here.*

Lily swam over, and the two of them hovered side-by-side against one of the darkened faces. The sub was on the other side, which meant that the irregular hump of the Anomaly blocked some of the light from the headlamps. Anjali switched on the floodlight clipped to her wrist, illuminating the little hollow in the artifact's side, which the main seafloor floodlights had left in shadow thanks to the sharp relief around it. There was a divot at the bottom the same circumference as the sphere.

"Yes, yes!" cried Dr. Chang. "Perfect. Put it in there, please. And... yes, it looks like you're supposed to place it with that little mark at the bottom facing down, so that the bands of material are perpendicular to the seabed. Yes, exactly."

Gingerly, Lily reached forward and placed the orb within.

"Now what?" she asked.

"Now..." Dr. Chang began.

One of Lily's hands was resting against the surface of the

Anomaly. Before Dr. Chang could answer, she felt the material start to vibrate, as though it was an engine that had just been switched on.

"We've got seismic activity down here," she said.

"She's right," Anjali said. She'd put her hand to the surface of the artifact as well. "It's vibrating."

"That's odd," Dr. Chang said.

It sure as hell is. But then Lily realized he wasn't talking about the vibration they were reporting. He was talking about whatever text he was referencing.

"This says that it will take time... *urkītu,* yes, that's right, that means at some point in the future, but I don't—"

"It's a clock," said Munroe.

"Are you sure?" asked Dr. Chang. "Because I don't see anywhere that it says... *What the hell was that?*"

Lily winced and put her hand to the side of her head. "What do you mean?"

"There's something in the water with you!" squealed Dr. Chang. He really was a very excitable man.

Anjali chuckled. "It's just shadows, Doctor, like we told you."

"See," said Lily, turning to show him a panorama of the sea floor. "It's just—"

She only made it about ninety degrees before she saw the reflection of something silver moving through the water beside her. Lily froze.

"Did you see that?" asked Dr. Chang.

"There's nothing to see," Anjali assured him.

Moments ago, Lily would have spoken with the same confidence as her colleague—but now, for the first time, she found herself frightened of the darkness.

You've gone on night dives before, she told herself, trying to calm her nerves. *You know that low visibility makes you nervous.*

Even as she thought it, she saw another flash of silver and let out an involuntary squeak.

"Not you too," chuckled Anjali.

"No," said Lily, "shine the light over here, there was something..." She extended her arm to point.

"Don't panic," said Dr. Hansen. "We've studied the biology of this ocean, and there's nothing to be worried about."

Probably hoping to humor her, Anjali turned the floodlight away from the artifact, toward the dark water where Lily was pointing.

It took Lily's brain a moment to process what she was seeing. At first, it looked like a ring of needles nearly four feet in diameter. Something glinted black on either side of the imperfect circle.

Eyes. The dark reflections were eyes.

Lily understood that the needles were teeth less than a second before they closed over her arm, piercing her suit and severing the limb from her body in a single powerful bite.

————

ANJALI WATCHED in horror as Lily's arm was ripped from her body.

"But there's nothing *alive* down here," she whimpered. "We've scanned before... we've reviewed the samples..." She could see the truth for herself, but that didn't mean that she'd accepted it yet.

"Get back to the ship," said Dr. Hansen.

"But—"

"*Anjali*," she said. "*Now.*"

Anjali reached toward Lily. "Come on," she said.

It was stupid—not just foolish, but genuinely idiotic—to slow herself down by hauling Lily with her. The other woman was already convulsing. Between nitrogen narcosis, blood loss, and hypothermia, she'd be dead long before they reached the ship.

But if Anjali knew one thing, it was that she wasn't the type of person to leave her friends behind. Everything else she knew to be true had just been proven wrong, but this was a *fact*.

She kicked up through the water, hauling Lily along with her. Holding onto her colleague's arm meant that she no longer had a free hand for the floodlight, but they were closing in on the submarine now, and she could rely on the ship's lighting.

It was probably a symptom of her panic, but the water seemed to be vibrating, as if the movement of the artifact had somehow extended to the whole sea. Lily had gone limp in her arms.

Anjali had almost reached the sub when she was cut off by a flash of scales. The creature passed before her, long and thin and pale.

Not silver. Which meant that it wasn't the same thing that had gotten Lily.

There's more than one, she thought frantically. *Whatever it is, there's more than one.*

She finned desperately toward the submersible, praying that she'd reach it in time. Lily slipped slightly, and Anjali pulled her closer, holding her in place with one arm while reaching for her flashlight, hoping to get her bearings for reentering the lockout chamber. Instead of *Moby Dick*'s familiar profile, however, she was met with the sight of a seething mottled grey mass.

"Hansen?" she breathed.

"Are you on board, Anjali?" the doctor's voice replied.

She swallowed, sweeping her light across the length of the sub. The surface was totally obscured by a swarm of crustaceans, each as long as her arm. *Isopods*, she thought, *or something like them.*

"Can you see my camera?" she asked.

In answer, she heard the sharp intake of Hansen's breath. "What the...?"

Anjali was still floating there, stunned, when a huge black bulk passed directly above her, headed for the ship.

"Hansen!" Anjali began. She was prepared to cry out in warning, but it was too late. A creature as large as a blue whale opened its massive jaws and caught the vessel between its sharklike teeth. Hansen screamed into the mic as isopods scattered.

Then the lights went out, and it was only Anjali in the darkness. Lily hadn't moved in ages, and Hansen's channel was dead.

"Anjali?" asked Dr. Chang. "Are you there?"

She felt something brush past her leg, and she swallowed hard. There was no ship, and no way back to the surface.

When she'd signed up for the space program, her family had told her that she was crazy. She hadn't been afraid; she'd *wanted* to see the wonders of space. For her whole life, Anjali had thought of herself as brave.

This was her moment of truth, and she didn't like what she saw inside herself. In her mind, if she was ever faced with a crisis, Anjali had believed that she would fight until the bitter end and face her death bravely.

Nothing was as she'd thought it was. Not even this.

In the total darkness of an alien sea, she clung to the corpse of her colleague and friend. As the massive beast that had destroyed the sub circled back, Anjali switched off her light so that she wouldn't have to see its final approach.

8

"WHAT THE *HELL* DID YOU DO?" Lowell demanded, stomping toward Munroe as Anjali's dying screams echoed through the speakers. His heart was pounding in his throat, and he could feel himself shaking with anger.

The lieutenant didn't even bother to look toward him. "Settle down, Private. This isn't your concern."

Lowell grabbed him by the shoulder, spinning him around and advancing on him until he had Munroe backed against the wall. "*Hansen* was my concern. *Lily* was my concern." Even as he said it, he felt the old pinch of shame. He had failed. Again. And he couldn't even remember either of the women's full names. He'd been so careful to keep his distance in case something happened, and he'd been standing *right here*, unable to protect anyone.

Munroe might not have held the gun that killed them this time, but he was responsible for the scientists' deaths all the same. There would be another cover-up, another handful of deaths swept under the rug, another cluster of mourning families who'd be fed another line of BS about equipment malfunctions or enemy attacks.

And Munroe would walk away from it.

Again.

"She trusted you," snarled Lowell through gritted teeth. *She trusted me.* "And you let her walk right into a deathtrap."

Munroe grabbed his wrist, bending Lowell's hand back until the nerves pinched and the joint of the suit grated against bone. "Do you really think I give a damn, Private? I had a job to do here, and it's done. If you know what's good for you, you'll stick to your lane."

How many times had Lowell told himself those very words? Dozens, probably. Had Munroe been the one to say them first?

If anyone deserved to have been ripped apart, it was Munroe.

"Are you going to stand down?" asked Munroe. Any glare of light on the polished helmet made it difficult to see the face of the person inside, but standing only a few inches away from his old commander, Lowell could see his expression clearly enough. He looked unshaken, completely at ease with his role as murderer.

He looks like a goddamn golden boy, thought Lowell furiously. *Like shit doesn't stick to his shoe.*

The sound of rifles being unslung behind him drew his attention to the fact that Munroe had two other men standing in the room who wouldn't hesitate to shoot Lowell in the back. If they were good little soldiers, like he'd been, their trigger fingers were already itching.

"I should have taken care of you on Mars," Munroe said in a low, smug voice. "We can correct that now." He nodded his head imperceptibly over Lowell's shoulder, as if he needed a reminder of the power dynamic.

Unlike Munroe and his men, Lowell didn't have a weapon.

And as small as the compartment was, it was large enough that he'd have to take at least two steps to get to the nearest man. Too long. He needed an advantage, and he didn't have one. Not yet, at least.

Reluctantly, Lowell stepped back.

"Good boy," Munroe said.

Lowell was still bristling when he heard a terrified squeak echo through his mic. He turned to find the linguist, Dr. Chang, bent over the bright silver tablet from which he'd been reading.

"*After a day, the sleeper will wake...* What sleeper?" he asked in a high, shaky voice. His finger was resting at the bottom of the tablet, but he was looking at Munroe. "You know what that means, don't you?"

Munroe chuckled. "Indeed I do. It means we've got twenty-four hours to get off this frozen rock."

Lowell's gaze flicked toward the clock; it was a little after 1400 hours. The station stuck to a 24-hour cycle, since most of the researchers came from Earth.

But a solar day on Enceladus was 33 hours. He assumed that Munroe had misspoken, but the linguist didn't contradict him. Then again, the tablet was from Earth, so maybe that solar day made sense.

Dr. Chang moved to stand.

"No need to get up," said Munroe, unclipping the holster at his hip and sliding his gun out. "I'm afraid you've reached the end of your shelf-life, Peter. Like I told you before, I don't waste time with dead weight."

The scientist whimpered and hunched his shoulders. If Lowell had ever doubted that the man was here under duress, those doubts vanished.

Everyone had bent over backwards to make sure that Munroe got what he wanted, and it was never enough. People were a commodity to him. Hansen had been a commodity. They were all disposable, as far as Munroe was concerned.

The bolt of white-hot anger that shot through Lowell at that moment was almost too much to contain. But it didn't cloud his thinking so much that he didn't see the opening that Munroe had presented him when he drew his weapon.

With a furious cry, Lowell drove toward Munroe, tackling the man before he could take aim. Dr. Chang shrieked as the two men toppled to the floor, so loud that static popped in Lowell's ears. He didn't let it slow him down, and instead drove his fist into Munroe's ribs.

In addition to protecting them from the cold and the unstable atmosphere, the hard shell of the suits provided a measure of physical protection. Still, Lowell knew them well enough to be familiar with their weak points. There was a soft seam between the chestplate and the backplate. Munroe grunted in pain as Lowell jammed his fingertips hard into the lieutenant's ribs.

Lowell figured he had exactly a nanosecond before one of Munroe's men put a bullet in his spine, so he took his old commander in a bear hug and rolled on his back so Munroe was above him, between himself and his lackeys.

The neck was another weak point. Lowell smashed his fist into the flexible joint over the other man's Adam's apple. As Munroe gasped and reached for his neck, Lowell spun him around and dragged him to his feet, still keeping his frame between himself and the rest of the room. Then he wrapped one arm around his chest and jabbed the barrel of the pistol up under his chin.

"Nobody move," Lowell barked.

The two recruits who had accompanied Munroe glanced at one another, their semis raised, prepared to open fire.

"What the hell do you think you're doing?" Munroe hissed.

"Saving the only person you haven't gotten around to killing yet," Lowell replied. "Dr. Chang, you're here against your will, aren't you?"

The man nodded. It was obvious from his posture that he was terrified.

"If you think you're going to walk out of this in one piece..." Munroe began.

"Do us both a favor and shut up," Lowell said, "Do you think I wouldn't *love* an excuse to pop this mask off your head and watch you die like those poor bastards on Mars?"

He felt Munroe go rigid, and the other man's breathing sped up. Yeah, he'd gotten the point, all right. Maybe he'd even heard something in Lowell's voice that proved his point.

How does it feel, Larry, to be trapped for once? All through the inquest, he'd grinned like the smug jackwad he was, knowing that nothing could touch him.

But the angels who watched over your proceedings aren't here.

"Whether I live or not doesn't particularly matter to me," Lowell told him. He felt a tiny twinge in his chest at the thought of Heather getting notice of his death, and of how Kylie would react to hearing that her mysterious Uncle Carp wouldn't be sending video messages anymore—but he'd never really imagined himself going back home, anyway.

His dad would probably just sigh when he heard the news. He'd given up on his oldest son a long time ago.

Lowell tipped his head toward Dr. Chang. "Come on. You're with me."

Dr. Chang got to his feet and hurried to Lowell's side, clutching the tablet to his chest.

"Open the door," said Lowell. "We're getting out of here."

Chang put his hand to the wall sensor, and it slid aside. The hatch would automatically open when approached, but Lowell wanted it open before he and Munroe moved. Lowell didn't really have a plan other than trying to stay alive.

Lowell started backing toward the hatch. Munroe grumbled, but Lowell only tightened his grip. If he'd been alone, he could have fired then and there and been done with it. Even knowing Munroe's men would blow him to bits, he had to fight the urge.

After Mars, Lowell had felt lost, without purpose. Now he knew: he was the only person on Enceladus who could see through Munroe's bullshit and stop whatever the hell he was trying to do.

·

9

PETER WAS PRETTY sure that the gun-wielding madman who'd just saved his life had a death wish, which wasn't hugely reassuring. On the other hand, he wasn't actively trying to murder anyone, which meant that he was Peter's best friend at the moment—and his only bet for survival, it seemed.

That's a pretty low bar, thought Peter, but it was probably the best he was going to get.

As they backed out the hatch, Peter kept his eyes on Munroe's men. *Although what's the point? If they try to shoot us, it's not like I have a weapon. Maybe I can use the tablet as armor...*

They'd only just stepped out into the narrow passageway when Peter felt the floor shaking.

"What's that?"

"I'm going to bet a lot of armed men running in this direction," Lowell said entirely too calmly. "Now get ready to close that hatch."

"Did you really think this little stunt of yours was going to be effective?" asked Munroe in a voice to match Lowell's.

I'm surrounded by sociopaths, Peter thought, closing his eyes and holding his breath as his hand hovered over the sensor on the wall next to the hatch.

Lowell released Munroe, then lifted one leg and kicked the lieutenant in the small of his back. "Now," he snapped.

Peter slapped his hand down just as Munroe stumbled and fell forward into the comm station. Peter heard a shot ping off the hatch as it closed.

"Can you run?" Lowell asked Peter. Without waiting for an answer—which would have been *no* in any case—he turned and grabbed Peter's arm, dragging him down the hall of the research station.

"Where are we going?" Peter exclaimed. Behind them, the hatch slid back open and Munroe lurched out, just as a group of soldiers came storming in from the opposite end of the corridor. Peter couldn't hear him or see anymore, because they raced around a sharp turn in the narrow passageway, but it didn't take an advanced degree to work out what was going on.

"Your guess is as good as mine, Dr. Chang," Lowell informed him.

Peter whimpered, already panting for breath. "I'm not even a real doctor."

"Then we'd better not get shot," Lowell replied. Either it was a joke, or he really didn't understand the hierarchy of academia.

A few weeks ago, Peter had drunkenly whined to his friends that he would kill to get his doctorate early. He hadn't banked on risking life and limb for an honorary title.

They rounded another corner. Lowell reached overhead and slammed a heavy steel door behind them, latching it. Unlike the other hatches he'd seen, this one clearly wasn't automatic.

"That'll slow them down for a minute," he grunted. Then he turned and reached toward Peter's helmet.

"Don't take it off, I need that!" Peter exclaimed.

"Hold still," said Lowell impatiently. "I just want to switch your channel. Munroe can still hear us."

Sure enough, Peter heard a soft curse through the mic, and then a distant *beep* as Lowell finished messing with the settings.

"There we go," said Lowell, after fiddling briefly with his own helmet. "Now we're on a private channel."

"Great," Peter said, his voice coming out high and shaky. "Except that we're still trapped in a settlement in deep space, and the entire US military wants us dead."

"Not the *entire* military," Lowell corrected, setting off down the hallway at a brisk trot. "Just the Space Corps, if I had to guess."

"Is that supposed to be a joke?" Peter sputtered.

"I'm really not sure," Lowell said over his shoulder.

Peter hurried along in his wake, looking back over his shoulder at the door; he could distantly hear someone pounding against it, but so far the heavy latch had held.

"We have two advantages," Lowell said as he hurried along. "Munroe's guys are competent, but they don't know the station as well as I do. The other guys who *do* know the station are all idiots."

"Great," said Peter weakly. "Let's pretend that we do somehow get out of this station alive. What then?"

Lowell grunted. "You ask a lot of questions."

"Pertinent ones," Peter muttered, but he was out of breath from the effort of keeping up. He'd never been big into cardio, and he felt on the brink of a heart attack anyway, after what had happened with the research team.

Giant fish. Living fossils. *Alien life.* Peter would have been thrilled to be around to witness the discovery, provided that the circumstances had been different. He'd never felt so bad about being *right* before.

Talking had become too difficult, and given Lowell's attitude, there didn't seem to be much point anyway. Peter found his mind wandering to the footage of the sea monsters that had trashed Dr. Hansen's ship, and the mysterious Anomaly itself. If only he could see the markings on that smooth silver surface, he might stand a better chance of figuring out what the heck they were up against.

He was so deep in thought that when Lowell stopped, Peter crashed into him.

"Sorry," he mumbled. "What's going on?"

They had come to a crossing corridor, and Lowell was looking first one way, then the other.

"Armory's that way," said Lowell, pointing to the left. "But the pods are to the right. I've only got two guns on me. Are you armed?"

"No," said Peter.

"You know how to shoot?"

Peter flinched. "Well, I *do* hold a high score in *Fallout: Mars...*"

"For Christ's sake," Lowell muttered.

The words were hardly out of his mouth when something pinged off the wall above Peter's head. It took him a moment to realize that it was bullet, but by then Lowell was already moving to the right.

"Okay," he grunted, "pods it is."

"Won't they try to cut us off before we get there?"

"Probably," Lowell admitted. "But if you've got a better idea for how to get out of here, I'd love to know."

Fair enough.

Peter had been right: a second group of men cut them off before they reached the hall. When he saw their guns pointed at him, Peter froze, remembering how Connor's head had blown apart against the tent canvas.

A hand closed over the back of his neck and shoved him down. Peter's chest hit the floor just as the men behind them opened fire.

He closed his eyes—he still hadn't gotten used to the disconnect of only having partial audio. He couldn't hear the report of the pistols, but he could feel them in his chest each time one of the soldiers pulled the trigger.

After what felt like a very long time, Lowell hauled him back to his feet. "Come on," he said. "We should keep moving."

Peter took a shuddering breath and looked around him at the two clusters of fallen soldiers. One of them was still moving, limbs flailing as the person tried in vain to cover the bullet holes in their suit. As Peter watched, their movements slowed, then stopped altogether.

Lowell dropped the gun he'd taken from Munroe and snatched up a replacement. Then he stepped over the bodies, still headed toward the pods. "Keep up, Chang," he barked.

Peter tried to obey, but he kept looking down at the corpses scattered across the floor of the hallway. Inside each one of those suits was a person who'd deserved better, someone like Amira or Jana or Connor.

Someone like me.

He let out an involuntary gasp and sank back to the floor as his trembling legs gave way beneath him. Halfway down the corridor, Lowell paused and looked back.

He's going to leave me here, Peter thought bleakly. *We don't have time for this. Munroe was right about me. I'm dead weight.*

To his surprise, he heard Lowell's sigh echo through the mic, and then the big man came jogging back, bending down into a crouch in front of Peter.

"Listen," he said. "I know this is too much to handle. You got dragged into this, right? You don't really strike me as a fighter."

Peter shook his head, unable to form a reply. If he tried to talk, he was probably going to end up crying like the big, stupid baby that he was.

"I can't promise we're going to make it out of here alive," Lowell said, the bouncing of his leg the only thing that gave away his eagerness to keep moving. "And even if we do, we might end up stuck on this godforsaken moon. But you know what I can promise?"

"A glorious death?" Peter asked, trying to perk himself up with a lame joke.

Lowell barked a laugh. "Nah. But I can promise that we're going to piss Munroe off, right to the bitter end." His voice turned serious. "And even if I don't make it home in one piece, I'm going to do my damnedest to stop whatever sick plan he's got going."

If I don't keep moving, Peter thought, *then my friends died for nothing. This is bigger than me, and Lowell is right—someone needs to put Munroe in his place. That's what a hero would do.* He might not know much about fighting, but after a lifetime of movies and video games and even the occasional novel, he knew all about heroes. The good guys weren't always fearless, but they weren't quitters, either.

Peter nodded, then climbed to his feet, clinging to the tablet like a lifeline. "I can get behind that." An assurance of success would have rung hollow, but Peter had always hated disappointing people: his father, his teachers, his friends. If a badass like Lowell thought that Peter was worth coming back for, then Peter owed it to him to at least try to keep up.

"Great," said Lowell. "Now, let's go ruin this bastard's day."

10

THE MORE LOWELL thought about it, the less confident he felt that the two of them were going to make it off of Enceladus alive. That was a shame, especially as far as Chang went. If he could spare the nerd, maybe he'd find some peace in whatever waited after death.

But Lowell forced himself to look at the big picture. A team of scientists had been killed on Mars half a decade ago for the purpose of securing the orb—and even then, the Chinese military had been sniffing around in the hopes of tracking down the same thing. Whatever they were after was *big*, and today, Munroe had set it in motion. Four years ago, Lowell had failed. Now he had a second chance to fix whatever his old commander had broken.

All this time, Munroe had been working toward this moment, toward whatever the hell had happened with the Anomaly less than an hour ago. If the Space Corps and the Pentagon were this invested in whatever the end result was supposed to be, enough that they were willing to give a rabid dog like Munroe a long leash and no consequences...

Then Lowell wanted to make sure it didn't happen.

Does that mean I'm actively committing treason right now? he mused. Either way, if the higher-ups got their hands on him now, they were going to nail him to the wall. They had almost reached the pod bay when Lowell made up his mind.

There was no point heading skyward. Munroe would find them anyway. Lowell was going to find the Anomaly, and he was going to stop whatever was happening, if it was the last thing he did in his life.

"You ever heard of sailboating?" Lowell asked.

"Like, with a yacht?" asked Chang, cocking his head. "Yeah, my stepdad owns one."

"No, not like—" Lowell rolled his eyes. "God. Forget it. If you zig-zag when you run, you'll make yourself harder to hit." He put his hands on the door handles, then hesitated. "And listen. You might want to grab your own pod, okay? We should probably split up."

"What?" Chang yelped. "No. No way. You want me to fly a spaceship?"

"I'm going to the Anomaly," Lowell told him. "You're probably better off on your own."

Peter blanched. "But you saw what happened down there."

"I sure did," Lowell said. "And it started with whatever the hell Munroe had them doing. So I'm going to go undo it."

Peter let out a long hiss like a deflating balloon, then stepped closer to Lowell. "You're not going to get very far without a map," he said, indicating the tablet. "You need me—and besides, there's no way I'm going to be able to pilot a ship on my own. I don't even have my driver's license."

"Suit yourself," Lowell told him. "Doesn't matter to me either way."

Still, when he flung the doors open, he couldn't help smiling to himself. The guy might be a bit of a nerd, but he was a *smart* nerd, and apparently he had more guts than Lowell had given him credit for.

The near-spherical hoverpods were parked in rows, resting on rubber bumpers that kept them upright in the research station's enhanced gravitational field. Out on Enceladus' surface, they were able to easily skim above the ice, taking advantage of the moon's low gravity. A large portion of the cockpit was encased in tinted glass, so that its pilots could observe the landscape around them without being blinded by the reflection of the icy landscape.

"Head for number forty-nine," Lowell said, then lifted his pistol. "Look for cover, and stay low. And don't forget to weave. Go!"

After a slight hesitation, Chang bolted past him, running with his head down toward the nearest pod. He let out a sharp noise of surprise when a bullet hit the ground next to his feet. Lowell turned in the direction from which the shot had been fired. If he'd had a *real* gun, a semi or an assault rifle, he would have fired off a dozen shots right then, but he hadn't exactly brought heavy artillery with him. He waited until he saw movement from the far end of the bay, and then fired at the dark square of the gunman's face shield. The glass shattered, and the figure dropped.

Chang had already reached the cover of the nearest pod and had taken shelter behind it. Lowell could hear his heavy breathing echoing through the mic.

"You're doing great," Lowell told him, calculating the distance between himself and the place where Chang crouched. He'd need roughly eight seconds to cover the distance.

I could really use some backup, he thought. The thought made him chuckle. *Although, honestly, when was the last time I had someone on my side? Chang might not be an asset in a gunfight, but moral support is better than nothing.*

No time like the present. Lowell bent forward like an Olympic runner preparing for the hundred-yard dash, then shot out into the open.

Six seconds into his run, he felt something graze the top of his helmet. He threw himself forward, rolling toward where Chang was hidden as he tried to pinpoint the shot's origin. It had come from the open walkway above the bay. There were two figures along the railing, each holding rifles. Lowell lifted his pistol; the first shot hit one of the snipers square in the face, sending him toppling over the railing to land in a broken, writhing heap on the floor below. The next shot pierced the throat of his companion, who fell backward into the wall.

God, I wish that had been Larry Munroe, thought Lowell. *I wish I'd killed him when I had the chance.*

I should have.

"We're headed there," he said aloud, pointing to where his pod waited in the middle of the fleet. "You go first, and I'll cover you. Pick a random path, so they won't be able to predict where you'll be coming out."

Chang nodded, then ducked between the pods, head down and weaving, just like Lowell had told him. Shots pinged off the exteriors of the pods around them as Lowell followed. He paused twice to squeeze off another shot, but on the third, the gun jumped uselessly in his hand.

Out of ammo. Without a second thought, he dropped it to the ground, then yanked the Glock VX out of its holster at his waist. No point in carrying an empty gun with him. There would be no resupply of ammunition where they were going.

When they were both crouched next to Hoverpod 49, Lowell handed the gun to Chang.

"What am I supposed to do with this?" the scientist

demanded, holding it out at arm's length, as though it might bite him.

"Just cover me," Lowell said. "I need my hands free."

"But how do I...?"

"Point." Lowell mimed aiming. "Pull." He imitated pulling the trigger. "You can read dead languages, Chang—you can fire a goddamn gun."

As Chang sputtered, Lowell dipped between the pods and mashed his thumb against the keypad on the door, typing in the passcode needed to activate the little ship. He had just hit *Enter* when something collided with his head.

Lowell fell, expecting to hear the hiss of air spilling out of his suit, but it hadn't been a bullet that grazed him. Instead, he found himself staring up at two familiar faces.

Wilcox and Horne stood above him, rifles slung across their chests. Horne looked smug, but it was Wilcox's expression that turned Lowell's stomach. The young man's usually smarmy grin had become feral.

Twerps like him think that shooting someone is revenge for getting their butts kicked, he thought. *God, it's going to be freaking pathetic if one of these idiots offs me.*

Lowell had logged off of the open channel, but he could see Wilcox's face well enough to read his lips as the young recruit mouthed the word, *Snitch.* He pointed his rifle straight unto Lowell's face and winked.

A second later, Wilcox's eyes went blank and glassy as a bullet tore through his neck. Horne spun, gun raised, and then went down as a second bullet passed through the soft seam between the armor plating.

"Oh, fu—" Chang said into the mic, and then retched.

Lowell sat up, looking in surprise at the scientist, who was still gagging at the sight of the dead men. "Good shots," he said, genuinely impressed. They'd been at close range, admittedly, but perfectly aimed.

"Thanks," said Chang, then gagged again. "Oh, God, I could see his *face*..."

Lowell got to his feet, kicking Wilcox's legs aside. "Come on," he said, as gently as he could manage. "You're doing great. Get in the pod."

11

I KILLED SOMEONE.

I killed someone.

I killed someone.

Peter crawled into the hoverpod alongside Lowell, and dropped heavily into a seat. The door swung closed after them, mercifully blocking the view of the two corpses Peter had left in his wake. After all of his righteous indignation about Munroe's behavior, it had turned out that he was no better.

He was capable of murder, when he wanted to be.

"You're okay," said Lowell's voice. "You did what you had to do. You're not going to freak out on me now, are you?"

"No," Peter gulped.

"Great," said Lowell as his hands flew across the hoverpod's controls. "Now buckle your seatbelt. I'm going to break some speed laws."

Peter was still fighting with the seatbelt when the pod roared to life. As he clung to the chair, the silver tablet slipped out of his hands and tumbled around on the floor beneath his feet.

"You'll have to keep your helmet on for this part," Lowell told him, as if he thought that Peter was entertaining some wild fantasy about removing it. "If the hull of the pod is breached, the engines will keep us going, but you'll be SOL on air. If we make it out of the station without blowing up along the way, you can remove it."

"Comforting," Peter told him.

"Something to look forward to, right?"

They took off, shooting straight up unto the air at first, then zipping above the surrounding pods. Being higher made them an easier target, and Peter flinched as the windshield was peppered with gunfire. To his great relief, the glass—or whatever it was—didn't shatter.

"No need to panic yet," Lowell assured him. "These babies were designed to withstand space debris. They can take a few hits."

The note of manic glee in his voice made Peter's skin crawl. "How can you be so upbeat right now?"

"We're not dead," Lowell informed him as they zipped toward the large doors at the end of the bay. "What's not to celebrate?"

"Uh, Lowell?" Peter asked through gritted teeth as he braced for impact. "Doors. Object permanence. *Please slow down.*"

"We're fine," Lowell assured him, reaching up toward the ceiling of the pod and pressing a button.

"What the hell is that?" Peter demanded, squinting. "It looked like a garage door opener."

"Basically," said Lowell. "Don't forget: there might be a military presence here, but the station itself is privately funded. The security here is..." He held out one hand, waggling it back and forth. "Iffy. It's not like the bigwigs at NASA are worried that the place is going to get robbed, and they probably weren't counting on a firefight."

Sure enough, the bay doors opened, and Peter raised his arm to block the flood of blinding white light reflected off the ice outside.

Peter knew well enough that they weren't safe yet, but that didn't stop him from breathing a little sigh of relief as they emerged from the walls of the research station. They'd made it a hell of a lot farther than he'd expected.

And he'd been *useful*.

"You okay over there?" Lowell asked.

"Maybe." Peter nodded, bending down to pick up the tablet. "Yeah, I guess. It's a lot to process, but..."

"But for a guy who's just watched a whole bunch of strangers die, you're coping?" Lowell asked wryly.

Peter frowned down at the tablet, not really seeing it. "Not just strangers."

"Sorry," said Lowell. He reached up to the back of his helmet, undoing the clasp. There was a hissing through the mic, and then he pulled the helmet away.

When he'd tried to imagine what Lowell looked like, Peter had envisioned someone bald and chiseled and possibly sporting facial tattoos. Instead, Lowell just looked tired; he had dark circles under his eyes, close-cropped dark hair sprinkled with grey, and the beginnings of a five o'clock shadow peppering his chin. He set the helmet down beside his chair, then said something. It took Peter a moment to realize that he couldn't hear because they were no longer linked by the radio channel.

After a brief struggle with his own helmet, Peter pulled it free. "What was that?"

"I said I'm sorry about this whole thing. I know Munroe, and he's a real tool."

"Yeah," Peter said, resting the helmet in his lap. "I gathered. So you two know each other?"

"Hmm." Lowell grunted; he seemed to grunt a lot. Apparently,

being stationed on an icy moon didn't give the man a lot of opportunity to improve his conversational skills. "Yeah, you could say
that. He killed some folks we were supposed to protect a few years
back, and he messed up my career in the process."

"Sounds like his style," Peter muttered.

He was prepared to ask more questions, but Lowell's eyes
suddenly turned flinty, and he glanced into the little mirrors inside
the spherical pod's walls. "Oh, hell. Hang onto something."

Peter twisted around in his chair to find three more pods on
their tail. "Oh, good *God*," he muttered. "How are we supposed to
lose them?"

He barely knew Lowell, and for most of their acquaintance,
he'd had to rely on the tone of his voice to know what the other
man was thinking. Even so, when a wide grin spread over Lowell's
face, it didn't take a doctorate to know that it was probably a
warning sign of something dangerous to come.

"I might know a way," Lowell said. "It's a little unpredictable,
but what do we have to lose?"

12

ACCORDING to the scientists Lowell had spoken to, roughly two miles of ice stood between the surface of Enceladus and the salt sea below, as far as *most* of the moon was concerned. The ice at the southern pole was thinner. It had cracked open, giving the moon its characteristic 'tiger stripes'—the long canals that breached the ice to reveal the surface below—and plumes of water from below often burst free along the fault lines.

Hansen would have been able to explain it better, but she'd spent years on Earth studying physics, and then months on Enceladus making sense of the readings. Lowell's understanding of the phenomenon was based entirely on explanations that he had, for the most part, tuned out. All he knew about the plumes was how to navigate them without getting blown off-world.

The southern pole was where Anjali had come to take samples, which had verified the presence of amino acid chains in the plumes and sent the whole research station into an uproar. Lowell had been part of her escort, and he'd navigated the fault lines and the artificial vents the scientists had bored into the ice.

Getting too close to the plumes could send a little weak-motored pod shooting straight into space, much less a person in a suit trying to take vapor samples. Being rocketed unexpectedly into orbit by the force of the plume wouldn't kill a pilot, but the pods' thruster system didn't work very well in space, and nobody wanted to be the guy who had to get towed back to the surface.

I hope it's Munroe's guys on my tail, thought Lowell. *They're not gonna know what hit them.*

"Is this thing meant to go so fast?" asked Chang, who was looking a little down at the mouth and green around the edges. "Because it seems like we're going *really freaking fast.*"

"You want me to slow down so they can shoot us?" asked Lowell, hooking his thumb over his shoulder toward the vessels that were in hot pursuit.

"No," his companion grumbled. His mop of black hair had been flattened by his helmet, and he had the expression of a man who hadn't slept in weeks. He had the slightly malnourished look that was common among the younger scientists who still had something to prove. In spite of all of that, he managed a fairly nasty glare in Lowell's direction. "Of course I don't want to get shot."

"Then hold onto your hat, Chang."

"Peter," he said. "I'd prefer if you called me Peteeeeeeerrrrr..." His teeth rattled and he broke off into a screech as Lowell accelerated; they were closing in on the stripes, and if they were lucky, the folks on their tail would have no idea how to deal with them.

From this distance, the jets looked more like mist or heavy smog than anything else. One of the troubles with navigating deep space was that the usual combat skills most soldiers relied on— smell, sound, even subtle differences like pressure shifts or changes in the wild—were stripped away by the layers of protective gear needed to navigate the hostile environment. Lowell had learned early on that he could primarily rely on things he could *see*. Even that was tricky, because a condition that *looked* like something mundane on Earth could, in reality, be something entirely different out here. Mist could decrease visibility, but it wasn't generally associated with the force of a high-pressure geyser.

Just before they reached the first fault line, Lowell banked right to avoid the chasm, then swerved left.

"Zig-zagging again?" Peter called about the roar of the engines.

"That's what I want them to think," said Lowell.

He glanced at his mirror just in time to see one of the pursuing pods dip into the chasm as it tried to go straight across and then, seconds later, rocket skyward.

Lowell cackled. "Good luck with that, you son-of-a—"

"Duck!" Peter cried.

The other two pods had followed Lowell's trail, and one of them fired a laser blast that threatened to take the top off of their vehicle. Lowell cursed. The lasers weren't meant for combat; they were intended to cut core samples from the ice. He wasn't sure precisely what would happen if they were hit, and he didn't want to risk finding out.

Peter physically ducked in his chair, and Lowell looked over at him in disgust before banking hard to the right, turning so hard that their seats were nearly parallel with the ice.

"'*Duck?*' What the hell good is ducking going to do?" Lowell demanded, righting them.

"You said we'd survive if the hull was compromised!" Peter exclaimed.

"Not with your helmet off, you won't."

Peter immediate bent over and began rummaging around on the floor.

Despite the risks, Lowell left his off. His hands were busy, and besides, it was easier to rely on his peripheral vision when his helmet wasn't getting in the way.

If Munroe's men were going to misuse the equipment, then so was Lowell. He leaned into the steering, spinning the pod one hundred and eighty degrees until their pursuers were locked in his sights. They weren't really meant to drive backwards, but who was going to stop him?

"Watch where we're going!" Peter exclaimed. He was clutching his helmet in one hand, but it hadn't made it onto his head yet. He'd gone deathly pale.

"Keep your eye on the rear camera," said Lowell, taking aim. "Shout if you see anything."

Peter made a strangled noise as Lowell fired. He didn't aim for the pod itself, instead blasting a hole in the ice between them. The shot was clean, and the resulting crack immediately opened like a blowhole, blasting a concentrated geyser of pressurized water directly into the air.

The other pilot had just enough time to react, swerving around the new plume just in time to avoid being launched skyward. They were close enough to the spray, however, for their windscreen to be covered in a fine mist of water droplets. Within moments, the water iced over, obscuring their view of the landscape.

I bet you'd like a de-icer now, thought Lowell. Baring his teeth, he fired on the other ship. The laser cut a perfect core through the center of the windshield, and the pod crashed a moment later, sending the crew tumbling through the glass. One of them had kept their helmet on, but the other—probably the pilot, hoping for a little increased visibility just as Lowell had—must have removed hers. As Lowell sped away, he could see her lips turning blue while she clawed at the front of her suit, gasping for air. If her crewmember got her helmet to her fast enough, she might get lucky and survive, although her vision would never be the same.

Eyeballs froze pretty quickly at −324°F.

Only one more pod to go. Lowell was adjusting his aim when Peter jabbed a finger at the rear camera display.

"Fissure. Fissure. *Lowell. FISSURE.*"

He glanced down at the screen and uttered a soft curse. Peter was right: they were coming up fast on another rift in the ice.

Lowell slammed on the controls so fast that they both lurched back in their seats. A vertebra popped in Lowell's neck, but there was no time to whine about it, as the lone surviving pod was coming up on them fast. He switched to forward acceleration and laid on the throttle, propelling them forward directly toward the enemy pod.

He could feel the smile forming on his lips. For the last four years, he'd been a good boy, playing by the rules while the men around him followed their own selfish codes. He'd tried to keep his head down and walk the straight and narrow. Now that he'd finally given up on that game, he could breathe a sigh of relief and let loose.

13

PETER HADN'T FELT this motion-sick since his parents had taken him to Disneyland as a kid. As Lowell spun them around on the ice, Peter tried to keep his eyes fixed on the horizon. He doubted that a tough guy like Lowell would be impressed with a polite request to drive more smoothly. He clung to his helmet, holding it under his chin like a bowl, just in case.

As they jetted directly at the other pod, Peter braced for impact—but at the last second, Lowell changed course, and they barely clipped the other ship before speeding along parallel to the nearest tiger stripe.

"Is this a combat strategy?" asked Peter breathlessly. "A way to get in their heads? Or do you just have a death wish?"

Lowell swung them around a plume without so much as blinking. "If they catch us, we're dead. If we crash, we're dead. If we get shot into space and Munroe tows us in, we're dead."

"You're not really painting a comforting picture."

"Sorry," he said, shrugging indifferently. "Just being honest."

Back on Earth, Peter had spent most of his life thinking about his doctorate, and his thesis, and whether he was going to have some free time on the weekend for once. He hadn't spent a lot of time mulling over his mortality, at least not until he'd watched the dig team die. Now, it was at the front of his mind. He'd been prepared to be shot along with Connor, or to have Munroe end his life once his usefulness ran out.

All in all, dying in a fiery crash on a distant moon was actually kind of...well, not *cool*, but at least *interesting*, and it would be on terms other than Munroe's.

Still, they had to try something. It seemed to Peter that this last pursuer knew their tricks and it wasn't like they could outrun them.

"Question," Peter said.

Lowell raised an eyebrow. "Is this really the time?"

"I was just looking at the plumes," said Peter, fixing his eyes on the steady spray from the tiger stripes. "I know those geysers are constantly sending ocean material up into space to form one of the rings of Saturn. So I'm guessing that the water is pressurized because the sea's warmer than the surface—well, okay, duh, because it's still liquid down there, which means the core's got to be active—"

"Get to the point," Lowell interrupted, spinning sideways just in time to avoid laser fire from their pursuer.

"The point," said Peter, jabbing his index finger at the window, "is that any opening into the ice is going to be pressurized. So how did the dive team take the sub into the water without letting out a plume of their own?"

"Oh, for *Moby Dick*? They had to take a huge core out of the ice under the station. It was this whole pain in the ass—" Lowell looked up sharply at Peter. "Damn, I'm an idiot." He quickly adjusted their course.

"What?"

"There's a smaller stabilized opening not far from here. They opened it so that they could safely run tests. Anjali and Hansen were taking comparable samples from a bunch of sites, trying to prove some theory about how the tiger stripes were formed and why the southern pole was more geologically active than the northern end."

"That was modeled years ago," Peter said excitedly. "There was this really great article…"

Lowell rolled his eyes and revved the pod's engine—presumably to increase their speed as they reached a more stable portion of the ice, although it also drowned out Peter's explanation.

As they sped across the ice, Peter wondered what his father would have to say about all of this. He would have loved to talk with Hansen and the rest of the team, but that wasn't possible; it would have been nice—kind of—to have the *real* Dr. Chang here for reference.

It had been a long time since Peter had *wanted* his father around, but at least on the surface of an alien world, they'd have had something to bond over other than the various ways that Peter hadn't lived up to his expectations.

"That's it," said Lowell, pointing toward a small tower sticking straight up from the ice. "We can enter the ocean there."

They were closing in on it, keeping steadily ahead of the last pod. Peter's heart was racing with excitement—*We can do this, we can make it, we might actually not die in the next two minutes.*

"While we're asking science-type questions here," Lowell shouted over his shoulder. "How likely is it that there are more of whatever attacked the dive team down there?"

Peter paused, wincing as he remembered the footage from the camera in Lily's helmet. He'd been trying not to think about it. He was more consumed with getting away from the men shooting at them.

But it was obvious that the answer to Lowell's question was that whatever was happening was only going to get worse. And that included whatever had attacked the dive team. Peter still hadn't satisfactorily translated the last part of the tablet, but he could tell it was bad news.

"Probably very likely—"

"Are you *kidding me?*" Lowell snarled.

Peter followed his line of sight toward the sky, but there was nothing there. He opened his mouth to ask a question when he saw something shimmer against the blue expanse above.

"What is that?" he asked, squinting. Another plume of some kind?

A moment later, the spot of shimmering nothing coalesced into a sleek black ship.

"Looks like the Chinese military upgraded their cloaking device," Lowell muttered.

Before Peter could respond, the other ship opened fire.

14

LOWELL HAD NEVER THOUGHT of himself as some great patriot. He hadn't joined the Marines because he believed that his nation was unequivocally better than all the others. Rather, he'd believed in the ideal that serving his country would, in some way, make the world a better place. He'd believed wholeheartedly in his ability to make a difference.

Yeah, right. Back when I was young and stupid and had no idea how the world worked.

Ultimately, he would have been perfectly happy to come to an understanding with an international crew, so long as he was convinced that they were working in the best interests of the human majority. Unfortunately, he'd been fired on by Tiān Zhuānjiā forces one too many times to think that they were a purely benevolent force.

He braced for fire and reached for his helmet in the hopes that, even if his pod took a direct hit, there would still be time to pull it on. If they used a sonic cannon, most likely his organs would be torn to shreds from the inside before he could take another breath.

But the little surface vessel never shuddered under a direct hit, and it was the pod behind him that careened off madly across the ice as its pilots succumbed.

Peter's scream, on the other hand, was so loud that Lowell had to lift one hand to cover his ears.

"What did they do? The other pilot practically exploded!"

"It's a sound cannon," Lowell mumbled. "Although they could probably weaponize your voice, too, good *Lord*..."

Lowell glanced up through the glass. The Chinese pilot was gesturing at him through the glass. He seemed to want Lowell to stop.

"Faster! Faster! We have to get away or they're going to—" Peter pointed wildly out the window. "They're going to do whatever they did to those guys! They'll sound-cannon us into *spam*."

Lowell sighed, but contrary to Peter's instructions, he slowed down.

"What are you doing?" Peter demanded.

"Look, they could have killed us if they wanted to, but they didn't. They aren't attacking now." Indeed, the Chinese ship was hovering over their pod, tracking their movements but holding its fire. Besides, Lowell's pod only had the laser, and it wasn't even technically meant to be a weapon. In a firefight, they didn't stand a chance.

Might as well see what they want.

"You're just going to pull over for an enemy pilot?"

"We're not at war with China," Lowell reminded him.

"So they're the good guys?" Peter asked nervously.

Lowell—who had gotten through years of combat by telling himself that he was acting as a hero—said, "There's no such thing."

He brought the pod to a stop and turned down the thrusters to the same idle setting he'd have used if he was doing maintenance on the research equipment. He kept the power just high enough to stop the spherical transport from toppling over.

Peter rubbed his temples. "Are they our allies, at least?"

"Couldn't tell you." Lowell shrugged. "Officially, yes, but the last time I ran afoul of these guys, they tried to kill me."

Peter grimaced.

"That was also the time Munroe murdered members of our own research team." Lowell shrugged and lifted his helmet, preparing to pull it back on. "I guess my definition of how to tell an ally from an enemy isn't all that clear-cut these days."

Peter considered this. "That was back when Munroe first found the stellar key, right? The orb? On Mars?"

Lowell snorted. "You're seeing the pattern, too. When Munroe shows up, trouble follows." He jerked his head toward the Chinese ship. "Specifically in the form of these guys. Wherever Munroe gets his information, they're getting it, too. I wouldn't be shocked if they monitor our work out here."

As the Chinese vessel landed, Lowell pulled his helmet on. Peter did the same, then moved to open the door of the pod. Before he could, Lowell grabbed him by the back of the suit and yanked him away from the handle.

"What the heck?" Peter yelped.

"Your helmet's not sealed right," said Lowell. "Let me fix it."

He adjusted the helmet, then secured the seal at the back. When he let go of Peter, the linguist turned toward him with an ashen visage.

"I could have died," Peter breathed into the mic.

Lowell shrugged and reached to open the door. "Not right away."

"Comforting," Peter muttered.

The curved door of the pod popped out on its pawl, releasing the seal, then slid along the track so that the whole side of the vessel stood open. Peter watched Lowell carefully, then did the same.

The kid's observant, Lowell noted. Every time he started to think that Peter wasn't firing on all cylinders, the guy proved him wrong.

The Tiān Zhuānjiā and the Space Corps were technically allies, in the sense that they'd generally agreed to turn a blind eye to whatever the other one got up to out here. Even so, Lowell was pretty sure that stepping out of his pod to have a friendly chat, especially after watching the ship fire on another American pod, might very well count as treason. On the other hand, he'd probably committed a hundred forms of treason by now. The brass might have stripped him of his pride after the inquest, but if they got their hands on him now that he'd openly fired on his own troops, they'd gut him like a fish. *Hypocrites. They didn't do squat when Munroe went rogue...unless he was following orders. Either way, nobody's going to give me a pat on the back and a pension, what with all the dust I've kicked up today.*

Talking to an enemy, even if they were your ally on paper, was a little harder in a hostile atmosphere. Lowell couldn't exactly wave a white flag and ask to parlay. He didn't want to tune into the open civilian channel, either—for all Munroe knew, Lowell and Peter were already dead. He might as well keep it that way and buy a little time.

Peter clambered after him, only to immediately slip on the ice. He caught himself on the edge of the pod doorway.

"Problems?" asked Lowell wryly.

"I'm fine," Peter grumbled, trying and failing to get his feet under him. "I'm just not used to this."

"We should have grabbed you some treads." Lowell watched with amusement as Peter pulled himself almost upright, tried to take a step, and immediately toppled over again.

"Oh, yeah, in all of our free time." The linguist grunted irritably as he finally found his footing, then did an awkward series of hip-thrust-meets-foot-shuffle moves to scoot closer to Lowell. "Don't you think we have bigger fish to fry?"

"You talk like my dad," Lowell chuckled, then groaned. "Say, Mandarin wouldn't happen to be one of the many languages you speak, would it?"

"I can read it," Peter said. "Sort of. I prefer dead languages."

Lowell shook his head. "Well, that'll be helpful if these guys kill us."

"Yes, got it," Peter snapped, still shuffle-dancing until he reached Lowell's side, then grabbing his arm for support. "Very clever."

Unlike Peter, the Chinese crew had come prepared. Five figures strode down the gangplank, three of them carrying large guns—laser cannons, by the look of things. When they hit the ice, they didn't slip. The Space Corps' spacesuits were a silvery blue, except for the flexible navy material between the armor's seams; the Chinese uniforms, however, were sleek and black, standing stark against the gleaming permafrost around them.

They had left the plumes behind, along with the mistier portion of Enceladus' atmosphere. Even this far out, though, frozen hailstones still drifted down around them, pinging off Lowell's helmet like raindrops. If Enceladus had anything like Earth's gravity, this part of the moon would be subjected to a near-constant hailstorm. As it was, the loose ice pellets made the ground even trickier to traverse, but didn't land hard enough to do any damage.

Lowell raised a hand in greeting as the little envoy approached. They walked with their shoulders pulled back and their heads held high, as if they were at any ordinary naval parade. Not one of them slipped.

"Showoffs," muttered Peter, who was still struggling to remain upright.

The nearest figure held up a fist, and the other four stopped, falling into a V formation with their leader at the point. Their commander gestured again—*probably talking through the mic, we're just not on the same channel yet*, Lowell reasoned—and one of the other soldiers stepped forward. They held a flattened rectangle in both hands and twisted the knobs on either side. Then they lifted the item aloft.

Lowell couldn't hold back the bark of laughter that escaped him as he realized what he was looking at. *It's a rich man's Etch-a-Sketch.* Low-tech, but clever. The Space Corps was still trying to hack a reliable writing tool for their mission staff, but for the moment they were still using digital options, even though they tended to go haywire in the harsh conditions and the batteries were always dying.

On the screen, the soldier had written, *Channel 444.* Four, Lowell knew, was considered an unlucky number in Chinese culture. This probably didn't bode well for his prospects when it came to negotiating.

Lowell tuned in, then reached over to adjust Peter's channels as well.

"Can you read us?" he asked.

"You're coming in clearly," said a woman's voice. Her words were crisp and precise. He must be hearing the voice of the person who'd written out the channel number, because as soon as she'd finished speaking, she tucked the object under her arm. "I am He Ming, and I will be translating today."

Lowell's gaze flicked toward the commander, whose face was invisible through the helmet. "And they're on a private channel, right?"

He could hear how tight-lipped she was when she said, "Yes."

Well, that sure as hell wasn't what I wanted to hear, he thought grimly. How was he supposed to get a sense of the commander's tone if he couldn't hear it for himself? Lowell had worked with enough translators to know that they could take liberties when they liked, but beggars couldn't exactly be choosers. *Especially when the beggars aren't armed.*

So be it. The Space Corps and the Tiān Zhuānjiā had never exactly seen eye to eye, but there was no harm in talking. "I'm Lowell," he said, "and this is Dr. Chang."

Peter waved.

We must look like a couple of buffoons out here, Lowell thought. His gaze roamed over their surroundings. They were painfully close to their destination; he could see the stabilized hole in the ice from here. It was big enough that the pod should be able to fit through, but the Chinese vessel probably couldn't.

Of course, that would be a moot point if Lowell's organs were all but vaporized before he could reach the entrance.

"It is a pleasure to meet you, gentlemen," said He Ming in a voice that sounded distinctly as though she wasn't smiling. "Could you provide your full names and ranks?"

Lowell sighed. "Private Carpenter Lowell."

"Peter Chang," said Peter, "grad student."

The interpreter nodded. "And are you currently in possession of the stellar key?"

Peter sucked in a breath, and Lowell was sure he was about to play dumb. *What key?*

But Lowell was done playing games. "As a matter of fact, Miss He, we aren't." He cocked his head. "Interested in helping us get it?"

15

THE CHINESE TRANSLATOR glanced at Peter and he just shrugged. He was glad for the spacesuit and helmet that hid his expression. He assumed that Lowell had a plan, but couldn't fathom what it might be.

"I will relay this to my commander. Pardon me." He Ming switched back to her other channel, and what felt like a long conversation ensued.

As they stood there, Peter could almost feel Lowell simmering with potential energy. He was clearly checking his surroundings, considering tactics, planning his next move... If it wasn't for him, Peter would be dead five times over by now.

Peter hadn't kept up with politics in the last few years. If it didn't impact a dig site he was headed to, he basically didn't care. He could have waxed poetic on the nuances of Mesopotamian temple economies, recited the list of Egyptian pharaohs in order of their rule, or drawn a map of the Ancient Greek colonies while explaining the nuances of their relationship to the homeland of Hellas... But as far as modern military alliances went, he didn't have a clue. He couldn't even ask Lowell to explain without the translator overhearing.

After what seemed a very long time, Ming turned back to them. Peter wished he could see her face to know what she was thinking. As it turned out, he didn't need to see her expression to understand that.

"Are you the same Carpenter Lowell who was stationed on Mars four years ago?" she asked, in a voice so frigid it made the landscape around them seem positively tropical by comparison.

"Yeah," said Lowell. He crossed his arms and nodded. "That was me."

The three figures behind He Ming and the commander lifted their weapons into position as one. Whether it was because of Lowell's answering nod, or just because he'd moved, Peter couldn't tell—either way, he hurriedly lifted his hands skyward at once, slipping a little the second he let go of Lowell.

Lowell was right, apparently. *Allies* was a relative term.

"Then there's no point in playing games, Private Lowell. You will either tell us where to find the stellar key, or you will be killed the moment we return to our ship."

Arms still crossed, Lowell cocked his head to one side again. "Tell you? I'll do you one better than that, Miss He. I'll show you."

Peter's mind went completely blank for approximately three seconds, which was exactly enough time for Lowell to swing around, arm extended, and shove him in the chest so hard that he fell over and slid across the ice back toward the pod. The ground wasn't perfectly level, but with the lower gravity of Enceladus, there wasn't enough drag to bring him to a stop until he crashed into the little transport.

"What the—" he began, and looked up to find Lowell skating toward him on a collision course with all the grace of an Olympic figure skater. Peter's eyes widened.

Just before he reached the pod, Lowell twisted sideways and dropped to his knees, bumping into its side next to Peter.

"Get up," he growled, hauling Peter up and shoving him through the door.

Two of the soldiers had opened fire with what appeared to be laser guns, sending bright beams of energy arcing through the air. When Peter turned his head, he saw that the third armed man had jumped toward them. Unburdened by the moon's low gravity, he leapt high into the air, gun aimed right at Lowell's back.

Not a chance in Hell, Peter thought grimly. *I'm not going to watch another friend die.* He reached for the gun strapped to Lowell's hip and yanked it free of its holster, then lifted it in front of him. There was no time to aim—it wasn't like Peter knew what the hell he was doing anyway. Still, he had a clear shot, and was firing point blank. Just as the Chinese soldier opened fire with his laser rifle, Peter squeezed the Glock's trigger. The force of the gun's report jolted him back hard into the side of the pod, and the force of the bullet's impact carried his enemy back into the air.

The laser shot went wide as the soldier drifted back to the ice, landing on his back. He wasn't dead, but Peter watched, entranced, as the other man tried to plug the bullet hole in his chestplate with a finger. *That can't possibly work...*

"Nice shot," Lowell said, dragging Peter back into the cockpit. He slammed the door shut on its tracks behind him.

"Where are you going?" cried He Ming. "Surely you know you cannot escape."

"I told you," grumbled Lowell. "We're going to show you where to find what you're looking for. We're taking you to the key." Without another word, he slammed on the throttle, and the pod roared to life beneath them.

16

LOWELL WATCHED the Tiān Zhuānjiā soldiers in his rear camera. He'd expected them to stay behind and see to their downed crewmember. Instead, as the soldier Peter had shot flailed amid the hailstones, the ship took off in his wake.

Shit. They left the pilot on board in case we bailed.

"Nice shooting, kid," Lowell said, wondering if those would be the last words he'd ever say.

"Are you kidding? I've started an international incident." Peter was panting into the mic. "I'm going to be the reason we go to war with China, millions will die…"

"Nah," drawled Lowell. He braked suddenly, sending Peter flying forward into the controls as the Chinese vessel swooped overhead. He wanted to stay out of range of their cannons, and piloting like an absolutely nutjob would at least make him hard to hit. "This is special ops territory, am I right, Miss He? This is all going to get swept under the rug."

"I don't believe you faced any serious consequences for

shooting down *our* ships, did you, Mr. Lowell?" she asked drily. "Your government made that all disappear."

Yeah, but they weren't saving my bacon when they did it, Lowell thought. *They were cleaning up after Munroe.*

The stabilized hole in the ice wasn't technically designed for ship entry. There were special pressure-stable canisters, made for sample collection, that Anjali had sent down on the automated sample retrieval track—but Lowell was pretty sure that the hole was wide enough that a pod could fit. It was certainly wide enough at the top. Hopefully it was the same size all the way down.

I guess we'll find out.

"Hold onto your helmet," Lowell said, throwing the pod into forward motion again. Ahead, the enemy ship was looping back to take another shot at them. All he had to do was stay out of the other ship's sights long enough to make it through the ice.

Peter squinted at the hole as they approached, then reached over to grab Lowell's arm.

"Do we have a plan in case what happened to the dive team happens—"

"Hey, hey," Lowell interrupted. "We're not the only ones in this conversation, remember?"

"Can we even survive down there?" Peter asked. "Lowell, what if we drown?"

"This thing is airtight. It's spaceproof. It's *fine.*"

"Will the engines still work underwater?"

"Chang, read my lips," Lowell said. "It's an all-terrain vehicle. It has underwater thrusters. I've piloted these things through air, water, gas, and even a nebula cloud. You want to know how the individual components work? Read the manual and *stop distracting me.*"

Peter didn't let go of his arm, and Lowell found himself

holding his breath. If the hole wasn't big enough, or if the aircraft fired its sound cannon before they were deep enough...

The only way out is through, buddy boy. No point in dwelling on the possibility of disaster. If it came right down to it, he'd rather be shot down by an indifferent foreign military than by a stone-cold bastard like Munroe.

Just before they reached the hole in the ice, Lowell felt the strange sensation of standing too close to a massive speaker, the bass thrum of a poorly balanced stereo accompanied by a flickering static, as if he was video-scrubbing the world around him.

It's the cannon, he thought as the sensation intensified. He unconsciously lifted his hands to his head, abandoning the controls, desperate for anything that might allow him to hurt just a little less, even for a moment. *They got us.*

A second later, the world dropped away.

The moment the pod fell through the hole in the ice, the pain eased. The humming pulse of the cannon gave way to a gut-wrenching freefall. Lowell looked up in time to see the black bulk of the Chinese warship blot out the sky. Its relative size might be an advantage in a firefight, but it also meant that the ship couldn't follow them through the hole.

"Take that, suckers!" Lowell cackled, extending a middle finger toward the ship, even though there was no way it could see them.

Then the pod hit the first stabilizing ring and the seawater restrained below. The force of their drop nearly flattened Lowell back into his chair.

"You are not as clever as you think you are," said He Ming through the mic.

"Maybe not," Lowell told her, letting himself go limp with relief for just a moment. "But I'm not dead yet, and that's something."

He changed the channel before she could threaten them further, tuning back into the private channel he and Peter had been using earlier.

He could feel that they were still sinking, and so far, the hole hadn't narrowed. If he fired the thrusters, he could take them further and faster, but he wasn't in any particular rush to get to the depths. After all, Peter had a point: there were monsters down there, apparently. Some of them were big enough to take down a goliath like *Moby Dick*; the pod would be snack-sized to something like that.

Lowell checked the clock on the pod's dash. It was almost 1800 hours, which meant that they'd stormed out of the command center only four hours ago. Lowell felt like he'd aged a hundred years in that time.

He reached up to remove his helmet once again, then lay back once more, staring at the roof of the pod. Everything had been happening so fast, he'd barely had time to think. What were they going to tell Heather? Would she buy whatever lie the Space Corps sold her, or would she know, deep in her heart, that he had gone down fighting? He almost hoped that she wouldn't—it would be easier for her to believe a convenient lie. *The power went out on the research station, and everyone died instantly. We're so sorry, Mrs. Godfrey. No, we weren't able to recover the body. At least it was painless.*

The really sick part was that, aside from his sister and possibly Kylie, there was no one on Earth who would give a damn he was gone. Well, Collins and Vasko, maybe, but they didn't really count.

His father wouldn't have much to say, that was for sure. He probably wouldn't even come to the funeral.

"What now?" Peter panted, startling Lowell out of his self-pitying spiral. "We've got two armies after us, and we're diving into an ocean with living fossils, apparently, who will view us as lunch."

"I guess we've got twenty hours to figure that out." Lowell sat up, then maneuvered the ship so that they weren't tilted backward anymore. The mere fact that they were upright again made him feel calmer, more in control.

A thought struck him. "Hey, why is it a 24-hour day and not a 33-hour day?"

"What?"

"When you read the inscription, you said the sleeper would wake in a *day*. But a solar day here is 33 hours."

Peter shook his head. "The cuneiform symbols provide a visual representation of an Earth day. It's clear that whatever was triggered would culminate in that period."

Lowell frowned. "Did you tell Munroe that? Because he immediately knew we had 24 hours."

Peter shrugged.

"That bastard knows way too much about what's going on," Lowell grumbled. "Meanwhile, we don't know where we're going or what we're doing."

"We have *some* idea," Peter corrected. He bent down between his feet to retrieve the shining silver tablet. "After all, that's what Munroe wanted me for in the first place. I'm the only one here who can read the map."

17

"SOME MAP. It wasn't super helpful the first time around, was it?" asked Lowell, cocking an eyebrow at him. His face seemed to be trapped in a perpetual scowl, the type of expression Connor would have called 'resting asshole face'. "All you really did was tell them what to do with the key."

"That's because Hansen already knew where the Anomaly was," Peter pointed out. "They probably had coordinates on file, since they'd already found it during one of their research missions. We, on the other hand, have absolutely *no* idea where we're going from here." He tapped one finger against the tablet. "But the map knows, and it all makes a bit more sense now. *The giantess* probably refers to Saturn itself, and the *great plume* is that phenomenon we just navigated. It's like I thought when I looked at it the first time: these are landmarks. They're just not landmarks on *Earth.*" Peter's excitement was mounting with each passing moment, and he hovered over the tablet, feeling the familiar rush of adrenaline that came with understanding.

This is how Lowell feels during a firefight, he realized. Combat, so far, made Peter sick to his stomach, but Lowell probably felt amped up and punchy, just as Peter did now.

"Okay, so this thing can tell us where to go?" Lowell frowned. "How? There aren't even pictures."

"But there are *words*," Peter argued.

Lowell leveled a steady glare at him. "Don't get smart with me, Chang. I can read just fine, but I can't make heads or tails of that crazy chicken-scratch. You can dial back the smugness, or I'll hit the ejector button and launch you back topside to deal with the Chinese soldiers we just pulled aggro on."

"There *isn't* an ejector button, is there?" Peter asked, looking around nervously.

Lowell's face was completely blank as he met Peter's eyes. "Is there? You tell me."

"I'm not trying to be a pain in the neck," Peter assured him hurriedly. "I'm just saying, we both have our skills. You can fly this thing, and I can be the navigator. Teamwork, am I right?"

Lowell sat back in his seat, still eyeing Peter narrowly. "Sure," he said. "Sounds like a plan. Where do we start?"

Peter swallowed, gaze still skimming over the controls to see if there really was an ejector button somewhere. "We're not that far from the plumes, right?"

"You mean the tiger stripes?" Lowell asked. "Nah, we're pretty close. Enceladus isn't all that large, and I can tell you what direction they're in. We're not going to want to go under them, though. If we did that, we'd..." He mimed a cork popping out of a bottle, smacking his lips for emphasis.

"Right." Peter looked down. He unconsciously tried to nibble his thumbnail the way he did during important exams, only to realize he was still wearing his gloves. With a sigh, he lowered both hands to the tablet, using one to hold it and one to follow along as he read. "Okay, this says... hang on, what does this even *mean?*"

Lowell turned his attention to the controls. "Ejector. Button."

"No, no!" Peter exclaimed. "This is just really... I mean, it's so *odd*. This makes it sound like there are all sorts of landmarks. But you were there, right, watching the live feed from Hansen's ship? You saw that the floor was almost completely smooth."

"It's an old map, right?" Lowell shrugged. "I don't know much about geology, but it's possible that the sea floor has changed in the last few thousand years, isn't it?"

Peter sighed, throwing his hands in the air. "Then the map is useless!"

"Don't panic yet," Lowell told him, accelerating so that they sank faster. "After all, yesterday, Hansen would have sworn up and down that there was no vertebrate life in these oceans, just... you know, proteins or whatever. Things change, and as we've seen, they change *fast*. There's something up with this moon."

"*This is no moon*," Peter said, then chuckled at his little joke.

Lowell barely dignified that comment with an eyeroll.

The pressure kept building, and Peter had to continue clearing his ears as they descended. His father had read all the journals, but Peter only retained snippets of what they'd discussed over dinners in the apartment. Visiting his dad had always been an exercise in patience. They never talked about anything *real*—it was easier to swap stories and statistics about life on other worlds. Now, Peter wished he'd paid closer attention to some of the scraps of trivia his father had tossed his way, rather than spending his nights resenting the lack of real communication.

"How thick is the ice?" he asked at last.

Lowell shrugged. "More than two miles, anyway. It's thinner at the south pole, which is why the plumes burst through there."

"North and south are arbitrary out here," said Peter archly.

"If you don't like the names, you can take it up with the

management. Pretty sure Munroe's the one in charge at this point, and he'd *love* some feedback on possible improvements."

"All right, all right," Peter grumbled, looking down at the tablet again.

"Radar says we're almost at the bottom."

Peter was still feeling salty when the thick layer of ice gave way to an open expanse of dark water. He was suddenly and desperately aware of the scale of things: the ocean was vast and uncharted, populated by hungry beasts that had no name.

"You okay?" asked Lowell, glancing over at him.

Peter nodded. "It just sank in."

"What did? The ship?"

"Reality." Peter laughed warily. "How deep we've put our feet in it," he gasped. "Can you, uh, turn on some headlamps or something?"

"Not sure I should," Lowell said. "We might attract something. Maybe we should just stick with the radar." He glanced over at Peter again. "You're looking a little sick, kid. You wouldn't happen to be claustrophobic, would you?"

"Maybe a little," Peter whimpered.

"Fine. Let's give it a shot." Lowell hit a button on the controls, and the floodlights at the front of the pod came on. There was nothing to see, and Peter felt himself relax. The worst part about floating around in an ocean full of hidden leviathans was not knowing where they were, but at least he had some sense of where they *weren't*.

"Thanks," he said, "that's better—"

His eyes widened as a dark red ribbon as big as a tree trunk undulated across the space illuminated by their floodlight. It took a full six seconds to pass, and Peter just stared in wonder until the rounded tail followed.

"What was—" Lowell began.

As he spoke, something huge and pale darted past, its uneven jaws opened wide to reveal serrated, translucent teeth. Peter only had time to make out the creature's eye, a lightless black orb set in taut white flesh, before Lowell's hand slammed down on the controls, turning off the headlamps and smothering them in darkness once more. They sat there, breathing hard, the only light coming from the LED backlighting on the controls.

"Maybe we should stick with the radar," Peter suggested once he was fairly confident his voice wouldn't crack.

"Sounds like a plan," Lowell replied. For the first time since they'd met, he sounded truly rattled, and Peter couldn't blame him.

18

"I HATE FISH," Lowell muttered, trying to keep it together. "Disgusting, scaly, cannibalistic little buggers..." He'd spent the last few years looking for the bright side when it came to his posting, and the lack of venomous wildlife was a big plus for him. The sheen was starting to wear off of the silver lining now that he was surrounded by creatures big enough to eat him in a single bite.

"I think they're cool," said Peter. "In an aquarium. I love aquariums. Love the fact that I can stop at the gift shop on my way out. Love the fact that I *can* walk out. You think He Ming would still be open to a chat about our options?"

"Are you panicking again?" asked Lowell, finally getting his hands to stop shaking enough that he was comfortable putting them back on the controls. He didn't mind admitting that he was afraid, not when he was faced with something like *that*, but he didn't think saying that to Peter would be the best idea. So long as Lowell kept his act together, he could be the grounding rod for the kid. If he went off the rails, he had no doubt that Peter would follow soon after.

"No more than the situation calls for," Peter replied. He let out a shuddering breath that echoed around the enclosed space. "But here's a question for you: how am I supposed to read the map without a light?"

"Good point." Lowell hooked one thumb toward the back of the pod. "There should be a night-vision visor in the back. It usually installs over a helmet, but you can probably figure out how to use it on its own."

Obediently, Peter twisted around in his seat and dug through the equipment Lowell had stashed there. Most of it was tools that he used on his rounds repairing the equipment, but some of it was old special-ops tech he'd kept his hands on just in case. Nobody had officially recalled it, and Lowell had a *better safe than sorry* policy when it came to the Space Corps. After all, he'd been dumb enough to let himself get stabbed in the back once. He had no intention of repeating that mistake.

While Peter searched, Lowell used the pod's radar to take them deeper, while avoiding the heat signatures around them. There were monsters everywhere, he now realized, and although the pressure at the bottom of the moon's ocean would probably test the limits of what the little pod could endure, that was where any landmarks would likely be found.

"Ouch," Peter muttered, gripping his nose and squeezing his eyes shut. "Whew, these pressure changes are killing me. How do they not bother you?"

Lowell shrugged. "They used to. I got over it."

"You deep-dive through the ocean a lot?"

Lowell shook his head. "We just had to go through all kinds of physical training before we were deployed. You switch atmospheres enough out here, and it stops bothering you so much. What I hate are the gravitational changes. Most of the places I've been to have a much lower gravitational pull than Earth does."

"Does it mess with your sense of balance?" asked Peter sympathetically.

"Nah." Lowell smirked, remembering Peter's haphazard struggle across the ice. "Just my aim."

Peter winced. "Yeah, makes sense. Didn't think of that."

"Yours isn't bad," said Lowell encouragingly. "If you've really only ever fired a gun three times, you've got a perfect kill record so far."

He meant it as a compliment, but Peter seemed to wilt. It was hard to tell in the diffused light of the controls, but it looked as though he was frowning.

Vasko would give him hell for that attitude, thought Lowell, remembering his old friend. The thought made him tired. Vasko and Collins were pretty much the only reason he hadn't been discharged back in the day. They'd put their careers on the line to take his side; if he could still be said to have friends in the Space Corps, theirs were the only names that would make the list. Part of him wished they were here instead of Peter. Vasko in particular drove him nuts, but he'd have made some set of wisecracks about the critters swimming around them that would have eased the tension a little. That had never really been Lowell's strength.

Instead of ragging on Peter for not being more bloodthirsty, he focused on taking the pod down smoothly. Little blips of life showed up on the infrared scanner, but he had the sneaking suspicion that there were plenty of creatures that the system wouldn't flag. That worm thing, for instance. Did invertebrates give off a heat signature? Lowell had never thought to ask.

"You were right about this ocean teeming with life. I can't get over it."

"That makes two of us," Peter said.

"But how? I just don't get it. How could this all just show up?"

Peter shook his head as he kept digging in back. "I'm no

oceanographer, but I have to assume that much of this was living deeper in the trenches and has migrated up here for some reason. This ocean is many times deeper than any on Earth."

"So something's scaring all the alien lifeforms up from the deep? That sounds ominous."

At last, Peter lifted something out of the back, holding it up to the controls. "This is the only thing that feels like a screen. Is this that visor you were talking about?"

Lowell glanced over and nodded. "Yup. Strap goes behind your head, and then there's a button on the top right... Dude, tighten it. You look like an idiot."

"You can't even see me," Peter said. "Where's this button supposed to be?" He shuffled around for another moment, then gasped. "Oh, wow, that's *weird.*"

"Typical civilian," said Lowell airily. "So easily impressed."

"Who's being smug now?" Peter said. "Knock it off, or I'll hit the ejector button on you."

"There is no ejector button."

"I knew it!"

Lowell chuckled, trying to keep his voice even as he watched a particularly large dot on the radar approach. *That must be whatever took out Hansen's ship*, he thought. No point in telling Peter it was coming. There was nothing they could do about it now.

To his great relief, it passed them by. Whatever it was must have been either a long way over or under them, too far away to sense the hum of their engines.

"This is perfect," Peter was saying when Lowell relaxed enough to pay attention again. "I can read just fine. And you can't see the light, can you? I shouldn't attract any attention?"

"Nope. Read away."

"Cool, cool." Peter tapped the metal surface. "So we're looking for a rock garden."

Lowell frowned at him. "Come again?"

Peter's finger rested on the tablet. "That's what it says, right here: *Behold the rock garden.*"

Lowell stifled a sigh and pinched the bridge of his nose. "There's nothing *but* rocks down there, Chang."

"Well, I don't know what to tell you," said Peter, exasperated. "That's what it says right here. "*Kiri* means garden, and *bulalum*, that's stone...'precious stone,' actually. So maybe gemstones?"

"Yeah," Lowell grumbled, "maybe there's a diamond mine at the bottom of the ocean. Maybe we can throw one of these creepy fish a couple of bucks and they'll let us mine our own gems." He growled, shaking his head. "Is that really the best you've got?"

"Oh, I'm sorry, is my translation not good enough for you?" Peter said, yanking the night-vision visor off of his head and thrusting it toward Lowell, along with the tablet. "Let's see what you can make of this. Maybe your *encyclopedic knowledge* of dead languages outstrips mine. Huh?" He waggled the tablet, bumping Lowell's arm with it. "Come on, show me what you've got."

"Poke me with that one more time and I'll turn the headlamps back on," Lowell said. "We'll see what *you* make of *that*."

"I've made my point," Peter sniffed, tugging the visor back on. "So are we going to keep our eyes open for a rock garden, or are you going to get snippy with me again?"

"You haven't seen me snippy. But at least I've figured out why Munroe wanted to shoot you."

Peter rolled his eyes. "You wouldn't happen to suffer from low blood sugar, would you? My stepdad gets like this when he's he hasn't eaten in a while. You're being tetchy."

Lowell whipped his head around, baring his teeth, ready to put the fear of God into the little nerd in the seat next to him, when Peter's eyes widened. He stood up, leaning closer to the glass in front of him.

"Can you see that?" he asked, tapping the glass with one finger.

"I can't see squat." Lowell squinted at Peter's expression. He didn't look like he was about to go bananas at the sight, which at least meant that whatever he could see probably wasn't the size of a city bus with teeth as long as Lowell's forearm. That was something.

"There are bubbles," said Peter. "At least, I think they're bubbles."

Lowell stared out into the darkness. "Hansen was always on about these hydrothermal vents. You think it could be from those?"

"I wouldn't think so. How close are we to the bottom?"

"According to the radar, pretty close." Lowell bit his lip. "Maybe I *should* turn the lights on again. Just for a minute. What do you think?"

Peter cleared his throat, and both men were silent for a long moment.

"I think if we're going to stop Munroe, we're going to have to take risks," said Peter at last. "And I'd rather take a chance on attracting a giant fish than let the clock run out and let whatever's going to happen...happen. You know?"

"I know," Lowell agreed. "And I think I'm with you on that. Okay, Chang, here goes. One...two...three..."

No fish, no fish, please, don't let there be a single fish in sight, he prayed to nobody, and switched on the lights.

Peter sucked in a breath. "They *are* bubbles."

Sure enough, millions upon millions of tiny bubbles danced through the water before them, rising in uneven trails toward the surface. They appeared to be coming from strange lumps on the seabed that looked almost like mushroom-shaped corals.

"What are they?" asked Lowell in wonder.

Peter was still staring out the glass, an expression of surprised puzzlement on his face.

Lowell snapped his fingers. "Hang on, Chang, I think that's your rock garden."

"They're not rocks," said Peter, blinking rapidly. "I've seen them before. They're alive."

19

"YOU'VE SEEN LIVING ROCKS BEFORE?" Lowell asked, switching the lights back off, just in case.

Peter nodded. "Back on Earth. They're call stromatolites. My dad took me to Australia when I was a kid, and he got *so* excited about being allowed to visit the stromatolite gardens. They're basically living fossils." He turned back to the tablet. "*Precious stones* indeed. What do you know, some of the stuff we talked about is coming in handy."

I'll tell him, Peter promised silently, *if I ever get a chance.*

"I guess we're lucky you know all this crap," Lowell said. "So you think that this is one of the landmarks you're after?"

"It seems likely." Peter sank back into his seat, frowning. "But it's weird, isn't it? That life on one of Saturn's moons evolved parallel to life in Earth's oceans? That's a pretty massive coincidence."

Lowell scoffed. "Somebody made that map, and somebody buried it on Earth. That's not coincidence. There's obviously a connection here."

Peter was practically vibrating with excitement. "You think aliens were involved?"

"Somebody or something that mastered spaceflight, anyways, yeah," said Lowell, as if such a thing should be obvious. "I mean, clearly."

Most people Peter met seemed to fall into two camps. They were either totally dismissive of even the barest concept of alien life, or they were so credulous that they believed everything they heard. Peter was used to being either mocked for his theories, or bombarded with accounts of people who claimed to have been abducted and probed themselves. He'd never had someone as jaded as Lowell agree with him outright—except his father, of course.

It took him a long moment to realize that the vibrating sensation was only intensifying. Maybe it *wasn't* just excitement.

"Do you feel that?" he asked.

"Yeah." He could make out Lowell's outline as the other man pressed his hands to the controls. "Yeah, I feel it. And I don't think it's your rocks that are doing that, either. What's the next landmark?"

Peter turned his visored face toward the tablet. "Right, let's see. This says something about a chasm, I think? But that could also mean a mine, or even just a hole..."

"Peter?" said Lowell in a low voice.

"Hm?"

"Read faster."

Peter could feel the floor shuddering underneath him. Now that Lowell had called his attention back to the present, it was hard to concentrate on anything else.

"What is that?" he murmured. "It's almost like—"

"Sonar," said Lowell abruptly.

Peter looked around sharply. "You think the Chinese crew figured out a way to follow us? Or is it Munroe?"

"I don't think it's manmade," said Lowell nervously. "Listen, I'm going to move us somewhere else, and we can figure out what we're doing next when we—"

He didn't get a chance to finish; something bumped against the side of the pod. Peter shrieked, then covered his mouth, feeling pathetic for being so high-strung. He was still wallowing in his embarrassment when something bumped them from the other side. He dropped heavily back into the seat.

"There are five of...whatever they are on the radar," Lowell said. "Can you see them? Do I even *want* to know what we're dealing with?"

Peter risked a quick glance through the glass, and instantly regretted it. The night-vision visor allowed him a clear view of the thing that had bumped them. It had a long, narrow snout, and its back fins were split, almost as if they'd once been legs.

Whales evolved to walk on land, but then returned to the water. But if these things are like whales, then when were they ever on land? Lowell must be right. Someone must have put them here. But why?

"Well?" asked Lowell.

"How do you feel about dolphins?"

"Dolphins are okay."

"I agree," said Peter. "These things are like dolphins, but with scales, and about ten times as many teeth. And smaller eyes. And bigger mouths. So far, they're only looking at us. They don't seem to be interested in attacking our—"

As if it could hear them through the water and wanted to disagree, one of the long-nosed beasts slammed its nose into the pod, sending it shooting off through the water.

"That didn't seem friendly," said Lowell, reaching for the controls. "Let's see if the laser works down here."

"Who knows what else you're going to attract with the light?"

Lowell shook his head emphatically. "It's our only weapon. We don't have a lot of options at this point."

Something struck them from the other direction, and a second later the laser went off, illuminating three of the creatures as they darted around the ship in a glow of red light. One of them spun around, following alongside the pod, its nearest eye fixed on Lowell only inches from the glass, reflecting the dim light of the backlit controls. It looked hungry.

Or maybe Peter was just projecting.

"Well, hello, you big ugly bastard," said Lowell conversationally. "Sorry to tell you this, but I kind of hate being the foosball in this little game."

In answer, the sleek beast banged its snout against the glass, clearly puzzled about why it could see Lowell, but not take a bite out of him.

"Is that how it's going to be?" Lowell asked.

The fish bashed against the glass a second time, so hard that it knocked the pod off-course.

"How much of a beating can the glass take, again?" Peter wheezed.

"Enough," Lowell said. "But *I* can't take much more, so let's finish this."

He accelerated, then spun the ship around and fired at the spot they had just pulled away from. The beam hit the creature broadside, searing a clean hole through its side and nearly severing its head. It opened its mouth, and Peter felt the ship vibrate again, clearly the result of whatever sound it was emitting. That was what had vibrated them before: it was essentially whale song. The thought would have made Peter sad about killing it, if the fish hadn't been the instigator.

Lowell flashed the lights on for just a moment to see if he'd hit his target. As black blood spilled out into the water, the dying fish's four companions circled back. His shot hadn't killed the creature outright, but as it thrashed in the water, its school tore into it, sending chunks of gore drifting down to settle on the seabed below.

"What did I tell you?" Lowell demanded, eyes fixed on the foul sight before them.

Peter swallowed hard. "That they're cannibals?"

"Damn straight. Unethical, backstabbing little buggers." Lowell shook his head in disgust. "In another life, Munroe would have made one hell of a fish."

20

LOWELL TURNED the lights off as they left the bloodthirsty school of sea creatures behind. At least they knew that the laser still worked at depth. It probably wouldn't be enough to take down some of the bigger creatures they'd encountered, but it was better than nothing.

The chasm Peter had speculated about was a lot easier to find than the rock garden. It appeared on the radar as a gouge in the seabed, a trench so deep that even the pod's mapping system couldn't reach the bottom. It cut across their path, and as they approached the lip of it, Lowell felt a harrowing combination of claustrophobia and kenophobia. The sea was too damn big, and the pod was too damn small. Without his helmet on, if the pod was damaged now, he'd be instantly crushed by the pressure of the water as it flooded the cockpit.

It's no different from being in space, he told himself. *The atmosphere can kill you out there, too.* But it felt different, no matter what he told himself.

"Where now?" he asked.

Peter tilted his head. "Head toward the, um, giantess's face?" he said, not sounding in the least bit confident. "So far, the giantess has referred to Saturn, but..."

"That's easy, then." Lowell turned to the left. "Enceladus has a locked orbit—the same side always faces Saturn, so that would work as a clear direction no matter what time of day it is."

"Oh." Peter perked up. "Okay, that makes sense."

Lowell pursed his lips thoughtfully. "Maybe they should just have said north or south."

"Nope. Apparently the ancients were smarter than the Space Corps."

Lowell chuckled. "What's the next thing we're looking for?"

"We're looking for a tunnel, or a passage of some kind. It could mark the entrance, but that won't be until we're closer to the Saturn-facing side."

Lowell grunted. "So you think we can follow this most of the way there?"

"Seems like it." Peter rubbed his hands together in anticipation. "We've still got almost eighteen hours before our clock runs out. We should be good—of course, who know what happens next, but we make a great team, don't you think?"

It had been so long since Lowell had felt like part of a team that Peter's words hit him in the gut. The guy was right, too. The fact that they'd made it this far was a pleasant surprise, and in spite of being an unapologetic geek, Peter was actually coming in handy.

"There are some MREs in the back," Lowell said, still reluctant to reinforce any sense of team identity that Peter might be fostering. "And if you think you can, you should get some sleep. Just tell me what the next landmark is."

"Sleep?" Peter scoffed. "How am I supposed to sleep at a time like this?"

"You should try." Lowell leaned back, setting the pod to autopilot. "We've got a little downtime now, and if you don't at least nap, you'll be a wreck later."

"What about you?" Peter asked.

"I could go for some food, but I don't need sleep," Lowell assured him. "I can stay awake for three days at a clip, or longer if I have to. I've had plenty of training."

Peter rummaged around in the back until he produced a box of MREs. "What's good?" he asked, reading the labels.

"None of it." Lowell snorted. "It's all awful. Give me a ham bar."

"A *what?* That can't be real." Peter shuddered. "Oh my God, you weren't kidding." He handed over a package, and Lowell tore it open with his teeth and started eating.

"We're in deep space," Lowell pointed out. "What, did you think we'd have a vegetable patch around the back of the research station?"

"So how often do you eat this crap?"

"Every day."

Peter gagged. "And does it ever get better?"

"Nah," Lowell said. "And that's not the worst one, either. I'd rather starve than eat the lentil powder."

"You know what I could really go for?" Peter sighed, settling back in his chair. "A fruit plate. Just cut fruit. Is that crazy? Oh, and some sushi. Something just really *fresh*, you know... Oh, God, or a cheeseburger right off the grill... Although actually, my mom makes this awesome green chili chicken—"

"Peter?"

"Yeah."

"Go to sleep."

"But—"

"If you say one more word about food," Lowell said, "I won't need an ejector seat. I'll shove you out of the airlock myself."

"Right."

"Perfect."

"... Lowell?"

"Yeah?"

"Thanks for saving my life, like, fifteen times today."

"Think you did the same for me a couple times, kid." Lowell grinned into the darkness. "And the night is still young."

————

LOWELL WATCHED the clock as Peter's breathing slowed and deepened. Despite his protests, the linguist was out like a light within ten minutes of settling back in his chair.

He had no sense of how fast they were going, but he was already pushing the limits of what the pod could do, and he didn't want to risk stranding them down here without enough power to keep the thrusters going.

Even before being transferred into the Space Corps, Lowell had trained to stay awake for days on end. When he wanted to, he could fall asleep on command, but he'd also learned how to enter a state of controlled half-sleep, the human equivalent of low battery mode. With his eyes fixed on the radar and the soft wheeze of Peter's breathing in his ears, he let his mind wander.

As usual, his mind slid to a dreaming place, lucid but aimless in its journey. He found himself thinking of his father.

What are you going to say, Dad, when you see me again?

In the dream, his father looked the same as he had when Lowell had enlisted, roughly the age Lowell was now. He'd seen his father at the inquest before his demotion, but he hadn't recognized the bitter old man watching the whole rigged proceeding unfold.

I don't know, son, this kinder version of his father replied. He was sitting on a bench on top of the hill near the house Lowell had grown up in. Lowell could feel a breeze. He'd almost forgotten about breezes. *A lot can happen between now and then. You remember what I told you?*

Shoot first and ask questions later.

His father laughed. *No. The other thing. The important thing. The difference between you and that asshole Munroe.*

Lowell considered this. It was important, or he wouldn't be thinking about it, but he couldn't remember what he was missing.

'*The only man who never makes mistakes...*' his father prompted.

'*... Never does anything.*' Yeah, *I remember.*

Lowell's father wagged a finger at him. *This could very easily be a mistake. If you make this about getting back at Munroe, you're going to get your butt kicked. You're going to lose sight of the big picture. This isn't about Munroe. Don't do it to get back at him. Do it for Keating. Do it for Peter. Do it for you. Oh, and Carpenter? Watch out for the shark.*

Lowell jolted in his seat, eyes suddenly focusing on the screen in front of him. The huge red dot that had bothered him earlier was back. It was right next to them, all but overlaying their current position on the digital map.

He felt his heart stutter in his chest and his breath catch in his throat. Whatever it was, it was swimming parallel to their ship, right next to them.

It was waiting in the trench.

21

HE MING HAD SERVED as a translator for the Tiān Zhuānjiā since she was seventeen years old. She'd been recruited from her classroom after showing exceptional skill in half a dozen distinct language groups. Following a rigorous training regimen, she'd been assigned to work for General Wu for the last five years.

English came easily to her, but all the same, she intensely disliked working with the Americans. More often than not, they were condescending, rude, indelicate, and had all the subtlety of a jackhammer. They also never seemed to employ their own translators, instead relying on the other fleets to provide their own.

If nothing else, she reasoned, they offered her job security. That was where her exceptions began and ended.

When the American ship hailed them, Ming hurried over to the general's chair and took her place by his side moments before he accepted the video call.

"Good afternoon," said the American commander, smiling so widely that his teeth showed. The Americans were always smiling. It was an exhausting habit.

"Good afternoon," Ming replied, folding her hands in her lap. "I don't think we've worked together before."

"We haven't. I'm Lieutenant Munroe," he said. He had a square, masculine look about him, with blunt features that would have been at home on the so-called silver screen. Another woman might have thought he was handsome, but Ming had spent as much time learning to read people's body language as she had spent mastering their languages.

He wasn't her type. Ming liked honesty.

Despite her instant mistrust of the man, she gave no indication of her wariness. "I am translator He Ming, speaking on behalf of General Wu." She smiled politely, keeping her lips closed.

"We're looking for a ship. Small one, two men in it..." His blue eyes narrowed slightly. "You wouldn't happen to have seen them?"

Before Ming translated this question, General Wu spoke up. He turned his eyes away from the screen, speaking to Ming rather than to the man in front of them.

"This man, Munroe, used to command the force that Lowell served in," he told her in Mandarin.

Ming kept her features perfectly composed, knowing that Munroe would be watching their every move. "The one that shot down your son's ship?"

"Precisely." General Wu kept his emotions beneath the surface, but Ming recalled the day that the announcement had come through about the two vessels shot down on the Martian surface, and how the general's face had crumpled when he read the brief. His two minutes of quiet weeping had meant more to Ming than a hundred American smiles.

"What shall I tell him?" she asked.

Before he could answer, Munroe cleared his throat. "Seems like a pretty straightforward question, doesn't it, ma'am? Yes or no: Did you see the ship?"

"The general is trying to remember," Ming told him. She turned back to Wu. "Sir? What should I tell him?"

"The truth," said the general. "That we fired on two of their hoverpods." Once again, his expression remained perfectly blank. There was always the possibility, even with the Americans, that someone else would be listening in to the conversation, double-checking her translation. Any communication between them must be subtle. Unspoken. Understood. This was the benefit of working with the same crew for so long: over time, it became almost possible to read one another's thoughts.

Ming nodded once, then turned back to the screen. "The general says that there were two hoverpods engaged in a firefight near the tiger stripes. We fired on both of them."

"That's a violation of our treaty," said Munroe.

"Considering what's at stake, Lieutenant," she said evenly, "it would be foolish not to consider this a war zone."

Munroe's lips curled back, and all semblance of friendliness vanished in an instant. "Tell General Wu that if your ships haven't cleared out by the time my people are ready to launch, I have no problem opening fire on him."

"The lieutenant is making threats, sir."

"Tell the American that it would be a pleasure to kill him myself."

So much for diplomacy. Ming was debating whether or not to soften the general's message or to translate literally when the quandary was resolved for her. Munroe disconnected.

For a moment, she and the general sat staring at the screen, eyes fixed on the blank black glass.

"I look forward to having the opportunity to kill that man," General Wu said at length.

"And what about the other two?" asked Ming. "They're

working against their government. Perhaps they would be useful allies."

General Wu shook his head. "That man, Lowell, is a tool of the Space Corps, and a tool only has one purpose: to be used by the one who wields it. If he works for Munroe, I do not trust him. If he has bitten the hand of his master, I still do not trust him. There is no middle ground. They will die, just as my Aiguo died. We will complete our mission."

Ming nodded. She didn't care, in the end, what became of either man. Individual lives meant nothing in the grand scheme of things.

The fate of mankind was at stake, and whoever won this battle would, very likely, secure a last victory for their nation on a scale of which few people could even dream.

22

PETER WAS DREAMING about his father when Lowell jostled him awake.

"Hey, Chang?"

Peter rubbed his eyes and sat up. Lowell was piloting the pod, but he kept looking at the screen before him and frowning.

"'Sup?" Peter mumbled, stifling a yawn.

"How much do you know about biology?"

I know I'm going to have to use the bathroom at some point, but I don't think that's what he has in mind, Peter thought, stretching and yawning again. He hadn't been sleeping well since he'd been kidnapped, and he could feel that lack of rest taking its toll. "What kind of biology are we talking?"

"You know how we were saying that it's no coincidence about those living rocks being similar to something that exists on Earth?" Lowell asked. "I'm wondering what you can tell me about ancient biology—dinosaurs, extinct fish, that kind of thing."

"Well, I'm an archaeologist, not a *paleontologist*," Peter informed him. "They're different disciplines, so I haven't studied fossils officially, but I watch a lot of documentaries and nature programs."

"Of course you do," Lowell muttered.

Peter huffed indignantly. "What's that supposed to mean?"

"I think you know." Before Peter had a chance to retort, Lowell carried on. "Okay, so let's go by secondhand knowledge. There wouldn't, by any chance, happen to have been some kind of insane ancient shark I should know about, would there?"

"Oh, sure." Peter sat up in his seat, already excited about the prospect of further speculation. "I mean, megalodons are probably the best-known..."

"And, at a guess, how big are we talking with those puppies?" Lowell's gaze flicked back to the controls.

"Fifty, sixty feet?" Peter shrugged.

"Hm," said Lowell.

It was entirely possible that Peter hadn't been fully awake before. Now he found himself looking over at Lowell, his stomach sinking. "Out of curiosity, why do you ask?"

Lowell cleared his throat. "You remember that thing that took out *Moby Dick*?"

"Captain Ahab?" Peter shook his head, smacking his temple. "No, sorry, you mean the submarine that Dr. Hansen was—" He choked at the end of the sentence. The research sub had been a heck of a lot bigger than the pod he and Lowell now sat in, and it hadn't fared well against that unidentified denizen of the Enceladean sea. Whatever had shown up on Anjali's final transmission had been well over sixty feet long, perhaps a *lot* over.

Lowell's nervous expression suddenly made a lot more sense.

"Oh, shit," Peter mumbled. "How far away is it?"

"Hard to say." Lowell abandoned all pretense of acting as though they were speaking in the abstract, as opposed to the painfully pertinent. "The radar says it's close, but it doesn't say *how* close. I'm not getting an accurate depth." He glanced at Peter. "Listen, I know this might be asking for trouble, but I'm turning the lights on again. Just for a minute. We've got to figure out if we should be aiming for this...whatever it is, or if we should be running like hell."

Peter had a nasty feeling that they should be doing the latter, but he didn't want to whine in front of a tough guy like Lowell.

"Ready?" asked Lowell.

Peter braced for whatever was coming next, his shoulders climbing toward his ears. "Ready."

The pod's lights came on. Peter blinked, wincing away from the glow, and looked at Lowell. He hadn't flinched from the light. His wide eyes were seemingly transfixed on a point beyond the glass in front of them. His jaw was slack.

If I turn my head and there's a giant shark out there, I'm going to drop dead right now and spare myself the trauma, Peter promised. It took more force of will than he would have believed to make himself turn his head. He was braced for blank eyes and teeth like spears, or as braced as he could get. Memories of late-night reruns of the 2054 *Jaws* remake and *Sharknado XVI* danced through his head.

It was still worse than he'd imagined.

When he'd watched Connor die, Peter had experienced a sort of out-of-body lightness, a weightlessness that had made him feel as if he was watching a gruesome VR film rather than living a nightmare. Call it adrenaline, call it self-preservation, but the end result was that he had felt outside of himself, not quite capable of processing the reality of the moment.

It was the same as he stared at the leviathan rising from the depths of Enceladus' underwater trench, illuminated in the glow of their floodlights. Tiny pinprick eyes, much too small for the gargantuan size of its body, were set deep in its dappled grey head.

Its armored skull looked as if it had been carved from stone, not birthed or grown. Instead of teeth, its jaws were lined with razor-sharp plates made for shearing bone.

Or for cutting a ship in two like it was warm butter.

"Lowell?" Peter squeaked. "I think we should find those tunnels now."

Lowell sat frozen in the seat beside him before finally letting out a tiny groan.

"Lowell?" Peter shook the big man's shoulder. "Get it together. I don't know how to drive or sail this thing, or whatever, and I swear to God, if you lose it now, I'm not going to be able to salvage this."

The Space Corpsman shuddered before finally turning his head to look Peter in the eyes. "I don't know if I've told you," he said, "but I really, *really* hate fish."

23

THERE WAS something fundamentally different about facing down a man who wanted to kill you for personal reasons and fighting a massive fish that was just looking for a meal. When it came to people, Lowell was pretty good at outsmarting them and using the terrain to subvert their expectations.

Predators were another matter.

Besides, who the hell knew what a shark was thinking? Only the shark.

Technically, the giant fish didn't look like any shark Lowell had ever seen. It was more like every nightmare he'd ever had about the ocean's mysteries rolled into one horrible beast, nothing but beady eyes, pointed fins, and gaping mouth. If Lowell had been a religious type, he'd have forsaken his faith there and then. No loving God would have designed a horrorshow like this.

As the armored fish swam toward them, Lowell couldn't strategize. He couldn't plan. The only conscious thought running through his mind was, *We're in her territory, and we're no match for her.*

"Lowell?" Peter repeated. "Maybe you should turn the lights off?"

"No way," he said. His voice echoed distantly through his ears. "I'm not taking my eyes off that thing. That damn fish can see right into my soul."

It was foolish, and he knew it. The shark was coming up behind them. It wasn't like the forward floodlights would matter, but it was the damn principle of the thing. *If she's taking me out, she's going to have to look me in the eye while she does it.*

"I'll give you the damn night vision visor, just turn off the lights. You have the radar."

Lowell cursed. Peter was right. He turned the lights off, and everything went pitch black outside the pod. He grabbed the visor and hastily fitted it over his head.

It was pretty cool, or would be, if it didn't show him the shark now gaining on them fast, only in a red tint that looked even more menacing.

He slammed the controls and fired the laser. In the visor's view, a red blotch blossomed on the side of the shark's armor plating, but it seemed to have no real impact at all. The great beast banked to one side, stalking them, and Lowell saw that there was now the faint impression of a perfect circle on her cheek. His one sorry excuse for a weapon had barely marked her. If she held still, and he leaned on the controls indefinitely, he might eventually punch through all that plating to get at the soft and squishy bits beneath.

Maybe. But I'm not holding my breath.

The idea of a sixty-foot fish had been bad enough, but if this beast was under eighty feet in length, Lowell would eat not only his helmet, but Peter's, too. He growled and threw them into reverse, spinning around to follow her movements.

"You see any weak points?" Peter asked. "Like the seam in the space suits?"

Lowell shook his head.

"If this creature is anything like its Earth counterpart, there are weak points around the head and jaw."

"These things exist on Earth?" Lowell demanded. "I *knew* it. This is exactly why we should stay out of the damn ocean."

"I mean, they went extinct about three hundred and sixty million years ago," Peter pointed out.

"Sure." Lowell jerked his chin toward the glass. "Tell that to her."

He had to keep spinning the pod to keep the great fish in his sights, and he could tell that she was narrowing her circle with each rotation.

Lowell fired again, aiming for the space beneath her jaw. It was roughly the equivalent of the part of the space suits that were most vulnerable, too, the joint where the head met the body. Peter's guess made sense; on any armor, the parts that allowed for movement were always the weakest segments.

But to Lowell's lasting disappointment, the laser still didn't pierce the great fish's hide.

"What's this thing made of?" Lowell growled. "She didn't even *feel* that." He'd gone from petrified to irritable in the span of only a few moments. It wasn't fair—he hadn't wanted to start anything, and he *certainly* hadn't been craving a showdown with an apex predator. He was just trying to keep Munroe from killing even more people, and now every fish in the ocean wanted a piece of him.

I wish Munroe was here, Lowell thought bitterly. *I'd feed him to this thing so fast, he wouldn't even know what hit him. Then we could all go on our merry way.*

The thought jarred something loose in him, dispelling the last of his executive dysfunction. Peter was no slouch, but he wasn't going to be able to get them out of this one. That was on Lowell himself.

Which meant that he needed to get his act together if they were going to stand a fighting chance.

Lowell glanced at the rear cameras. The creature was less than a hundred yards away, and gaining fast.

Vasko wouldn't quit just because he didn't have weapons on him. He'd figure something out.

"Let's say I have an idea, but it's the kind of thing someone with a death wish would come up with. You in?"

Peter's jaw was clenched, but he nodded decisively. "If it's that or wave the white flag and get turned into chum, then yeah, I'm in."

"Remember you said that," Lowell told him. "No take-backs."

He reversed thrust suddenly and swung around to face the fish. He threw off the visor and switched on the floodlights. This was no time to hide. One beady black eye glinted, and her open mouth loomed ever wider.

"Lowell?" whimpered Peter.

He kept his eyes fixed on that gaping mouth, hoping to time it perfectly. If she closed her mouth while they were half-inside, Lowell had no doubt that she'd damage the pod beyond repair.

She's armored on the outside, Lowell thought. *So let's see what the inside is like.*

At the last moment, when the great creature's mouth was the only thing that filled his viewscreen, Lowell hit the thrusters, carrying them into the wet red darkness beyond.

Talk about finding yourself in the belly of the beast.

24

PETER WAS FAIRLY confident that he would never stop screaming.

"Why? Why? *Why why why*—"

"Knock it off," Lowell grunted. "You're giving me a headache."

"You just took us inside a sea monster *on purpose,* and you're worried about a *headache*?"

Their lights were still on, so Peter could clearly see when Lowell turned to him and rolled his eyes. "I've got a plan. This is part of it. Is screaming your brains out part of some plan on your end?"

Peter whimpered and shook his head.

"Then tone it down. You said you trusted me." Lowell leaned over the controls, an expression of intense focus on his dimly lit features. "So shut up and trust me. Think of it like that Bible story and have a little faith."

"We never really read the Bible," Peter wheezed. "Mom's Taoist and Dad's an atheist."

Lowell shrugged. "Okay, then how about that doll that came to life?"

Peter's eye twitched. "Annabelle?"

"Nah." Lowell snapped his fingers. "Pinocchio."

"What the hell are you talking about?" Peter groaned.

They slid down a fluttering deep-pink tube that suctioned to the glass as they slipped through. After what seemed a very long time, they finally plopped down into a larger space, slick with what was probably Devonian-era stomach acid. Remains of the creature's previous meals sat around them, slowly being dissolved by the corrosive sludge.

Peter shuddered when he recognized a familiar shape: the prone, slightly mummified body of one of Hansen's crew. The suit it wore was still largely intact, but its helmet was off, and after hours of being digested, its features were no longer distinct.

"Holy crap," he breathed as the pod came to a stop. "Now what?"

"This is about as far as I got," Lowell admitted. "I knew that we couldn't outrun her, and she was going to eat us either way, and here we are: in one piece. How about you, Mr. Scientist? Did any of your documentaries cover how to cut your way out of one of these things?"

"Weirdly, no!" Peter cried sarcastically, burying his face in his hands and breathing hard. "Didn't they cover this in Space Corps school?"

"Nah." Lowell crossed his arms. "Pretty useless, huh?"

"I can't believe you brought us in here with no plan," Peter groused. "I mean, you could always try the laser again. This is certainly one way to get through the armor plating."

"I'm never going to be able to cut a hole big enough for us to get out with the laser," Lowell began. Then his eyes unfocused, and one side of his mouth twisted into an unsettling approximation of a smile. Peter had the distinct impression that he was having an idea, and from where he was sitting, he didn't feel great about it.

But I don't feel great about sitting in here and being slowly dissolved by stomach acid while Munroe's plan unfolds either, he thought.

A slightly manic expression had taken up residence on Lowell's face. "Hey, Chang, did your dad ever take you fishing as a kid?"

Peter shook his head and forced himself to look away from the body. "Did yours? Is this karma?"

"Nah, but let's call it a lesson. I'm going to show you how to gut one of these suckers." He reached for a plastic cover at the top of his control panel and fiddled with one of the dials. "When we're working topside, we sometimes have to leave the pods in place for a long period of time. Sometimes they get frozen to the ice, and when that happens, we have to cut them free by hand. A couple of years ago, one of the commanders got approval to have them all upgraded, and..."

The pod began to vibrate, and dark chunks of what looked like fish meat splattered across the glass. Peter's gorge rose as he realized what was happening—the pod's upgrade was cutting a circular hole through the armored fish's stomach lining, scoring the meat with a rotary designed to combat ice. The result was a gory mess of tissue and meat that looked like it had been through a tenderizer.

I'm never eating sushi again, he thought miserably, covering his eyes and breathing hard through his nose. If he was sick to his stomach, Lowell would probably never let him live it down.

After several seconds, the pod began to shake violently. The shark, Peter realized, was thrashing wildly, and with the pod now seated in the ragged hole it was digging into the creature, it was getting thrown around just as hard. He wondered how much more it could handle.

"Take that, Sharkie, you big ugly sonofabitch!" Lowell howled.

A moment later, they burst through the creature's stomach and dropped through the open ocean, surrounded by shapeless lumps of meat and a cloud of dark blood.

"I thought you didn't have any more secret weapons," Peter wheezed. Their screen was still smeared with what looked like raw tuna salad, but he could see the undigested remains of previous meals slowly sifting through the water around them, drifting to the ocean floor.

As they sank, Peter leaned forward to watch the huge fish flail above them in agony. He didn't know a lot about anatomy, but he was pretty sure it was about to die—most things didn't take kindly to being sawed open from the inside.

"It's a shame," he said aloud.

Lowell turned to look at him incredulously. "What is? Killing that ugly bugger?"

"Scientifically speaking, there's an excess of humans in the galaxy." Peter pointed up to the silhouette of the animal above, which had gone still. "Who knows how many of them there are?"

"I can put you back in her if you want," Lowell offered, shaking his head. "In the meantime, we've got some tunnels to find."

"Right—tunnels." Peter turned his gaze toward the seabed. The mammoth fish was lost to sight, and the clock was still counting down. He'd need to focus if he wanted to stop whatever the hell Munroe's plan was.

I wonder if they'd let me lead a research team out here, he thought. *If Lowell and I get the key back and stall Munroe out, maybe we can find a way back to Earth, and I can come out here with a crew so that we can study the link between ancient marine life and the presence of dead languages. Maybe I could even stream a documentary about it to help with funding. This is going to mess with so many people's theories... Dad's going to have a field day with all of this.*

The thought of his father made him sigh aloud. There was one man who wouldn't be proud of Peter for slaughtering a scientifically significant animal just for the sake of preserving his own life.

He might be the only man in the universe to ever be disowned for murdering a fish.

25

"HELLCAT, DO YOU COPY?"

Lance Corporal Helena 'Hellcat' Moore stared at the wreckage of the American pod as she said, "I copy, Lieutenant."

"What have you got for me?"

"A wreck from another vessel." Helena's eyes swept over the rubble. "Two bodies, sir. I think it's Pearce and Gretlo, but it's hard to tell. I didn't see which ship they took, and there's not much left to ID them by."

"No sign of Lowell or Chang?"

"Nothing that I can find. No sign of the tablet, either." The landscape of Enceladus was desolate and bleak, a flat white world with no distinguishing features and nowhere for the eye to land. She had yet to visit the dark side of the moon, but even in broad, eternal daylight, just staring out at all that ice was depressing. *What a miserable place to die,* she thought. *It's like the Ninth Circle of Hell out here.*

"I knew the Chinese were lying," Munroe grumbled.

"Maybe these guys got blown off-world by the plumes, like

Tamsin's pod?" she suggested. "It's pretty miserable out here, sir. I don't know where else they could be. Not a lot of places to hide, unless you think the Tiān Zhuānjiā captured them."

Munroe chuckle darkly. "No, they didn't get them, or the general would have tried to bargain. I know Lowell. He's the kind of man who doesn't know when to quit. Trust me, Hellcat, he's out there. I'd bet my last dollar he's found his way through the ice. He's a petty man, and he'd do anything to make my life difficult." His voice sank lower, as if he was speaking to himself and not to her. "Four years later and he's still kicking up dust. I thought they'd buried him. Instead, some idiot sent him out here, the one place in the galaxy where he'd be guaranteed to be a thorn in my side."

Helena cocked her head, focusing on the important part of what he'd said. "You think he went underwater to try to sabotage the mission? No offense, sir, but that sounds extreme. Borderline treasonous."

"I'm well aware."

Helena glanced over her shoulder at her team. "I can't tell you where he is now, sir. Do you have the coordinates for the Anomaly?"

"Dr. Hansen's team had it all on record. I bet you can figure out which ship he took using their log—you might be able to track him."

"Then my team and I will head back to the research station and gear up, then use their entry point. If Chang and Lowell make it to the Anomaly, we'll be waiting. You're off-world already, right?"

"Everyone's out of there but your team."

"Works for me." Helena grinned. "I assume I'm authorized to terminate the targets?"

"With extreme prejudice. I never want to have to hear the

name Carpenter Lowell again. But you'll need to watch the clock." Munroe chuckled. "And mind the fish."

"I think I can handle a few guppies." Helena approached the wreck, prodding one of the frozen bodies with the toe of her boot. "What about Pearce and Gretlo?"

"Leave them," said Munroe. "You're working on a tight schedule. We don't have time to get sentimental, Hellcat. We're at war. I've spent the last half a decade working toward this moment, and nobody's going to stand in my way. Not Lowell, not Chang, and not the Tiān Zhuānjiā."

Helena turned and leapt back toward her ship, taking advantage of the low gravity. "You deal with the Chinese forces, sir." She swung through the door, buckled in, and reached for the throttle. "Leave the other two to me."

26

LOWELL'S HEART was pumping with excitement, and he found it difficult to sit still in his chair. He wanted a break for a round with a punching bag, or the chance to run a few miles and get some of the energy out.

Us: Two, at least. Asshole fish: Zero.

As odds went, they were pretty good—better than he would have thought possible at first. He'd almost allowed himself to forget that they were probably going to die down here, stranded in a pod that didn't have the juice to reach escape velocity.

Lowell took them low, keeping the lights on this time. If they were going to see the entrance to the tunnels described on Peter's nonsensical map, they'd need some visibility, even if it pulled things from the depths.

"Do you have a problem with me keeping the lights on?" he asked Peter when he noticed the young man nervously looking over the controls.

"I have a problem with every single thing that's happened to me in the last few weeks," Peter replied. "On the downside, I'm going to be paying therapy bills for the rest of my life—but since we might only be alive for another"—he checked the clock—"nine hours, the good news is I might not live long enough to seek out someone who specializes in alien-related PTSD."

Lowell snorted. "If you start talking about this with a shrink, they're going to write you off as a nutjob."

"Oh, you'd be surprised." Peter smiled wryly. "I'm sure my dad knows people who would eat this up. Of course, they'd probably suggest that I charge crystals under a full moon to ward me against evil presences, but at least they wouldn't think I was lying."

"Moon crystals might be your best option," Lowell pointed out. "Just keep in mind that if the government gets wind of you talking about all of this, they're either going to discredit you or bury you."

Peter turned away. "Believe me, I'm well aware. I've seen what Munroe and his people do to people they're finished with."

"Giving a shit about people," Lowell muttered, pointing a finger in Peter's direction. "That was your first mistake."

"You really think that?"

There was an edge of disgust in Peter's voice that didn't sit well with Lowell. He'd clearly missed the part where Lowell felt personally responsible for every crappy thing Munroe had ever done—or at least everything he'd done since Mars.

I should have put a bullet in him when I realized what he'd done. I could have saved a lot of people a lot of heartbreak.

Lowell cleared his throat. "Yeah. Too bad I've made the same mistake myself." At that moment, a name sprang unbidden to his mind: Francine Hansen.

Francine. That's it. I knew that I knew her name...

By unspoken agreement, they let the conversation die. The

punchy rush of success from earlier had faded. Lowell was back to feeling tired and battered and about a hundred years old.

Not everything in Enceladus' ocean appreciated their light source. At one point, they passed over a cluster of free-swimming nautiluses the size of German shepherds. The moment the beams hit them, they scattered.

A few minutes later, Peter jumped. "There's something underneath us," he whispered, as if speaking louder might alert the creature to their presence.

There was nothing on the scanner, and Lowell found himself imagining a hundred spineless, wriggling monsters that might be swimming around out here. He'd never thought of himself as a fearful man, but the idea of unseen predators made his skin crawl. He'd been wary of these critters before, and their little detour into Sharkie's stomach hadn't improved things. At this point, he'd far rather be safe than sorry.

Maybe we should blast it first and ask questions later, he thought.

A glance at the readout for the ship's systems disabused him of that notion; they'd be lucky if they didn't run out of juice before they found the tunnels. Lowell didn't relish the idea of running out of power underground, but better that than running out of power in an open space. Sharkie might be dead, but for all he knew, she had a brood of mini-monsters waiting for her in the trench, hungry for supper with a side helping of revenge. At least they had a strategy for fighting them now, but he'd far rather avoid another encounter than have to pull another stunt like that.

Their lights hit a small cloud of silver fish, and the thing below them darted out. It was a jointed crustacean, reminiscent of a sleek man-size lobster; it grabbed a few of the little fish in its myriad claws before sinking down to the sand to stuff them in its mouth.

"It's just shadow-hunting," Lowell sighed with relief. "Using our lights to target prey."

Peter nodded. "I'm fine with that, so long as *we're* not the prey. Hey, do you see that?" He pointed out to the sloped wall of the trench. "Up ahead. It looks like an opening in the seabed."

Sure enough, a black crevasse gaped in the side of the trench, right near the point where the level plateau dropped off into the abyss. It was more than large enough for their pod, enough that even the Chinese spacecraft could probably have fit inside—but to Lowell's relief, their piscine pursuer would have had a rough time squeezing her armor-plated head inside, even if she'd wanted to.

"I'm taking us down," he said.

Peter nodded and cleared his ears as the pod began to descend.

A dozen or so large crustaceans milled around the mouth of the opening, darting into smaller crevices as the pod approached. At last, they slid into the mouth of the tunnel, and Lowell breathed a little sigh of relief. It was always easier to defend a narrow space than an open one, especially when enemies could approach from above and below as easily as from the side. Instead of having to track a three hundred sixty-degree scope, he only had to keep an eye in two directions now: ahead and behind.

The walls of the tunnel were lined with vegetation. Eyeless fish and small shrimplike creatures moved among the greenery, harvesting their meals—well, relatively small. Most of them were the size of housecats, but Lowell was confident that he could take them in a fight. There was something placid about watching them busily at work, indifferent to the passing ship. It was a little like watching sheep graze.

"It's nice to know that not everything is out to get us," Peter observed, voicing Lowell's thoughts. "Even the predators aren't after us specifically—they're just going about their business."

"The rest of it feels like someone designed a hell specifically for me," Lowell agreed. "But this isn't so bad."

"What I don't understand is how all of these creatures ended up here, in the same time and place." Peter frowned through the glass. "The tablet was only left on Earth a few thousand years back, but some of these creatures went extinct hundreds of millions of years ago."

"On Earth."

Peter tapped his fingers against the glass. "What do you mean?"

"I mean that these things, or creatures like them, died out *on Earth* millions of years ago—but obviously, they weren't completely extinct. I also mean that you can throw out everything you think you know about biology, evolution, and space travel."

Peter snorted. "So how do you explain it?"

Lowell shrugged. "Aliens."

"That's usually my line. But why move sea creatures from Earth to some faraway moon over the course of millions of years? They must have made hundreds of trips back and forth over millennia."

"That's assuming these lifeforms started off on our world," Lowell said. "But even I know that there are all kinds of theories about the origins of life. I had to listen to plenty of arguments about it in the cantina. Nobody's been able to satisfactorily recreate the conditions in which life began. That was one of the reasons that Hansen and Anjali were going nuts over the protein strands. They thought that life might have come to Enceladus— and Earth—through things like meteor showers. Seeding, I think they called it. But what if they got the scale all wrong?"

Peter gaped. "You mean you think it started here? Instead of microbes arriving by meteor, something bigger came? Something that put lifeforms here on purpose?"

"Hell if I know," Lowell told him. "I just drive the ship."

A second later, their floodlights flickered. Lowell turned to the controls; the *low battery* alert blinked twice and then went out.

The engines followed.

"I spoke too soon," he grumbled. "There's nothing to drive. Sorry to break it to you, Chang, but it looks like we're dead in the water."

27

PETER SQUEEZED his eyes shut and prepared to suffocate, but long moments passed and his breathing still came easily.

"Why aren't we dying?" he asked weakly.

Lowell scoffed. "Jesus, Chang, when I said *we* were dead, I mean the engines. Quit being dramatic. You really think I'd risk running our battery down if we didn't have any auxiliary power?"

Peter opened his eyes, but it was so dark he could hardly tell the difference. He heard Lowell shifting around, and then fumbling between the seats for something.

Without the engines, the pod was so quiet that it made Peter uneasy. Once upon a time, he would have found the utter absence of background noise relaxing—but in those days, he hadn't relied on machinery for life support.

"What are we breathing?" he asked.

Lowell dropped something and swore under his breath, scrambling around on the floor. "Recyc. There's a backup system for if the main battery goes down. It'll come on in three...two..."

A soft buzzing filled the cabin. It reminded Peter of the way the lights in his old school had hummed back in the day, a faint high-pitched whine just gentle enough that he could almost tune it out.

"There we go." Lowell exhaled, as if he'd been privately worried that the system wouldn't kick on and had wanted to spare Peter any added concern. He sounded as if he was comforting himself as much as Peter when he went on. "The people who designed this thing might not have had combat in mind, but they've got some safety measures in place. We just need to give the battery a chance to recharge." Lowell finally found whatever he was looking for and turned it on. A beam of white light hit Peter square in the face; he burbled a noise of protest and tried to block his eyes.

"Sorry," said Lowell, averting the beam. "Hope I didn't blind you."

Peter blinked, shaking his head as he tried to get his sight back. Bright white spots danced across his field of vision. "How long does the battery take to recharge?"

Lowell shrugged. "Depends. An hour, maybe two."

Peter let out a huff of annoyance. "What time is it?"

"The clock's down, but last I checked, it was about 0700 hours."

With a groan, Peter dug the palms of his hands into his eyes. "Oh my *God*, we've got seven hours to get to the Anomaly, and now we're just going to get stuck here *waiting*..."

Lowell sounded utterly nonchalant when he said, "If you want to go face Sharkie again, my offer stands. Remember what I said about the ejector button." He shone the light behind their seats, then found another smaller flashlight, which he handed to Peter. "Don't turn that on yet. We might need it later, and you don't want to drain it. These guys don't self-recharge, and I don't want to have to plug anything into the pod if I can avoid it. We don't want to run it down twice."

Peter set the light on the floor beside his helmet and leaned back, crossing his arms. "So what happens now?" he asked. "Do we take a nap or something?"

"We could go for a swim," Lowell teased. He shone his light through the window, sweeping the bright beam across the small herbivores outside and throwing grotesque shadows against the cavern wall.

"Very funny." Peter slouched against his seat. Every time he closed his eyes, he saw the remains of that crewmember, skin slowly sloughing off before his eyes.

He tried to put the thought aside, and focused on Lowell's suggestion about seeding. His classmates had routinely made fun of him for his wild conspiracy theories, including his obsession with alien life, but this was too much to consider all at once, especially with the evidence staring him in the face. He'd always been fascinated with the idea of otherworldly life visiting Earth, and he'd spent hundreds of late nights poring over books and shows, scrolling through websites and social media pages dedicated to the topic. Some of the theories were wild, and he'd brushed many of them off as easily explained or downright ignorant. The pyramids, for instance: to suggest that only an alien civilization could have constructed them was just some racist crap cooked up by people who devalued early North African planning and design.

This was nuts. If he read about it on a forum, he'd flag himself for being too out there. On the other hand, they'd just sawed their way out of a veritable dinosaur. But if Lowell was right, who would have done the seeding?

He was deep in his own thoughts when Lowell's flashlight beam passed over something on the tunnel wall. Peter leaned forward in his seat. "Hang on. What's that?"

Lowell quickly swung the light around toward where Peter was pointing. "If it's Sharkie's granddaughter, I'm going to blow a fuse. What did you see?"

"It's not a fish." Peter reached out and guided the flashlight toward a strange shape in the rock face. "Do you see that?"

Lowell shivered. "Looks like a hidey-hole for some creepy critter."

"No, look closer. At the bottom. Do you see that?"

Lowell squinted. "It almost looks like steps."

"I think it is," Peter said. He was getting excited now. "It's like this tunnel—too perfectly round to be natural. I think it leads somewhere."

"Good for it," said Lowell sullenly. "Too bad we're not dumb enough to go exploring, right?"

"Would our suits work underwater?" Peter asked, already reaching for his helmet.

"No."

"I bet they would, and since our pod is stuck here for a couple of hours anyway..."

"*No.*"

Peter set his helmet in his lap and turned to his reluctant partner. "Are you saying *no* as in *no, our suits can't handle the pressure?* Or *no* as in *no way in hell am I going out there and you can't change my mind?*"

"The latter," Lowell grunted.

Peter donned his sweetest smile and leaned closer, making sure that Lowell could see him in the flashlight's beam. "Are you sure about that? Because earlier, you told me to trust you, and then you took me inside a *shark.*"

"I told you, I had a plan."

"I have a plan, too," Peter argued.

"Checking out a mystery tunnel does *not* count as a plan," Lowell grumbled.

Guilt wasn't going to work, apparently, but Peter had a backup strategy. He'd only known Lowell for a few hours, but he was fairly confident that it was going to work.

"Fine," he said with a little shrug. "I'll go on my own."

"Like hell you will," Lowell said at once.

Perfect, thought Peter. *Mission accomplished.*

28

HEATHER HAD TRIED for years to lure Lowell out into the surf, all to no avail. Trust Peter to do in two minutes what his sister had failed to do in a lifetime.

Lowell belligerently pulled on his helmet, securing it before checking Peter's. At least the kid had managed to put his on properly this time. "If we get eaten by giant sea bugs, I'm going to kill you," he muttered.

Peter's snort echoed through his helmet's mic. "In that case, you have my permission."

Lowell didn't often use the pod's pressurized escape hatch, but the vessel had been designed for use on a number of worlds, some of which were a lot less hospitable than Enceladus. Ultra-low temperatures could mess with the equipment, but the pods had been shot skyward more than once, and Enceladus wasn't the only heavenly body to boast both a watery atmosphere and a top-secret research station.

Lowell folded the seats up to reveal the circular port in the floor. "Careful," he warned Peter. "These little pods wobble easily, and if you tip this baby sideways on your way through, you'll flood the cabin. Good luck getting it bailed out in time if that happens."

Peter nodded. "No wobbling. Got it."

The scientist had been whining and moaning all day, but now that they were about to step out into the deep sea, with nothing but their suits in between them and, well, *everything*, Peter seemed almost relaxed. Lowell had never understood scientists. He had a private theory that they were all slightly insane, and that they all suffered from a kind of mass academic hysteria that drove them to do things that no rational human would agree to.

Lowell was a rational person. He knew better. Still, as Peter slipped through the port and down into the black water, Lowell braced his feet on either side of the hole and thought long and hard about what to do next.

You could just wait for him. Hang out here until he comes back, and if he doesn't, then just carry on alone.

Sure, he could—but when Wilcox and Horne had had him pinned, Peter had been the one to save him. If Lowell couldn't talk him into being sensible, he could at least have the kid's back.

"You coming?" asked Peter through the mic. "I haven't been crushed to death, and the sea bugs haven't torn me limb from limb yet."

Jovial. The idiot sounded *jovial.* That proved it: mass hysteria.

Lowell held his breath, pulled his arms close to his chest, and let himself fall through the hole feet-first into the sea.

At first, he flailed. He'd never been a big swimmer, even in pools and ponds. The sleek suit passed through the water too easily, making it hard to propel himself. The scientists, Lowell recalled, had always relied on fins, but he wasn't exactly equipped for a dip in the deep.

At last he righted himself and reached up to re-secure the hatch. If something bumped the pod while he and Peter were cavorting about in a death trap, at least they wouldn't come back to a flooded ship.

Peter was waiting for him beneath the ship. "Are you feeling okay?" he asked gently.

"I'm fine," Lowell snapped. "I just feel...squeezed." It was like someone was sitting on his chest, crushing his ribs. *Is this what a panic attack feels like?* he wondered. A few of the guys he'd served with in the Middle East had had panic attacks when they were under fire. Lowell had been able to take combat in stride, but a life-long fear of the ocean might take a different toll. His heart seemed to want to crawl out of his throat, and his eyes prickled. He couldn't catch a breath.

"It's the pressure," Peter assured him. "I feel it, too—the suit seems to be having a hard time down here."

"It might take a moment to readjust," Lowell told him. Sure enough, the squeezed sensation was already dissipating, and he found that he could breathe a little more easily. His heart rate hadn't slowed to normal, but at the very least, he wasn't going out of his mind with panic anymore.

Lowell struggled to swim, flailing his arms and legs, trying to right himself. The suit was able to help him a little with his buoy-ancy control, but he didn't seem to be making any progress toward the stairs.

"Do you mind?" asked Peter, holding out his hand. "I can take the light."

"Suit yourself," Lowell told him.

He watched in consternation as Peter accepted the flashlight, clasped his hands in front of him, and began to kick toward the hole in the wall. He cut through the water easily—not as easily as Sharkie, but with a heck of a lot more confidence than Lowell had.

"How the hell are you doing that?" he demanded.

"Using your arms at depth is a waste of oxygen, and you'll just tire yourself out faster. You make more progress with your legs. Fins would help, but this will do." Judging by his voice, Peter was barely breathing hard, but he'd already cleared half the distance to the steps.

Lowell mimicked the kid's posture. He wasn't as smooth as Peter, but the technique worked pretty well. "Where'd you learn that?"

"I got certified for an underwater dig off the coast of Greece," Peter told him. He laughed self-consciously. "I used to fantasize about finding something on the scale of the Uluburun shipwreck. I guess I wasn't thinking big enough, huh?"

"I don't want to know."

"Trust me, I wasn't going to waste my breath. It's pretty obvious you don't care about this stuff."

Peter reached the steps well ahead of him. When Lowell followed, he had to brace his arms against the walls to keep himself upright. Climbing steps underwater wasn't as easy as he'd have guessed. Peter just swam up the water above the steps until they reached air.

As Lowell dragged himself up out of the water, he looked around in consternation. There was a whole room up here, perfectly dry. The steps opened onto a wide corridor. There was a solid wall to his left, but he could see other gaps to his right. They must open up all along the underwater tunnel in a dozen or more access points.

But access points to what? he wondered.

"Hey, Chang," he began, but Peter was standing by the wall, his mouth open in wonder as he ran gloved fingers across the stone. Lowell stepped closer, cocking his head when he saw the cuts in the wall. His original point forgotten, he stepped closer, looking over Peter's shoulder at thousands of markings cut into the stone. "What is this?" he mumbled. "Writing?"

"Yeah," Peter breathed. "It's like the Anomaly itself—writing in dozens of languages. Some of them are from Earth, but others..." He hurried away, gesturing to swathes of text that meant less than nothing to Lowell. "Some of these I've never seen before. They're not all alphabets, either. This one looks like it's logographic, but this one's probably a syllabary, although I can't..."

Lowell cleared his throat. "Remember how much I care about this stuff?"

"I get that linguistics isn't your area of interest," said Peter, looking over his shoulder. Between the low light and the tinted helmet, Lowell couldn't see his face, but he had a sneaking suspicion that the kid was glaring at him. "But I'd think that you'd care that whatever's going on here is related to the Anomaly, and to the key. Which means it's *also* related to whatever Munroe is up to."

Lowell sighed. "Then maybe skip the bit with the rock-tographs and find a part you can actually read."

Peter backed up to an earlier part of the wall. The chicken-scratch wasn't the same language as the tablet—it looked like some kind of Asian script, but uneven and scrawling.

"What's this?" Lowell asked.

"Jaiguwen," Peter murmured. "Ancient Chinese script. Now be quiet and let me translate."

Lowell turned to look around the room. He couldn't see much, but aside from the long hall, it was mostly bare. Either whoever had made it hadn't planned to spend much time here, or they'd cleared it out when they left.

"I don't get this." Peter let out a frustrated sigh. "Some of these words aren't familiar."

"Maybe you're not as smart as you think you are."

"It's not that—I mean, not to brag or anything—but based on the context, I don't think I have the vocabulary. For all I know, these words mean *nuclear reactor* or *spaceship*. I wouldn't know the technical terms. Like, if someone in ancient Rome was writing about an airplane, I wouldn't have a translation for the word." Peter grumbled incoherently and shook his head.

"Can you get the gist of it?"

"It's slow going, and I can't quite follow..." Peter's finger froze under one of the images, and he trailed off.

"What?" asked Lowell. "Spare me the dramatics and just tell me what it says."

"*Weapon of war.*" Peter tapped his finger on the stone. "The cuneiform said *ariru.* I thought it meant 'magic,' or a curse. Some superstition, maybe. I didn't pay that much attention. But this is clear. It's not a curse, it's a *weapon.*" He turned slowly to Lowell. "Somehow, activating the Anomaly creates a weapon—put in the stellar key, wait a day, and then..." He shrugged helplessly.

"That's one impressive key."

"Well, *stellar* or *star* key can also be translated as *sun* key," Peter explained. "A term for ultimate power among the ancients. And the thing about translation is that I might be missing some nuance that would have been obvious back in the day. But yeah, this key is a big deal."

"In other words, the key is an energy source."

"Sure," Peter said. "That's a fair interpretation. It's more like a key that powers something up than one that just opens it." He paused. "But the orb is tiny, and it's not generating fusion energy like a star."

"You're the one saying this ancient relic is a *weapon.* Do you really think that we understand fully what's happening here? Based on what?" Lowell gestured to the wall. "A map, and...this? We're guessing about ninety percent of this stuff."

"Good point."

"No wonder Munroe wants to activate this thing so badly," Lowell said. "And no wonder the top brass was willing to sweep so much carnage under the rug. Heck, and the Chinese know…" As the implications sank in, Lowell's head began to spin. "How does it work?"

"I don't *know.*" Peter thumped his fist against the wall. "It doesn't make sense!"

"We've got to stop whatever Munroe's got planned. Whatever it is, the Space Corps has put four years' worth of personnel time and God knows how many dollars into this project."

"More than that," Peter said, stepping back. "We're not talking years' worth of effort, Lowell, we're talking *millennia.*"

As the scale of the project came into focus, Lowell felt as if he was shrinking to the size of an ant. He had to catch himself before he spun out. *This isn't all new, it's just new to you. You've been telling yourself for years that you can only trust the things in front of you. You've known that you can only believe what you're told. You thought you were on the inside, but you only had one small part of the bigger picture.*

"Okay," he said aloud.

"*Okay?*" Peter spun around. "*Okay?* How many people have spent lifetimes trying to prove, disprove, and catalog things that we might as well call a waste of time and just throw out? How many lives have been spent on projects that were, according to this place, a total waste of time?"

Lowell shrugged. "They were no more a waste of time than they were yesterday."

"Does *nothing* faze you?" Peter demanded. "Come on, this is practically *proof* that aliens are real!"

I guess he missed my fish-induced panic attack, Lowell thought. Aloud he said, "The idea of Munroe getting his hands on some galactic-scale weapon fazes me. We should get going. The pod will be recharged soon, and we don't want to waste time."

Peter led the way reluctantly to the stairs. Lowell would have bet a year's salary that he wanted to stay behind reading and translating, working out how to read otherworldly languages. That was one project he would have happily given his life to, wasn't it?

Instead, they slipped back into the water and down the stairs. A few large crustaceans had finned over and were crawling around the pod, puzzled by this new addition to their environment.

Peter was obviously still wrestling with his feelings, but Lowell felt blank, scrubbed clean by the reminder that, in the long term, the mission was the only thing that mattered.

It was the only thing that *ever* mattered.

This time, when they swam back to the pod, Lowell got there first.

29

MUNROE SAT in his command chair, drumming his fingers on the edge of the control panel. Below him, the blank white face of Enceladus stared back, marred only by the ribbing of the fault lines in the ice and the faint blur of seawater blown heavenward by the plumes.

One of his soldiers approached, hovering in the doorway. "Sir?"

"What is it, Grady?" Munroe kept his eyes fixed on the moon. Lowell was down there somewhere, getting up to God knew what, costing the Space Corps an unreasonable amount of money and wasting everyone's time. He'd already lost six men today, and would probably lose a few more when his quarry stumbled into the ambush.

It's a shame he never learned to follow orders. That man would have made an excellent second-in-command if he could have learned to control his impulses.

The private cleared his throat. "Sir, I'm afraid you should see this."

Munroe turned to find Grady standing nervously in the doorway. "What is it?" he asked, trying to keep his temper in check. One more setback, and he was really going to go off on someone.

These new recruits were better with the tech, but they didn't have the grit and fortitude of the old guard. In a fight between Lowell and this kid, Grady wouldn't last two minutes. It was a shame that more people weren't like Hellcat, a perfect mix of focused and ruthless.

Some days, it was all he could do to keep from shooting his weaker platoon members in the back, just for a chance to request new men. *If this all goes according to plan*, he reminded himself, *I'll be able to cherry-pick my team. I'll make O-9 overnight. Even if they don't promote me, who's going to get in my way?*

Grady went to the window and powered up the screen. The surface of Enceladus disappeared, only to be replaced by the image of a sizable craft against a starry background.

"What's this?" Munroe demanded.

"Our men circling Titan spotted it a few hours ago." Grady wouldn't meet his eye. The little twerp already recognized that this was bad news. *I wonder if they drew straws to decide who was going to come tell me?*

Munroe leaned forward, resting his elbows on his knees. "It looks like a Russian warship." His eye landed on the logo: a blue, red, and white oval speared through by a blue arrow. Without turning his head, his flicked his gaze toward Grady. "Is that what I'm looking at?"

"I'm afraid so, sir. Not only that..." Grady prodded the screen, which flipped to an image of a long, narrow ship ringed by a high-velocity energon wheel. The insignia on the side showed two overlaid parallelograms.

"The Germans, too?" Munroe rubbed his temples, squeezing

his eyes shut. *This can't be happening. Hasn't enough gone wrong today?*

"There's also talk of an Indian craft that left Earth's orbit about six hours ago. Command says there must have been a data breach regarding the current mission." Grady shuffled his feet.

"You heard from Command?" Munroe's eye twitched. "Why wasn't I informed of this immediately?"

"I came down at once," Grady assured him. At least he'd stopped shuffling his feet now. "What do we do, sir?"

"Nothing we *can* do," Munroe told him. He got to his feet and began to pace back and forth across the length of the small cabin. "If there's no backup in the area, we can't risk starting an armed conflict with any one of these people."

"Sir, our allies…" Grady began.

Munroe laughed, shaking his head. "Allies? What do you think a promise made by a group of politicians means out here? Nothing. *Less* than nothing." He gestured toward the moon outside, although it was no longer visible with the screen powered on. "We're already fighting our own men, and you think we can trust the Russians to play nice? Get real, Grady. I thought even you were smarter than that."

The young man shrank away from him, but Munroe was already weighing his options. The second someone opened fire, it would be a free-for-all. The press could spin anything, and if the Corps initiated action, the Pentagon would have his head.

On the other hand, if he sat idly by until he was outnumbered, and they lost control of the weapon as a result…

"Get out," he said, not even bothering to look back at Grady. He heard the man's footsteps withdraw, but the private hadn't bothered to power down the screen. When Munroe circled back, he was still faced with the image of the German ship.

"Five nations' worth of firepower," Munroe muttered. That

was assuming the Japanese stayed out of it, which was a long shot. He was certain that the Japanese forces wouldn't team up with the Tiān Zhuānjiā, and there had been a falling out between the Russian and Indian space forces a few years back, but even if they were all fighting independently, he would have his hands full.

There were very few times that Munroe rushed to cede power, but he had to admit that he was in over his head this time.

This isn't my call. I'm going to need confirmation on this. This might be a war zone, but until we have the weapon secured, nothing is guaranteed.

He reached for his helmet and set the channel number to his encrypted line with the Pentagon. The handshake took nearly ten minutes at this range, and when he was finally patched through, the wait time on the transmissions lagged. It was always best to get right to the point; the audio took another three minutes to reach Earth, and then he'd be forced to wait another three minutes for the reply. Who knew what time it was in Virginia—if it was the middle of the night, it could take even longer for someone to track down the people who would be able to issue the final word on the matter.

When the line finally connected, Munroe spoke quickly. "This is Lieutenant Munroe, reporting on Operation Cascade. I've got vessels from at least four nationalities approaching. It appears the secret is in the open. What are my orders?"

Time seemed to stretch, and Munroe sat there, staring at the image on the screen and waiting. They must have access to the blueprints for the German vessel. If he got a chance, he'd review the hologram of its layout and determine the best place to hit the ship to bring it down.

The line crackled, and then a voice said, "We are aware of the situation. Your orders have not changed. Complete the mission by any means necessary."

According to the clock on his helmet's readout, exactly six minutes had passed. The Pentagon must be on high alert already, which meant that Space Corps forces were likely on their way.

"Understood. Munroe out." He dropped the channel, knowing that he was unlikely to get more details at this point. They had told him what they thought he needed to know, and he was on his own now.

They could have warned me, he thought in annoyance, then checked himself at once. That was the sort of logic that had gotten Lowell into trouble. Munroe's job was not to know, or to think, or even to understand. His job was to bring back a weapon that would change the future.

A new call request opened up on his readout, and Munroe accepted it with a sigh of relief.

"Hellcat? I'm hoping you have some good news for me."

"I sure do," Hellcat replied, sounding almost cheerful. "We're at the Anomaly. There's no sign of Lowell yet, but there's a ton of activity down here. If he's lucky, something else will get him before he reaches us." She chuckled to herself. "But we've got all kinds of toys down here in case he shows up wanting to play."

He checked the clock again: 1230 hours. "You've got an hour and a half," Munroe told her. "If he doesn't show by then, get out of there."

"Sir? What about the Anomaly?" Hellcat asked.

"By that point it won't matter," Munroe said. He crossed the room, powering down the screen so that he could see the icy lunar surface below him once more. "Our Lowell problem will disappear —along with the rest of this godforsaken place."

30

FOR YEARS, Peter had waffled on the details of his thesis topic. He'd briefly considered the subject of ripple-flaked knives, then had spent a month reading about the connections between metallurgy in ancient Rome and China to see if that sparked his interest. He sometimes fantasized about being allowed to tie in one of the reigning theories on alien intervention.

Now he finally had the research topic of a lifetime, and nobody back home was going to believe him.

"I wish I could have taken a picture," he said. "Can you imagine what I could do with that? The minute I put it online, I'd win the internet."

"The government would stop you," Lowell said flatly.

"Not if I had *proof*," Peter insisted.

Lowell clicked his tongue. "Really? You think nobody has ever had proof before? You think that you're going to take a couple of scans of some rock wall and people are going to buy into it? Even if they didn't call your images fake—and trust me, they *would*—they'd be forced to rely on your translation of whatever it said.

Every step away from the original introduces doubt, and the top brass would dogpile on that. If you're lucky, they'd ruin your reputation."

"That's *lucky?*" Peter asked.

Lowell turned to look at him flatly. "You'd be alive."

"Where did you learn to think like this?" asked Peter, who'd been raised by a believer. According to his father, the proof had been out there for years, and Peter had flip-flopped between blind acceptance and deep skepticism.

"Space Corps Cadet Academy training." Lowell looked crossways at him. "They told us exactly how they'd discredit us if we decided to go public with any of our intel. It's what they've done in the past. You might kick up a dust cloud, but it wouldn't take. The only people you'd convince would be the ones who already buy into the current conspiracy theory."

Peter slumped miserably in his seat. "There has to be some way to get the word out."

"Why?" Lowell shrugged. "People like feeling comfortable. You're going to tell people that their life's work is based on a false assumption, and they're going to roll over and take it? No way. They'll call you a nutjob and blackball you from every academic position on the planet. Trust me, I've seen it happen. You can't take these guys on. They've got more money, more resources, and more motivation than you do. Don't kid yourself, Chang. You're out of your depth." He paused for a moment, then smirked. "So to speak."

According to the radar, they had almost reached the end of the tunnel, which accounted for the last of their instructions. The tunnel would dump them out somewhere near the Anomaly. It was a good thing, too, given their timing. They had just over an hour to get the key back and stop Munroe from getting his weapon. Peter still hadn't worked out precisely what it was, but he wouldn't have trusted Munroe with an old claw hammer, much less advanced alien tech.

Lowell cut the thrusters abruptly, his eyes fixed on the radar.

"What's wrong?" Peter asked.

"This doesn't make sense," Lowell muttered. He pointed at the radar. "According to this thing, it's a feeding frenzy out there."

"Didn't one of the techs say that the Anomaly seemed to be vibrating?" Peter asked. "If the key's causing some type of geological activity, this would be ground zero. Everything would be going nuts."

"Great," Lowell grumbled. "More freakin' *fish*." He shook his head wearily, then laid his hand on the throttle. "Okay, here's the plan. We're going to get as close to the Anomaly as we can, I'm going to stop just long enough to drop you out of the hatch, and then I'll lead whatever critters are out there on a merry chase while you retrieve the key. Let me know when you've grabbed it, and I'll circle back for you."

"*Me?*" Peter squeaked. "You're just going to dump me out there after what happened to those techs?"

Lowell rolled his eyes. "Sorry, I guess I should have asked. Would *you* like to pilot the pod while fighting a hundred sea creatures?"

"No," Peter admitted.

"Then stick with the plan." Lowell pointed to Peter's helmet, then reached for his own.

As Peter checked the seal, he found himself wrinkling his nose. Either the helmet was starting to stink, or his breath was getting rancid after that second ham bar.

Stop being an idiot, Peter. Personal hygiene is the least of your problems right now.

He got up from his seat and swung it back, kneeling on the floor next to the hatch. If he was going to be on key-retrieval duty, he wanted to limit his time in the water as much as possible.

"Ready?" asked Lowell.

"Ready as I'm going to get."

"I'll seal it when you're out. You just focus on getting that key."

Peter nodded. He was hazy with exhaustion, thirsty, and wondering how he was going to be able to keep things together long enough to survive this mission.

"You're good to go, Chang," said Lowell's voice in his ear. "I believe in you."

"That makes one of us," Peter chuckled nervously. "Let me know when we're close."

Lowell took them out of the tunnel, pushing the little pod so fast that Peter almost overbalanced.

"What if we run the battery down again?" he asked.

"Then we'll either die, or we'll figure it out then," Lowell replied.

"You should have been an orator," Peter grumbled. "One more rousing speech like that and you'll move me to tears."

"Just focus on the miss—" Lowell began.

He was cut off abruptly when something smashed into the side of the vessel.

"No more dolphins," Peter groaned. "No more sharks or coelacanths or liopleurodons..."

"This isn't an animal," said Lowell, his voice sinking low and dangerous. "It's much worse."

31

TWO HOURS AGO, Helena Moore would have said that she had run missions in all kinds of conditions, but even she had to admit that the circumstances on Enceladus were unique. Before the Space Corps had recruited her, she'd worked security detail for a rich dentist who'd had more money than sense. During a hunting trip off the South African coast, she'd had to spear an eighteen-foot great white shark at close range to keep the idiot from meeting his maker.

At the time, she'd been struck by the size of the beast. Some of the critters out here were big enough to see a great white as an *amuse-bouche.*

Helena's team was outfitted with some of the best equipment available, with all the bells and whistles released in the new wave of Space Corps tech that DARPA could come up with. Their jet-scooters had been designed for travel and combat in Saturn's gaseous atmosphere, and the low-drag harpoons had been upgraded with ballistic tips that burst apart on impact. Four of her eight team members were already in position, while the rest of her crew manned the two armored ships.

Helena tuned into her crew-wide channel and watched the radar. The wildlife was going crazy out there, and it would be difficult to tell a ship's heat signature from everything else—but the station's log had said that Lowell had been assigned to Hoverpod 4. When NASA had commissioned the pods, they'd been equipped with tracking devices so that the command towers could track the comings and goings of their team, and locate transports if the pilots reported an accident. Now that she knew what she was looking for, Helena had been able to lock their ident into the radar. She'd been able to confirm that the pod was no longer on the surface of the moon, just as Munroe had suspected.

The trouble was, she didn't seem to be able to find them at all.

Where are you hiding, Lowell?

Her eyes were fixed on the readings when Simms hailed her from the other ship.

"Do we have a bead on the target?" Helena asked.

"We've got a weak reading at five o'clock," Simms replied. "The signal keeps cutting out, though. I'm not sure why."

The ship's engines had been designed for efficiency, with the explicit intention that they wouldn't disturb equipment readings. The fact that they were nearly silent, even in an atmosphere other than the one they'd been designed for, was an added bonus, one that Helena appreciated fully as she took her ship closer to Simms'. The fish were out of control, but they didn't seem to care much about her presence as she slipped through the fray.

From her new position, Helena could see that her second-in-command was right. There was a weak signal reading, almost as if something was blocking the tracker.

"Where the hell are you?" Helena murmured. It was almost as if the little ship was underground somehow, stopped not quite beneath them, unmoving for a long moment. *It's going to be ironic as hell if it turns out they're in the belly of one of these monsters,* she thought.

And then, suddenly, the signal came in clear.

"Are you all getting this?" she asked.

Half a dozen voices replied in the affirmative.

"You know your roles," she barked. "Let's complete the mission and get off-world. We've got fifty-six minutes before our clock runs out. Watch out for the native life."

As the rest of her crew aimed their harpoons, Helena handed over control of the ship to her navigator and then headed for the weapons station. She was a good pilot, but when it came to following her passions, her Hellcat heart was always poised to draw first blood.

Ballistics were fine, but she had something a little bigger in mind for her quarry.

32

LOWELL GRITTED his teeth as the second shot struck the side of the pod.

Of course Munroe couldn't make this easy on me. I should have seen this coming—probably would have, too, if I hadn't had my hands full with all the fish.

"What do you mean, worse?" Peter asked.

Instead of answering, Lowell fired the laser. He wasn't aiming at anything in particular, but the shot had the desired effect: in the faint light of the red beam, he could see the outlines of four figures clinging to bullet-shaped vehicles the size of a man's torso.

"Looks like your friends are back," Lowell grunted when the light went out again.

"They're your friends, not mine," Peter argued. "What are we going to do?"

Lowell glanced down at the radar. There was nothing nearby anywhere close to the size of Sharkie. He'd be taking a risk, for sure, but time was running out. If there was ever a time to get reckless, it was now.

"We're going shadow-hunting," he said.

Peter made a little noise of disbelief when Lowell turned the lights on, and one of the incoming Space Corpsmen raised an arm to block the light from their eyes.

A moment later, a beady-eyed fish the size of a smartcar took the protective arm clean off.

Lowell didn't waste time watching that man die: he had three more targets in his sights. He fired the laser at one of the other soldiers, missing by a hair's breadth.

I need some real weapons, not a research pod and a gun with two shots left.

He was preparing to fire again when the radar caught his eye, and two larger heat signatures closed in.

Combat vessels.

"Dammit," Lowell grunted. He turned to look at Peter, who was hovering uncertainly by the hatch. "Listen, Chang, I'm going to need you to trust me and do what I tell you. No second-guessing my orders. Got it?"

"All right," Peter said in a shaky voice.

"Here's the plan. We're going to—"

He was cut short by a terrific *bang*, and the whole pod rocked to the side. A serrated blade as long as Lowell's arm sheared through the side of the vessel, stopping just short of the back of his neck.

A moment later, water came pouring in around the metal tip of the weapon.

"Oh my God," Peter moaned.

"Your helmet's on," Lowell told him. "You can breathe even if the pod's compromised. We've still got a few minutes, we just—"

The pod lurched again, and Lowell swore. They hadn't just been hit by an oversized harpoon—now they were being winched in. As they were dragged along, the plating around the puncture point began to fold in. *I wonder how much PSI we're under... and how much we can take before this pod buckles like a soda can beneath a bootheel.*

"Screw the plan," he said, throwing himself off of his chair. "Open the hatch." Outside, the three remaining soldiers were still contending with the writhing mass of sea creatures, which seemed to be multiplying by the second. *And we're going out there... Great. Just what the doctor ordered.*

Peter's hands fumbled with the mechanism, and Lowell shoved him aside. As he threw the hatch back, he saw Peter reach for the tablet, the silver brick of trouble that had started it all.

"Leave it," he said.

"But..." Peter began.

Lowell grabbed his crewmember's arm and thrust him toward the opening. "*Leave. It.*"

"My friends died for that!" Peter cried. "I can't just let it *sink.*"

Lowell grabbed the kid by the back of the neck, holding him in place with a firm hand. "If you don't keep your hands free, you're going to die for it, too. You said you were going to follow orders. That starts now, or I leave you here."

Peter whimpered, and Lowell wondered if he'd crossed a line, but there was no time to worry about that now. He shoved Peter toward the opening at the bottom of the pod and dove out after.

He'd been right about the winch. In the bobbing illumination thrown by the pod's floodlights, he could see the line leading back to the ship like an umbilical cord. That squeezed sensation returned, and Lowell went limp for a moment, paralyzed with something that felt uncomfortably like fear.

No time for that, he told himself. It had been one thing to panic in the tunnel, but they were in the open ocean now, surrounded by enemies and hungry animals, and being pulled by the current. He could feel the way the ocean tugged at his limbs, drawing him inexorably down.

I'm going to end up in the trench if I don't get it together. I need to be strong for both of us.

"Okay, Chang, are you with me?" he asked, as if they were taking a hike through the forest and Chang was lagging a little bit behind.

"Yes," Peter said weakly.

"You're a stronger swimmer than I am," Lowell told him. "I'd pull you if I could, but I'm going to need you to keep up. We're going back toward the divers. Got it?"

Peter made a little noise of agreement.

Lowell began to swim. He could no longer see Peter, or much of anything else around them. He had to rely on the fact that he could hear heavy breathing in his mic, the only indication that Peter was following instructions and doing his best to keep pace. He quelled the urge to paddle with his arms and focused on kicking, relying on smooth and steady strokes rather than short, frenetic movements.

"You're doing great," he said.

Peter laughed miserably, gasping for air as he struggled through the water at Lowell's side. "We're going to die down here," he said, as if it was already decided, as if he'd already given in.

"No," Lowell grunted back. "I don't accept it."

Peter's laugh was a little stronger this time. "Don't throw my words back at me..."

"You might be right," Lowell said. They were closing in on the divers. "We're in trouble, kid. But the one thing I can promise you is that, if we're on our way out, we'll take as many of these guys down with us as we can."

33

I CAN'T BELIEVE *I lost the tablet.*

It was probably a sign of exhaustion, or possibly just insanity, that Peter couldn't let go of the fact that he'd lost the greatest archaeological find of his life to the depths of an alien sea. In the grand scheme of things, it was just an object, a little scrap of material whose sole purpose had been to get them here. If the point of an object was to be used, it had done what it needed to do.

But Peter was an archaeologist, and a romantic to boot. He believed in treasures.

He'd managed to shove the night-vision visor over his helmet before his graceless entry into the sea, so even the parts of the tableau before him that weren't illuminated were still clearly visible. It wasn't exactly an inspiring sight. Three enemy soldiers, two ships, and an untold number of living fossils seemed determined to take out two men armed only with a gun and a gift for reading dead languages.

I'm glad I flunked out of statistics, he thought grimly. *I doubt I'd like those odds.*

Lowell, however, seemed to have gotten his second wind. He was flying along, kicking furiously. A few hours ago, he'd been ready to accept his fate, but his sense of purpose appeared to have returned in full force.

"Do you see that empty scooter?" Lowell asked, lifting one arm to point off to his right.

Peter turned his head. "Yeah." It was the vehicle that had been used by the unfortunate diver who'd died in front of them only moments ago. The scooter was sinking fast now that it had lost its rider. If it wasn't for his visor, he wouldn't have been able to pick it out.

"Grab it," Lowell said. "See if you can figure out how to use it. The second you can, I want you to dive. We must be close."

"What about you?" Peter asked, even as he changed direction. He wasn't about to be accused of talking back again.

"The plan is the same," Lowell said. "You're going to get the key, and I'm going to secure us a ride. You worry about your end of things, and I'll handle mine. Once you've got the key back, Munroe's clock stops. All we have to do after that is survive."

"Got it." Peter swam out to the sinking scooter. He could see where his hands were supposed to go, but he'd never used one of these things, and certainly nothing this high-tech before. "Any idea how to make it go?"

"I'm sure a smart PhD candidate like yourself can figure it out," Lowell said drily.

Peter put his hands in place, but the scooter was still sinking, dragging him down with it. Something brushed his leg, and the pressure was building in his ears.

I hate this, he thought as his anger returned. *I hate that I should be digging in the Iraqi dust, and instead I'm trying to figure out to work a military-grade underwater transport.* He squeezed his hands around the grips in frustration.

And then he held on for dear life as the scooter shot through the water.

"I figured it out!" he called.

"You get a gold star," Lowell grunted. "Now be quiet. I've got some guys to kill."

Peter adjusted his course, heading for the seabed. Below him, he could see the silhouette of the Anomaly, its outline brilliant against the sandy rubble. It was even more beautiful than it had looked in the video feed from *Moby Dick*, and he could feel the subtle vibration in the water as he approached.

The skeleton of the *Moby Dick* lay nearby. It looked as if it had been down there for a century rather than a day. Crabs and spiny sea stars had reclaimed it.

Even with the grim reminder of the wreck below him, Peter's gaze kept being drawn back to the Anomaly. It may have jump-started the destruction of the submarine, but that made it no less enthralling. Like the tablet itself, it seemed to call to Peter, a wealth of hidden knowledge just waiting to be revealed. He tried to imagine what it would be like if it was ever hauled out of the ocean, framed in a case inside some vaulted museum, how it would glimmer in the light.

And my name would be on the plaque, he thought.

He was so lost in his vision of fame and grandeur that he didn't see the dark shape closing in on him.

34

LOWELL HADN'T BEEN TRYING to keep things light with his 'gold star' sarcasm to Peter, but he wasn't kidding about the killing part.

He reached the first of the divers just as the soldier fired a spear into the side of something that looked almost like an over-sized lobster. The man was so distracted by the flailing of the giant crustacean that he didn't notice Lowell approach. He was prob-ably on the crew's channel, and if he said anything to alert the others to Lowell's presence, he'd lose the element of surprise.

Which meant he'd have one shot at taking the guy out cleanly.

The Glock could fire at this depth, but it wouldn't have much range; the drag from the water meant that the bullet would only be deadly at a few meters. Lowell decided to hedge his bets. He swam closer, shoving aside a pony-sized trilobite, and wrapped one arm around the man's torso. At the same time, he lifted his gun to the back of the man's neck, right in the weak point of the seam, and fired.

The front of the soldier's helmet blew to shrapnel, and the man instantly went limp in Lowell's arms.

Lowell re-holstered his gun. He only had one shot left, and he'd need to make it count. Keeping his arm around the dead Space Corpsman, he retrieved the man's knife and took his night-vision visor.

Finding nothing else readily available, he dropped the man's body and grabbed hold of the empty scooter. He'd never personally used one before, but he had a good idea of how to make it work. The harpoon mount was another matter.

As he clung to the scooter, looking for any sign on the controls, he realized that something was moving toward him from below. Refocusing his eyes, he saw the large form of an eel twining up toward him, mouth open and needle teeth parted to reveal a long gullet.

Oh no you don't, buddy. I've already been eaten once today, and I'm in no hurry to repeat the experience.

On instinct, Lowell tensed his arms, pulling the grips of the scooter toward him as his chest pressed against the body of the machine. The machine made a dull *whump* noise, and a three-foot bar shot out of the front of the scooter and sailed right down the eel's throat.

Less than a second later, the eel blew apart, as though it had swallowed a stick of dynamite.

"Perfect," Lowell chuckled, baring his teeth. "Hey, Chang, if you need to fire your harpoon, just point it where you want and pull the handles back toward you." *Smart thinking on the part of whoever designed this thing—there's almost no recoil. I wonder how much cash they dropped on these things?*

He swung toward the other two divers, lining up his next shot. The addition of the night-vision visor gave him a clear view of his targets, and he fired on the first one before the poor guy even knew what was happening.

This guy didn't die right away. The bolt pinned him to his scooter, but he thrashed for a long moment—long enough that he caught the attention of the final diver and probably shouted a warning over their radio channel.

A second later, the final diver spun to face him. With the assistance of the visor, Lowell could see her face through the helmet. There was rage there, and disappointment. He recognized her from a long time ago as a woman named Hatchett. She'd been part of the team back on Mars, but he'd never spent much time around her. They'd worked opposite shifts.

You think I'm a traitor, he thought sadly, and her eyes narrowed in disgust. *But I wish I could ask you what the hell you saw in Munroe that made that bastard worth dying for. How can you write off everything he did?*

How close did I come to being the kind of person who would roll over and accept whatever the commanders told me to do?

Lowell fired, but either Hatchett was ready for him or his heart wasn't really in it, because she jetted out of the way just in time.

This is no time to get sentimental, Lowell. She's part of the crew that killed Chang's dig team. She's had every chance in the world to get wise to the way this works, and she's still playing along with one of the vilest men you've ever had the displeasure of meeting. If you're going to commit to treason, there can be no half measures.

Hatchett had the same weapons, the same training, the same tactical advantages. He wasn't going to be able to strong-arm her, the way he had with Wilcox and Horne.

"Sorry," he said aloud, wondering if she could read his expression. Then he reached for his flashlight.

When the beam hit the visor of her helmet, Hatchett recoiled, momentarily blinded. That was all Lowell needed: he pulled his arms in, firing a bolt right through her chest with such force that it carried her bodily away from her scooter. As she flailed, the fish around her closed in, drawn by the beam of the flashlight. Lowell clicked the light off to spare himself the sight, forgetting that the visor would allow him to bear witness anyway.

He hovered for a moment, watching as someone he knew became fish chow.

Sometimes I wonder if I'm that much better than Munroe. I certainly seem to have no problem killing the people who get in my way.

The changing minute on the digital clock inside his helmet array startled him back to the present. Thirty-six minutes to go.

"Are you close?" he asked aloud.

"Nearly there," Peter told him. "I'm maybe a hundred feet away."

The kid was holding up his end of things, which meant Lowell had his own work cut out for him. *Time to score us a ride,* he thought.

Good thing the Corps had been thoughtful enough to send *two* ships. It never hurt to have backup.

35

HELENA GRITTED HER TEETH. "Hatchett? Prichard? Do you copy?"

When there was no answer, Helena slammed her palm down on the controls and uttered a wordless snarl. Her aim with the grappling cable had been dead on, and the pod was flooded, but there was no sign of bodies within. Judging by the sudden radio silence of her crew, she was down to two ships and missing half a crew.

Who the hell is this guy?

She'd never met Lowell before. Munroe had never explicitly said so, but Helena had a feeling that she'd been hired to fill the spot he'd vacated on the team. Whenever the old guard talked about the traitor, they all but spat at the mention of his name—but Munroe didn't respect many people, and it sure seemed like he respected Lowell.

Helena was beginning to see why.

"The divers are gone. What have you got for me, Simms?" she asked.

Simms' voice crackled back through her mic. "It looks like they split up. One of them is down here by the Anomaly. He's got one of our scooters."

He's going for the key.

"Hellcat, do you think we should contact the lieutenant?" Simms asked.

"No," she snapped immediately. "There's nothing to say." Helena was in no hurry to admit defeat. She was done underestimating this guy, and she clearly couldn't trust other people to handle the problem.

Time to get serious.

"You take the one down by the Anomaly—that's got to be Chang. Ice him, Simms. I'm dropping the drones."

"Roger that."

Helena turned to her controls. Her attack on the pod might not have taken Lowell out, but at least he was in the open now. It wouldn't take much firepower to compromise his suit. All she'd need was one well-placed shot.

She had three drones made for multi-element combat. They wouldn't be as effective at depth as they would off-world, but it wasn't like she was fighting a whole platoon. It was just two guys, one of which was a civilian without a clue. Simms could handle the kid.

Lowell, on the other hand, is mine.

36

AS HE CLOSED in on the Anomaly, Peter's eyes roamed over the surface. Being here in person was certainly different from seeing it on a screen, and he couldn't help wondering at the intricacy of the inscriptions. *How did the aliens make this?* he wondered. *We're miles below the surface. Did they make it down here, or transport it? Was there always water on the moon, or did they bring it here afterward? What was the* point?

His mind was filled with a hundred practical questions, all of which scattered the instant he became aware of the bulk moving alongside him.

"It's not Sharkie," he muttered, "so what the heck...?"

The faint vibration of the Anomaly was suddenly replaced by a throbbing pulse that tore through Peter's chest and sent him tumbling away from the scooter. He gasped for air, whimpering through a blur of pain. His vision turned red, and dark floaters danced across his retinas.

"Chang?" asked Lowell, his voice so close to Peter's ear that for a second Peter forgot that he was hundreds of meters away. "What's happening?"

"Hurts," Peter moaned. His ears were ringing, and he was dimly aware that he was sinking, but he could do nothing about it. His arms and legs seemed to belong to someone else, and all his concerns had become distant. The only thing that mattered was the pain.

"Sonic cannon," Lowell said, and there was panic in his tone. "Chang, can you breathe?"

"No," Peter said, although surely he could, or he wouldn't be able to talk. Nothing made sense anymore.

"Hold on," said Lowell. "I'm coming to you."

"I had orders," Peter mumbled. "Sorry I didn't follow them."

"Shut up and stay alive," Lowell growled. "*That's* an order."

Above him, Peter saw the dark shape close in on the scooter, then spear it with one of the oversized harpoons, drawing it back by the thick cable like the one that had claimed the pod.

I'm alone out here with no vehicle and no weapon, he thought. *This is it.*

And then, *I don't accept it.*

Little by little, his vision cleared. His mouth tasted like copper, and he could feel something warm and wet trickling down his stomach inside the protective layers of the suit, but he could move his arms again.

"Lowell?" he said.

"Don't you dare die on me, Chang," the other man said fiercely.

"They got my ride." He coughed, wincing. "You're going to have to come get me."

"I'm on my way, buddy."

"Not now." He took another breath, then rolled over so that he was looking down at the Anomaly below. "Come back when you've got a way off this frozen rock."

Lowell hesitated. "You sure?"

Peter coughed again, smiling through the pain. "It's an order."

Slowly, well aware that every move cost him, he began to kick. The Anomaly was close, and even if he did it with his dying breath, he was going to get that key back.

He'd lost one artifact. He had no intention of losing another, and there was no point in wasting time that they didn't have.

37

LOWELL HAD FIRED his share of sonic cannons over the years, but he'd never fired one underwater.

By his reckoning, Peter had gotten lucky. Just as the water slowed the trajectory of ballistics, it must have put a damper on the cannon. Otherwise, Peter would have been reduced to pâté inside his suit.

That would make my job twice as hard, Lowell thought, as if that was the only reason he cared about Peter's fate. He'd always been a crap liar, even when he was lying to himself.

He was tempted to swim down there and take charge of things, but either way, they'd still have two ships on their tail. If he kept the Space Corps busy far enough away from Peter, the kid would stand a better chance.

The other ship was approaching now, the speared carcass of Hoverpod 4 dangling from its hull. A scooter wasn't going to be able to take both of them down.

Guess I'm going to have to upgrade.

The ships might have superior firepower, but Lowell had

speed and maneuverability on his side. He stayed low, out of range of the top-mounted sonic cannons, and came up under the hull of the nearest ship.

There had been a few advancements in ship design since Lowell had gone into near-exile, but the basic design was the same as ever. Back in training, they'd been told that the ships' main engines were underneath, which allowed them to work within a planet's atmosphere and gravitational pull as well as off-world. At the time, the briefing had included this information as a warning to pilots to guard the undersides of their hulls from attack.

They probably didn't think we'd be using that information to sabotage our own crew.

It would have been easier, of course, if the crew hadn't seen him coming, or if the ship had been stationary. As it was, he soon found himself caught in the ship's wake.

"You still alive, Chang?" he asked.

"So far," said Peter. The kid didn't sound good, and Lowell winced in sympathy. They'd been put through all types of pain tolerance training before deployment, but he could only imagine how he would have reacted to that kind of agony, much less how a civilian like Peter might fare against a weapon that could cut your organs to ribbons with a direct hit. Not that he'd have been able to keep that from happening—he'd just had more experience in pain management.

If it hadn't been for his peripheral vision and the aid of the visor, Lowell would have missed the flash of movement on his right. As it was, he only spotted the drone seconds before it fired.

"You little son of a..." he growled, rolling to the side so that the bulk of his sea-scooter took the hit. He felt the impact all the way through his body.

Good thing I saw that before it hit me. I doubt even my suit's chestplate would hold up to that kind of damage.

He tried to turn sideways to get a shot at the drone with his harpoon, but the slipstream caused by the moving ship made it almost impossible. When he did finally risk firing a shot, the harpoon was swept away long before it hit.

"You don't have to sound so mad about it," said Peter weakly. "I can die faster if that would make you feel better."

"I'm not talking to you," Lowell informed him, rolling back so that at least his torso would be shielded by the scooter. Of course, if the drone shot him in the leg, he might not die instantly, but if the suit was compromised, Lowell would be instantly crushed by the pressure of twenty-some miles of ocean.

The teardrop-shaped drones were more aquadynamic than a man on a scooter, and from this angle would be almost impossible to hit. On the other hand, the slipstream would have little impact on the aim of its laser targeting.

Lowell had a tried-and-true method for dealing with information that he didn't want to have to cope with just yet: *don't think about it.*

Instead, he took a few precious seconds to weigh the pros and cons of sinking the entire ship. He could try firing a bolt right into the hull. He had no way of knowing how many harpoons he had left, but it might be enough to compromise the exterior.

Not worth it, he decided. If he took this one down, he'd still have to make it to the other ship if he and Peter were going to have even a faint hope of making it out of here alive. Time was running short, and even if Peter managed to get to the key in time, he was in bad shape. He'd need care, which meant Lowell would have to get to him before the kid bled out.

That settled it. He'd stick with this vessel and finish what he'd started.

Lowell looked straight ahead, trying to figure out where he was relative to the ship's weak points, and realized that there was another drone up ahead. It fired a blast of dazzling light a moment later, and Lowell pulled himself close to the scooter in an attempt to dodge the beam. Not only did it work, but it had the unintended consequence of firing a harpoon at just the right angle to knock this drone out of the slipstream around the ship. The machine swept past him and was lost to the open sea.

There's going to be more where that came from, and I can only fight so many battles at once. If you're going to fight, go all in.

"Hey, Chang," he asked aloud, "do you still trust me?"

"Do I have a choice?" asked Peter weakly.

Lowell chuckled. "Touché, buddy."

He pushed the scooter one last time for all it was worth, until it brought him so close to the hull of the ship that he could actually touch it. And then, with a word of prayer whispered to a God he'd lost faith in years ago, he let go of the scooter's handles and flew free, utterly untethered from everything.

38

"SIR, we just picked up something in the rear cameras," the navigator said.

Simms glanced over at the controls, then grinned. "It's that bastard's scooter. Hellcat must have taken him out with the drones."

Simms remembered when Lowell had been part of the crew. It had been years since the man had turned on them, and tainted two other perfectly good soldiers by association. Their platoon had been grounded for almost eight months after he'd testified at the inquest, and they'd been on half pay the whole time.

Sure, a couple of nerds got killed along the way, but there are casualties in every war, Simms thought. Take, for example, the kid he'd just blown away. He'd caused more trouble than he was worth. It would have been better if they'd just killed him back in Ur-An and hired someone privately to read that tablet. The stakes of the mission weren't entirely clear to Simms, but it didn't take a genius to see that these two had thrown a wrench into the works.

"Mission complete," he radioed to Hellcat. "I've got both scooters accounted for, and we hit the kid with cannonfire."

"I want a body," Hellcat replied. "In fact, I want both."

Simms checked the clock. "We've got fifteen minutes before we're supposed to be off-world. If we didn't stop for Pearce and Gretlo, why are we retrieving these two?"

"Because I want proof," said the lance corporal firmly. "I want to see Lowell's corpse with my own eyes. I want to *spit* on it. This guy took out ten of our people today. He's a traitor, Simms. I want his head on a pike."

"Sure," Simms sighed. He knew the lance corporal well enough to know that once she got her teeth into something, she wasn't going to just walk away. Most of the time, he appreciated her thoroughness.

But most of the time, he wasn't surrounded by monstrous fish or a satellite on the way out.

He was taking the ship down when he heard a muffled curse through the mic.

"What's wrong?" asked one of the navigators.

"I've got a drone on you," Hellcat snarled. "You've got a problem. Lowell's not dead."

Simms blinked. "But his scooter—"

"He's on the side of your ship," Hellcat said. "He must have ditched the scooter, and he's sticking to you like a damn barnacle."

"I don't know what you think he's going to do out there," Simms said.

Hellcat's voice became suddenly soft, laced with an edge of venom that made Simms' hair stand on end. "That man should be dead ten times over, and he's still out there. I don't know what his plan is, but I guarantee he has one. *Handle it.*"

"Yes, of course, right away," Simms stammered.

"I've got two drones on him," Hellcat said. "I'll keep him pinned. I expect you to do the rest. And when you do, I want his head as a trophy. He's going to rue the day he joined the Space Corps."

39

LOWELL CLUNG to the side of the ship for dear life, his fingers hooked into the seam between panels, and wondered briefly what his life would be like if he had never joined the Space Corps.

I'd still think Michigan winters were as cold as it gets.

I could be at home, drinking margaritas and celebrating Kylie's birthday.

I could still have a functioning relationship with my dad.

Lowell allowed himself exactly three seconds of crippling self-pity, and then he shut it down. Time was running out, and whining about his lot in life wasn't helping anyone.

The Space Corps suits had a rappelling function, designed primarily for people who were crazy enough to crawl around and make external ship repairs deep in space—Lowell, unfortunately, had plenty of experience with that. He was finding that it didn't work as well in water as it did in a low-gravity, zero-drag environment, but it was better than free climbing. So long as a fish or a drone didn't get him, he'd be able to make it to the access hatch on the ship's underbelly using the electrostatic bonding function between the suit and the ship.

Whether he'd be able to make it inside the timeframe was another matter altogether.

"How you doing, Chang?" he asked as he climbed.

"Not dead yet," Peter said stiffly. "That's something, right?"

"Could be worse," said Lowell, beginning his climb along the side of the ship. "Any day you're still aboveground is a good day."

"Does this count?"

"Sure as hell does," Lowell grunted. "Are you close to the key?"

"As long as nothing gets me first, I'll make it," Peter said. "Have you got our ride?"

"Working on it." A flash of movement to Lowell's right caught his eye, and he sighed. "Don't talk to me for a minute, okay?"

"Is something wrong?" Peter asked, sounding suddenly nervous.

Yeah, my teammate can't shut his mouth when I ask him to, Lowell thought. He didn't say it aloud, though. All things considered, the kid was doing pretty well. It wasn't Peter's fault that Lowell had a drone on him right now. The drone might only be the size of a housecat, but Lowell had no useful weapons, no shield, and no cover. He wasn't sure who was piloting the damn thing, but whoever they were had him square in their sights. Just in case it was Munroe, Lowell carefully removed one hand from the side of the ship and gave the drone the finger.

You'd better hope you kill me before I get to you, Lieutenant, because I have no intention of going quietly.

Lowell mentally calculated the distance to the hatch entrance, multiplied by the drag, divided by how many times a drone could shoot him before he reached the target. All in all, it wasn't looking great.

When have my odds ever looked that good? he thought dismally.

Nothing sprang to mind. He was getting mighty tired of being the underdog. Just once, he'd like to be the hotshot holding the big gun and making everyone *else* feel like inferior idiots.

A simpler equation was more useful, anyway: if the drone shot him, he *might* die. If Peter didn't get the key back and Munroe's plan went off without a hitch, they were *definitely* going to die. That put things in perspective.

Lowell ignored the drone and began to scramble for the hatch. A moment later, he realized that there was a second drone coming in from the other side. Maybe he shouldn't have been so quick to let go of the scooter and ditch the harpoon.

He checked his helmet display. Twelve minutes left.

Lowell crawled across the hull of the ship as one of the drones fired. Its ray missed him by a hair's breadth. Even a small puncture in the suit could spell disaster, especially this far from the hatch. Between the water pressure and the fact that his suit could flood, it was a dismal prospect.

Don't think about drowning. Don't think about being crushed by a few thousand bars of pressure. Just. Keep. Moving.

The fingers of his glove closed over the lip of the hatch as the second drone fired. He managed to roll his shoulders to one side to avoid a puncture in the seam, but a warning light inside the helmet informed him that the suit was compromised. It instantly became more difficult to breathe, and he could feel the saltwater of Enceladus' sea begin to seep in against his ribs. Within seconds, he was gasping—not only from the lack of oxygen, but from the sheer weight of all those miles of water pressing down on him. His ribs creaked, and a stabbing pain in his eardrums made him let out an involuntary yelp of agony.

"Lowell?" asked Peter through the mic.

Lowell didn't answer. He was too busy yanking at the hatch of the ship, well aware that he had only seconds left to get out of harm's way.

"Lowell!" Peter cried.

His vision swam and darkened; he could feel the blood vessels in his eyes bursting. With a sound more befitting an animal than a man, he grabbed the hatch in both hands and twisted. To his immense relief, it gave way. The water pressure would have held a more solid hatch in place, but like so many of ships used by the Space Corps, this one had been designed for use in a wide range of environments; the hatch's pressure seal circulator allowed for emergency removal even in extreme conditions.

Lowell said a little prayer of thanks as he launched himself through the hatch, dragging his dripping body up into the ship's hull. He slammed the lid of the hatch back in place to keep the drones from following him, and then collapsed onto all fours, fumbling at the latch on the back of his helmet with shaking hands. The moment it came free, he yanked it off, then collapsed onto the floor like a dead man.

His breathing came in short, staccato bursts, and he was trembling uncontrollably.

Come on, Carpenter. Get it together.

Lowell had survived firefights, mines, and even engine failure near one of the asteroids he'd guarded. He'd never felt like this, as though all of his life force had been drained from his body.

You can do this, he told himself, sucking in the ship's recycled oxygen for all he was worth.

In spite of his pep talks and years of commanders telling him to 'walk it off,' Lowell found himself lying face-down in the corridor of an enemy ship, unable to take a full breath or even focus his eyes.

He could only hope that Peter was faring better.

Nine minutes left.

40

PETER WAS UTTERLY ALONE. Even Lowell's heavy breathing no longer filled the mic.

What if they got him?

Peter could feel his strength flagging, but he was so close to the Anomaly, he could just about reach out and touch its brilliant surface. Down here, the humming was more intense than ever. It vibrated through Peter's already jostled organs like an electrical pulse or a heartbeat. When he finally reached out to lay his hand on the silver alloy, he felt the movement echo in every atom.

Even the largest of the sea creatures paid him no mind now. They seemed as agitated as their fellows, but ultimately indifferent to Peter's presence. He swam around the Anomaly, reading what he could as he looked for the cavity where the key had been placed. He remembered seeing it by flashlight, but everything was so much bigger in person, the landscape of the Anomaly so much more complex than he had previously realized.

"I'm almost there, Lowell," he said aloud. Maybe the other man's mic had shorted out; maybe he was unconscious or worse;

but if there was any chance of him hearing the message, Peter wanted him to know that it hadn't all been in vain. "I just reached the place the techs touched down. Not far now..."

For the first time since he'd been kidnapped, Peter felt almost at peace. There was nothing left to be afraid of. He had no ticket out of here, no plan of escape. The best he could do would be to grab the key and swim for the trench. He hadn't yet decided whether he would drop it or just dive. Maybe another creature like Sharkie would find him and he could swim through its jaws. Even if ancient shark bile didn't destroy the key, it would make the object almost impossible for Munroe to track down. Once it was lost forever, his work would be done.

I'm sorry, Dad, he thought. His mother would be out of her mind with grief when she got whatever fabricated report the military gave her, but she had a support network: friends, her husband, her big family. His dad would be all alone, with nobody to talk to, nobody who would know that when he said, *It's fine, I'm handling it better than I expected,* it would be total bullshit.

It would be such a relief to go back and tell his father the truth about the aliens, the government, the universe. If the two of them could come out here together, they would finally have something in common. A puzzle to solve as a team.

Too bad it was never going to happen.

Peter recognized the groove in the Anomaly's surface and followed it down. The cavity was only inches away, with the key glowing like a star inside.

All right, Peter thought, *let's finish this.*

41

LOWELL SAT UP WOOZILY, bracing one arm against the floor and resting the other on his forehead. His vision was still shot, but he didn't need 20/20 eyesight to fight a couple of guys. If there were more people onboard, they would have come after him already. If he was lucky, they'd come after him one at a time.

Right, because 'Lucky' is my middle name.

At least he could more or less breathe now. He got to his feet, reached for his helmet, and began to limp through the access corridor.

During his initial Marine training, Lowell had developed a mantra to help him get through the worst days. When they'd slogged through the boggy mess the cadets called the Peanut Butter Patch, he'd told himself, *I can survive anything for a mile.* When they'd climbed the sandy dune known as the Sugar Cookie under the blazing summer sun, he'd told himself, *I can survive anything for ten minutes.* When they'd handpicked him into the Space Corps program and started the conditioning routines that usually made the fresh blood puke, he'd told himself, *I can survive anything for an hour.*

Swaying down the corridor, pausing every few steps to brace himself against the wall, Lowell thought, *I can survive this until we defeat Munroe.* Whether it was true or not was immaterial. All that mattered was that he believed it.

Besides, if he didn't survive, who was going to be around to tell him he'd been wrong?

By the time he reached the ladder up toward the command center, he could manage a brisk walk unaided. Either his body had begun to recover from the pressure shift, or he was simply getting used to the pain.

He hauled himself up the ladder and had one elbow on the main floor of the ship when he heard something from the other end of the hallway fizzle and snap. When he looked up, he found himself facing one of his old teammates with a bulky gun trained on him: one of the new digital weapons that the Space Corps was rolling out, probably. They hadn't made their way to Enceladus yet.

I guess they have now, Lowell thought. He hadn't had a chance to fire one, but based on the charred crater at the other end of the hall, they were pretty effective.

The other man's helmet was off, and his close-cropped dark hair only partially obscured a long pale scar that ran from his chin across his lip, alongside his nose, all the way up to the crown of his head. Lowell remembered when he'd gotten that scar. They'd been disarming a downed Russian drone when it had self-destructed; the guy had been lucky not to lose an eye.

"Cushing?" asked Lowell, narrowing his eyes. "Still working for Munroe, huh?"

"Sure am." Cushing took aim. "You still a yellow-bellied traitor?"

"That's up for debate," Lowell told him. Then he launched himself up into the corridor.

Cushing fell back a pace, firing his electric gun, but Lowell's adrenaline had kicked in and he was moving fast. He held his helmet in one hand, and with the other he reached for the knife he'd taken from the diver.

Bringing a knife to a gun fight? he could practically hear Cushing snarling in his mind. *You always were an idiot, Lowell.*

Lowell dropped to the ground in front of Cushing, rolled forward, and with his full strength brought the knife down on the seam of the boot's ankle. The blade pierced straight through Cushing's foot and into the floor, and the man cried out in pain. Lowell rocketed to his feet, fighting a rush of disorientation—something was wrong with his inner ear, but he had no time to worry about that. As Cushing reached down to dislodge the knife, Lowell swung his helmet into the side of the man's head. Cushing fell, his foot still pinned in place by the blade.

Before he could take aim with his laser rifle, Lowell grappled the barrel and dropped his whole weight onto the gun. With an *oof* of surprise, Cushing let go of the weapon, and Lowell lifted it in one hand, pressing the barrel to Cushing's temple and firing simultaneously. Digital weapon or not, it was effective. Half of Cushing's brain ended up on the bulkhead as the rest of him slumped to the deck.

Lowell struggled to stay on his feet. The scuffle had left him lightheaded, but time was running out. He jammed the helmet back on his head, not bothering to secure the seal. If something happened to the ship, Lowell was screwed either way, but he didn't have any other way to get in touch with Chang.

"Hey, kid, are you there?" he asked, lifting the gun to his shoulder.

"Lowell?" asked Peter. "You're alive!"

"Just about. We've got"—Lowell's gaze flitted to the display—"three minutes before our time runs out."

"I'm there," Peter said. He sounded like he was on the verge of tears. "I can see it."

"Swell," said Lowell. "You keep working on that. I'm getting us a ride."

He hustled through the ship toward the cockpit, weapon raised. He hadn't encountered anyone besides Cushing, but that didn't surprise him. Most likely, there would only be one or two more crew members inside.

He reached the door to the cockpit and pressed his back against the wall, taking a deep breath before spinning into the room.

It was empty.

"Where are you?" he murmured.

"I told you," Peter said, "I'm right—"

A blow hit Lowell right between the shoulder blades, and a second hit to the back of his head sent him sprawling. The helmet fell off and slid away across the floor under the command center. Lowell lay on the ground, gasping for breath.

Stupid lungs. Stupid drones. He blinked furiously and rolled his head to one side until another familiar face came into view. *Stupid ex-crew still following in the footsteps of a homicidal megalomaniac...*

"I can't believe you got Cushing," said Simms, shaking his head. He stepped out into the main control center, laser rifle raised. "I thought that was the end of you, but it turns out that you have no problem offing your old friends."

Lowell coughed, and a spiderweb of pain radiated across the back of his ribcage. He glared up at Simms and panted, "I got him, all right."

"Too bad," said Simms. "He was a good soldier. Unlike you."

With a sudden movement, Lowell lifted his stolen laser gun, aiming right between the man's eyes.

"Looks like we've got ourselves a Mexican standoff," he said. He could taste copper on his lips, and he wondered how much damage Simms' shot had done.

I can survive anything for two minutes.

"Not really." Simms smirked and held up a small object the rough size and shape of his palm. "All of our electrical weapons are actually controlled remotely in case something like this happens. I think you'll find I've disarmed yours." He pouted sympathetically. "You know, I have orders to kill you, but I think Munroe might like a chance to say a few things to you himself. You really FUBARed his career, you know. He could have been in the top brass by now. If I were him, I'd definitely be holding a grudge."

Lowell pulled the trigger of the laser gun experimentally. Just as Simms had said, it did nothing.

"Didn't trust me?" Simms taunted.

Lowell shrugged. "It was worth a shot."

Simms chuckled as Lowell slumped against the floor. If Peter didn't have the key by now, it would be in his hands at any moment. He was counting on Lowell for a ride.

Lowell had no intention of letting him down.

"Now, I know I've got restraints here somewhere," Simms said, looking to the side. "Ah, yes..." He reached for the magnetic cuffs.

Lowell knew that this might well be his only chance, and he wasn't going to risk waiting for another one. His hand whipped out and grabbed the Glock at his hip, and before Simms could turn to him, Lowell fired the final bullet into the side of his head.

Simms dropped like a stone.

"That," Lowell muttered to himself, "is why I prefer analog weapons."

He rolled onto his knees and slowly got to his feet. He'd always been pretty good at using the terrain to his advantage, and the few times he'd been injured in his early days in the Marines, he'd had guys on his side who would cover him. Even on his worst days, he'd never taken a beating like this. Every breath required a colossal effort of will.

"I'm getting too old for this crap," he grumbled as he collapsed into the captain's chair. Although now that he was thinking about it, perhaps he shouldn't complain about his age. If Munroe got his wish, Lowell wouldn't live to be much older.

He didn't bother to reach for his helmet before he took over the ship's controls. He knew exactly where Peter would be, and it was his job to get there as soon as possible.

42

"SIMMS? SIMMS, DO YOU HEAR ME?" Helena pressed her hand to her earpiece, hoping for an answer, but getting none. She'd seen that one of her drones had managed a direct hit on the traitor, but Lowell hadn't gone down. Even with a compromised suit, he'd managed to get onboard.

She'd have been impressed if it hadn't been her job to kill the guy.

"I'm not getting an answer, ma'am," said Acosta. "Cushing isn't responding, either."

"What the hell?" Helena murmured. As a hit went, she'd done it all by the book—she'd thrown everything she had at him. It should have been overkill. Instead, Lowell just kept going, like some kind of clockwork machine whose batteries refused to die. "What about the other target?"

"Simms hit him with the pulse cannon," said the navigator, as if that made one lick of difference. "He's down."

"Yeah, right," Helena grumbled. "I'll believe it when I see it. Take us closer to the other ship."

"Munroe told us to be off-world within two minutes," said Acosta nervously. "Are you sure that we shouldn't be regrouping?"

"I'm not leaving until I see their bodies," Helena snapped. "My order stands."

"Yes, ma'am." With obvious misgivings, the navigator took them down. Everything seemed to take much longer than usual—she was used to fighting in zero-gravity when they were onboard. The ships worked down here, but they were so *slow*.

As Acosta brought them deeper, Helena redirected one of her drones toward the Anomaly. She wasn't entirely sure what would happen when her time ran out, but she knew that it wasn't going to be pretty. The orders she'd received on Operation Cascade had been so heavily edited as to be almost illegible, but she knew what was expected of her: secure the site. Eliminate the target. If Lowell had somehow gotten control of the ship, he'd probably try to stop the one she'd sent to check in on his partner.

It wouldn't occur to him that there was still one drone out there until it was stuck in his engines.

She'd never failed in a mission before, and she wasn't going to start now.

———

LOWELL CLOSED his hands over the depth control and aimed the ship toward the Anomaly. They could worry about the other vessel once he had Peter onboard. They weren't in the clear yet, but he had no intention of leaving his teammate behind.

"Come on, Chang," he muttered. "You can do this."

———

PETER'S HAND closed around the stellar key. He thought that some effort would be required to remove it, as if it might somehow have fused with the Anomaly in the last twenty-four hours. Instead, it came free easily in his hand.

Still, something changed. He couldn't say what, but the hairs on the back of his neck stood on end. No matter, though. He clutched the brilliant sphere to his chest. "Lowell, if you can hear me, we *did it*."

43

LOWELL CURSED LOUDLY as he saw one of the teardrop-shaped drones zip ahead of him as he approached the Anomaly. He was glad he wasn't wearing his helmet; he really didn't need to hear Peter panic over it.

Clearly, Munroe's team was never going to yield. They'd keep needling him right to the very end.

Lowell leaned over the controls, examining his weapon options. The sonic cannon was good for blanket targeting, but he had no intention of getting Peter caught in the crossfire. If he was going to take out the drones, he was going to need something with a narrower range.

Looking over the controls, he flicked on a targeting system. He wasn't sure precisely what it powered, but at this point, he was willing to try anything. The second ship was approaching fast, and he was sure that whoever was in charge of it would know exactly what every one of these buttons did.

The targeting system adjusted, locking in on one of the drones. Lowell jabbed his thumb at the firing mechanism, and let out a whoop of delight when a refractor beam powered on. By all appearances, it was a heck of a lot more powerful than the beam on the pod—when it hit the drone, the little device all but disintegrated.

"Hell *yes!*" he bellowed, thumping his palm on the controls. "Now that's what I'm talking about!"

There was still another drone out there, but Lowell didn't bother looking for it, and didn't waste time firing on the second Corps ship. He could worry about the other pilot once he had Peter on board.

As he pulled in, he targeted the other drone, scrambling under the seat for his helmet. "Chang, do you read me? I'm right on top of you."

"You stole a Space Corps vessel?"

"Yeah, buddy, hop onboard. There's an airlock on the side; I'll open it when you're there and let you in."

"Are you seriously telling me that they just let you onto that ship?" Peter asked.

"Not exactly," Lowell said, realizing he needed to warn Peter. "You're going to see a couple bodies. Just keep moving."

"Bodies," Peter repeated weakly.

Lowell watched on the infrared as Peter's form struggled up toward the ship. As he did so, a long, ribbon-like fish followed him up, another eel like the one he'd fired on when they first stole the scooters. Lowell didn't waste a second blowing it into chunks that reminded him unpleasantly of ceviche.

I don't have time for you, he thought, grinning madly to himself. *I've bigger fish to fry.* He pulled the helmet off before he started cackling to himself; he clearly wasn't in his right mind, but there was no sense in alerting Peter to the fact that he had most likely sustained all kinds of brain damage when his suit was hit.

The moment the on-board cameras showed him that Peter had

entered the airlock, Lowell started the auto-purge function for the chamber and leaned on the throttle. He wasn't sure what the other ship was doing, or where that last drone had gotten to, and he didn't want to hang around to find out.

Unfortunately, the enemy pilot had other plans.

The ship rocked as the other vessel fired their own refractor, and Lowell winced as the readings went haywire. The memory of the incredible pressure he'd experienced when the drone punctured his suit left him panicky and anxious—if the ship's envelope gave way now, he wasn't sure if he would drown first, or be crushed to a pulp. Either way, he wasn't thrilled about his options.

To his great relief, the ship didn't implode, which Lowell took as a good sign. He aimed his sonic cannon in the general direction of the other ship's engines and fired, but it seemed to have little effect.

They've probably been firing on me this whole time, and the water just doesn't conduct the vibrations well enough to do any damage, he realized. That explained why they hadn't fried him sooner—they probably hadn't put two and two together on the cannon yet.

The ships were identical, and the other small crew would have a tactical advantage in their familiarity with the controls. Rather than just sit still and take their fire, Lowell whipped away from the Anomaly, heading back toward the trench. He was having some trouble thinking clearly, but it seemed to him that if he could get back to an area he knew, he could figure out a plan.

A moment later, he heard footsteps, and then Peter came running into the cockpit, his suit dripping and the silver orb in his hand. His helmet was tucked under the other arm. "We did it!" he exclaimed. "And with only seconds to spare, too!"

Lowell looked back, and Peter stopped short, his eyes bulging.

"Good *Lord*," he asked, "what happened to you?"

"Popped a leak in my suit," said Lowell. "I guess the pressure got to me."

Peter just stared at him.

"Gallows humor," said Lowell with a shrug. "And possibly a blood clot. Hey, get over here and help me pilot this ship. Nice job with the key, by the way. Now, let's try not to die." Lowell patted the seat beside him. "I'm still figuring out the new weapons systems, and... *Whoa-ho-ho!*" The ship rocked sideways again, not from a blast of refractor fire this time, but from something getting stuck in their engine's propulsion system.

Guess I just found out where drone number three got to.

With a few muttered curses, Lowell began to purge the system, but dislodging the obstruction meant losing ground to their pursuers. To Lowell's great annoyance, the other ship began to gain.

"What do I do?" asked Peter anxiously, fluttering nervously around behind Lowell.

"Oh, for God's sake," Lowell grumbled. "Sit down and shut up. Let me finish this and I'll give you some instructions."

He flinched as the other ship fired again; somewhere below them, an alarm went off.

"That seems bad. Should we put our helmets on?"

"Go for it," Lowell grunted, finishing the purge on the engine.

"I won't if you aren't," Peter said bravely.

Lowell watched as the crushed remains of the drone shot away behind them, but he'd lost too much time. One more shot, and he had no doubt that they'd be done for. He leaned on the throttle, but even without an obstruction, the engine wasn't working properly.

Behind them, the other ship was closing in. Lowell let out a muffled string of curses that tasted like old coins on his tongue.

Peter opened his mouth to say something, but before a sound

came out something hit the side of the ship so hard that they were blasted away through the ocean as if the whole ship had been fired from a cannon. Peter lost his footing, and Lowell gripped the controls, knowing full well that it would have no effect.

He'd never experienced anything like it before.

The good news was that whatever had blown them away hadn't come from the other ship.

The bad news was they now had a whole new problem.

44

"WHAT HAPPENED?" Helena demanded, scrambling to her feet. She'd finally had Lowell in her sights, and she'd been so sure that she was about to end him.

And then victory had been snatched from her fingers. *Again.*

"It looks like the seabed is unstable," Acosta told her. He looked up from the readings, and expression of utter bemusement on his features. "We appear to have been hit by some sort of hydrothermal vent. Shifting tectonic plates can create a rift and allow water under the seabed—"

"Give it to me in layman's terms," Helena barked.

Acosta raised an eyebrow. "It's not that complicated. When a fissure opens up in the mantle, it can cause a heated vent to erupt into the ocean. Water. Heat." He held up his hands and mimed a cork popping out of a bottle.

Helena narrowed her eyes. "We just got hit by an underwater Jacuzzi jet?"

Acosta nodded. "Close enough, but the sudden presence of a new thermal vent could indicate that the sea floor is unstable. Out of curiosity, Hellcat... Did Munroe tell you *why* we needed to evacuate the moon by a certain time?"

Helena's eyes widened. "You think that he knew this would happen. Which means that Operation Cascade..."

Acosta nodded again. "Has been successful thus far."

Helena stood beside her chair, considering this. "In that case, I think we should follow Munroe's orders. It'll be difficult fighting on unstable ground, and my drone just did a number on their engines. I doubt they'll be able to make it off-world, but if they do, we'll be waiting for them. Head for the research station. We'll exit the ice there; it's the only way in and out of the ocean. We can head above the surface and watch for them, and if they show up..."

"We fire on them," said Acosta. "And if they don't, we can search the rubble for their corpses afterward."

Helena let out a sigh of relief as Acosta brought them around, taking them back to the station's coordinates. On the thermal sensors, Helena could see bright spots of warm water blooming all over the seabed.

She might not have gotten Lowell as quickly as she'd wanted, but they'd won in the end. All she had to do now was make sure Lowell had no chance to escape.

45

"I DON'T UNDERSTAND," said Peter, watching as the seabed of Enceladus began to fracture. Giant cracks opened up beneath them, and sand sifted down into the new fissures. *"After a day, the sleeper will wake...* That's what the tablet said. But I got the stellar key before our time ran out. Why is this happening?"

"We knew it was a long shot," Lowell said with resignation. "It was just that a long shot was the only shot we had."

"But I got it out in *time*."

"That 24-hour day thing never made any damn sense anyway," Lowell grumbled.

"It was in the cuneiform *symbol*," Peter said with exasperation. "I told you."

Lowell held up a hand. "I believe you. And anyway, a longer solar day would have given us *more* time, which makes this all make even less damn sense to me. The creatures. The seabed activity. Everything started going sideways from the moment we first got that damn orb near the Anomaly anyway—"

He stopped abruptly. So abruptly that Peter looked up, expecting to see something ahead of the ship. "What?"

Lowell looked as though he'd been brought back from the dead via a particularly rough necromantic ritual. The whites of his eyes looked bruised, and his face was mottled with blue-black veins. Despite his nightmarish appearance, he slapped his fist on the console in front of him with such force that Peter jumped.

Peter turned to stare at him. "Are you okay? Are you having an episode? A stroke, maybe? You know, divers can get the bends after extreme pressure changes, so it's possible that you—"

Lowell held up a hand to silence him again. "Remember when we checked out your little mystery tunnel and you realized the Anomaly was a weapon of war? You said the stellar key was an *energy source*. Those are your words. '*It's more like a key that powers something up than one that just opens it,*' you said."

Peter frowned. "Okaaay. What's your point—" Then it hit him.

"What if it was doing that this *whole* time?" Lowell asked. "Since the moment it was in place. That's why it needed a day. It doesn't open it up *after* a day, it powers it up over the *course* of a day. And that means..."

"Pulling it out at the last moment would barely matter," Peter said, completing his thought.

"It's basically finished with what it had to do, and it's set this whole mess in motion," Lowell agreed. He shook his head, and when he spoke again, it was almost in awe. "What kind of weapon needs a day of stellar energy just to activate?"

Peter squeezed his eyes shut. He couldn't think about those implications right now. They'd been wrong about so much already, there was no point in guessing. "So we went through all that for *nothing*. We got eaten by a shark for *nothing*." He gripped his stomach, wondering how much damage his organs had taken from the sonic cannon, and for what?

"Munroe wins," he murmured.

Lowell's shoulders went slack as he leaned back in his chair. "Yeah. I guess he does." He let out a soft puff of laughter. "Just like he always does."

"Can we at least get out of here now that we have a ship?" Peter asked hopefully.

Lowell pointed to the screen, where a dozen lights were blinking, warnings about various systems malfunctioning. Peter didn't know much about spaceships, but an electric short in his self-driving car back in college had resulted in him totaling the vehicle. He knew what it meant when every light on your dashboard flipped on at once, and it wasn't good.

"Oh, God," he groaned, "we're like your dad's old beater, with nothing left to lose."

"We're not dead in the water," said Lowell, "but the engines are damaged. We'll struggle to get back to the surface. Heck, we'd have been better off in the pod."

Peter rocked back and forth in his seat, shaking his head. "So that's it? We're just...done?"

"Unless you've got any better ideas," said Lowell.

They stared at each other for a long moment. *He looks as bad as I feel,* Peter thought. They'd both taken a beating today.

"Well, we tried." He managed a small smile. "And like you said, we gave Munroe a run for his money."

Lowell nodded. "I guess so. Cost him six guys and a ship. Not too shabby." He held out a hand, and Peter shook it.

They sat in silence for a moment, and Peter found his gaze traveling toward the dead man in the corner of the cockpit. In a weird way, Peter was jealous of the guy. *He already got the hard part over with,* he thought. *He doesn't have to wonder anymore.*

"Who are you leaving behind?" Lowell asked.

Peter dragged his eyes away from the dead Corpsman. "What do you mean?"

"Like a girlfriend...or boyfriend, I dunno. Family? Do you have people?"

"Just my parents," said Peter. The adrenaline high that had been carrying him since their escape from the research station had begun to dissipate, and he relaxed back into his chair. Maybe he could fall asleep here. That wouldn't be so bad, all things considered—he could just fall asleep and never wake up.

There were worse ways to go.

"You guys close?" asked Lowell.

Peter shrugged. "They have their own lives now. Mom's remarried, and Dad's a professor of astrobiology."

"Oh, so he'd have fit right in with the rest of the nerds." Lowell's low chuckle gave way to a wet cough, and it took him a minute to get it under control. "My family doesn't have anything to say about all this. Not that I can tell them much, you know. But they're not stupid."

"Oh, my dad would kill to be out here." Peter closed his eyes, remembering how animated his father got every time a new article about life on other worlds ran in the journals. "He lost his mind when they first found amino acid chains in the plume. He was like a kid at Christmas." Peter let his eyes flutter open, and the smile slipped off of his face. "Of course, he had no idea about the living fossils and... Oh, God, Lowell, we're *never* going to figure out what all those carvings mean! They're just going to be lost, and nobody's ever going to translate..."

He turned to Lowell, knowing full well that the military man wasn't going to lose sleep over how close they'd come to a groundbreaking theory, but hoping that the man would humor him.

Rather than rolling his eyes or cutting Peter off, Lowell was frowning. "I didn't think of that," he murmured.

"It's a travesty! So many questions are going to go unanswered. It's as bad as the destruction of the library at Alexandria. Worse, maybe." Peter tugged at his hair. "And people will just carry on with their research, never knowing that the mysteries of the universe could have been laid bare, if only we'd been able to translate the inscription. I should have taken pictures, just to see if we could transmit them back to Earth, just to see if we could salvage anything before—well, before Munroe gets his hands on the weapon."

Lowell's hands crept slowly toward the controls. "Yeah," he said vaguely, "yeah, it might be doable. What do we have to lose?"

"Really?" asked Peter, reaching out to grab Lowell's arm. "Do you think we can get a transmission out?"

Lowell jumped, then stared down at Peter's hand, his brow wrinkling in confusion. "What are you babbling about?"

"The inscriptions," said Peter. "In the cave."

"Oh, forget about those," said Lowell dismissively. "You said something about the plume, and it got me thinking."

"Thinking about what?" asked Peter, stung by the fact that, once again, Lowell had managed to quell his dreams with an eye-roll and a curt shake of the head.

Lowell's battered face split into a grin. "I might have a plan."

46

THE RUSSIANS HAD ARRIVED to join the fray, and just as Munroe suspected, the Japanese had shown up, too. Saturn's isolated little moon had never been so popular, and Munroe had begun to pace back and forth across his cabin again, watching the icy orb intently. He hadn't heard from Hellcat, and their time was up.

If Lowell ruins this for me... he thought grimly. Well, in that case, US law would cease to matter. This was a war zone, and Lowell was a traitor. The man was marked for death.

He was still stewing when a video request blinked to life on the screen. The Tiān Zhuānjiā insignia marked the caller's ID.

Oh, so the Chinese want to parlay now. With a huff of irritation, he called up the chat so that the image of the translator and her general filled the screen, projected larger-than-life into the room.

Usually, Munroe would be expected to jump through all the hoops associated with international negotiations: backup recordings, translator on standby, approval from the Pentagon. Today, he was done worrying about the rules. It was time for everyone to grow up and figure out the score. He had his orders. The rest was just history waiting to happen.

"How can I help you?" he asked brusquely, crossing his arms and spreading his feet.

The translator, who had introduced herself before as He Ming, offered an indifferent smile. Dealing with translators always drove Munroe crazy. They never seemed to mean what they said, and he always wondered what details they kept to themselves. It was worse when they played coy.

The general didn't speak, but He Ming said, "Our government has requested a statement of intent. Do you intend to honor our alliance should a firefight ensue?"

Munroe rolled his eyes. "Sure, like you guys have *honored our alliance* all these years? Get real. I'm going to do everything in my power to make sure that you don't get your hands on the weapon. You can tell your government that my intent is to win."

If they were coming to Munroe for an alliance, that probably meant that they had exhausted all of their other options. He'd been right when he'd guessed that they'd have trouble forming a coalition on the fly.

They know that we've beaten them to the punch, and now they're going to come running with their tails between their legs. Not happening. If the Pentagon wanted me to play nice with the allies, they'd have been more specific in the brief.

He Ming smiled slightly and turned to the general. She said a few words in soft Mandarin. She was probably trying to make him sound nice.

Translators were always meddling.

The general responded, and He Ming nodded, then turned back to the screen. "General Wu thanks you for your time, Lieutenant."

"See you on the battlefield," Munroe said, and powered down the call.

That would show them. After all these years, Munroe was finally going to get a chance to skip the BS and get right to the point.

Anyone foolish enough to stand in his way was going to regret it.

———

HE MING STARED at the blank screen, recalling the look of smug disgust on Munroe's face. Somehow, even when he was threatening them, he'd been smiling. "I'm not surprised by his response, General."

"Nor am I," General Wu replied, "but for the sake of appearances, the offer had to be made. Now we have his response recorded in case the ICC feels it necessary to investigate whatever happens here. I'll have the recording transmitted to Beijing for their records. Even if we're all killed, they'll be able to prove that we followed protocol."

"Then I suppose we shall be absolved if anyone asks, regardless of your family's history," He Ming murmured.

General Wu nodded. "Precisely."

After a moment's contemplation, He Ming reached for the comm again. "Shall I contact Ilin?"

General Wu nodded. "He should be apprised of the situation at once."

He Ming hailed the Russian ship, then folded her hands in her lap and waited for a reply. The blunt, square features of Major General Yevgeniy Ilin appeared on the screen a moment later.

"Good afternoon, General Wu," he said. His Mandarin was

heavily accented, but his grammar was impeccable. "Have you spoken to the American commander?"

"He has made his position clear," said the general. "The Americans have no interest in an alliance with us. They intend to keep the weapon for themselves."

"I wish I could say that I was disappointed," said Ilin. "However, I will have no regrets about firing on Munroe. That man has done more than his share of damage over the years, and I'm looking forward to repaying some old debts."

"We're in agreement, then."

"I look forward to our partnership."

Ilin smiled, but it wasn't like an American smile. He Ming didn't get the sense that he was trying to fool or mislead her. Ilin was genuinely looking forward to the prospect of paying back an old enemy for his past transgressions.

They all were.

47

LOWELL DIDN'T KNOW MUCH about geology or oceanography or whatever the hell else people had to study to understand the mechanics of heavenly bodies. What he understood was force. Brute force.

That, and how to use the terrain to his advantage.

"You have an idea?" asked Peter, sitting up. "As in, an idea of how to get out of here in one piece?"

"Keep in mind that it's a work in progress."

"So this is a plan in the same sense that going inside a shark was a plan," said Peter skeptically.

"Hey, we didn't die," Lowell pointed out. "I'd say the plan worked perfectly."

"That's certainly one way of looking at it."

"Look, if you don't like it, you can stay behind and try your luck with the beasties." Lowell pointed out into the ocean, where schools of agitated fish seemed just as taken aback by the change in geography as he felt. Creatures of all shapes and sizes were rising from the seabed, startled out of their holes and burrows by the sea floor's slow collapse. It was getting hard to imagine this had ever seemed like a lifeless place, even if a day ago he would have sworn by it.

"I didn't say that I didn't like it. I'm just wary." Peter crossed his arms. "But I'll try anything if it means we'll have a chance."

"Great. So do you want to learn how to fly, or how to shoot?"

Peter's eye twitched. "Wait, what?"

"You don't get to sit around and let me do all the work," Lowell told him. "I'm not your chauffeur. One of us is going to be using the weapons, and the other is going to be flying. Or...swimming. Driving. You know, steering the damn ship."

Peter licked his lips and stared down at the dashboard. "There are, like, eight hundred buttons."

"It's like driving a stick shift. No big deal."

"I've only ever used self-driving cars. The rest of the time, I take the bus."

Lowell bit down on his tongue and shook his head. "Listen, pick one: guns or steering."

Peter hesitated, and in that brief span of time, another jet of pressurized water hit the side of the ship, knocking them off-course. Below them, the seabed of Enceladus was falling away, cracking and splitting apart before their very eyes. Lowell hurried to right them, only to be buffeted by another jet of water from the opposite direction. A cluster of isopods flew past, thrown by the force of the thermal fissures' eruption.

"Guns," said Peter. "I'll do guns. How does it work?"

Lowell gestured toward the targeting system. "All right, that part's for the refractor. It kind of works like a giant laser, but it's a little more—uh, *combustible.* Once you're locked in on a target, fire. It's not like a gun; the positioning system will recalibrate based on our movement." He managed to get them back upright, then glanced over to point out another set of equipment. "This here's the firing system for the sonic cannon. This little guy's the intensity dial—dang, man, you took a hit on high and didn't die? Nice work."

"Thanks," Peter said weakly. "I try."

"Then fire with that." Lowell pointed to the button, but his eyes were already on their IPS coordinates. At this rate, he wasn't sure how much longer they had before the whole moon was destroyed. "Got it?"

"Point with this, fire with that and that." Peter nodded, pointing at each of the controls in turn. "Got it, I think. Hopefully. What exactly am I shooting?"

"Whatever gets in the way. You're going to make sure we have a clear path," said Lowell. "The ship is already damaged. If we get hit with something, it could puncture our hull, and there's no coming back from that."

"Okay." Peter frowned, then shook his head. "Sorry, but I'm not really following the plan. How are we getting out of the ice?"

"The engines are damaged, so they aren't strong enough to get us off-world." On the thermal imaging system, Lowell saw the faint glow of a new thermal vent forming seconds before it erupted, and he managed to course-correct before it went off. "But we don't need the engines to reach escape velocity. It's fairly easy, actually, once we're out of the water. Remember the pod that went over the tiger stripes and got knocked into orbit?"

Peter gaped at him. "You want to ride the plume out of the moon's atmosphere?"

"Why not?" Lowell asked with a shrug. "Those plumes send ocean water out into space all the time. They form the largest ring around Saturn—at least, that's what they told me when I got the grand tour when I started here. So why not get a free ride?"

"Are the ship's systems going to be able to keep up with that kind of pressure change?" Peter asked. "Can't our lungs rupture if the pressure drops too fast?"

"They might, or they might not," Lowell said with a shrug. "This thing is a lot newer than our pods, and those little things could handle it, at least in theory. DARPA knows their toys. I'm hoping that the ship's systems will be able to keep up with the pressure change. Either way, it's better than sitting around waiting for the moon to..." He paused. "Do whatever it's doing."

"I never realized you were a glass-half-full kind of guy."

Lowell shot him a quick glance.

"Gallows humor," Peter explained. "Thought I'd give it a try."

"Punchline needs work."

According to the radar, they were approaching the tiger stripes and the plume above. As more and more vents opened, Lowell watched the ocean's other inhabitants thrash and writhe; none of the predators seemed to be interested in coming after them now. Maybe they could sense that the end was near, and had given up on hunting.

In a way, Lowell almost felt sorry for them. Killing Sharkie had been fair play, but that was in earnest combat, and the apex predator had won. Plenty of the other creatures had just been going about their business with no sense of what was coming, and even the toothier critters were just going about their regular days.

Somehow, it didn't seem fair. Lowell wasn't about to lose sleep over it, or have a meltdown about lost research opportunities like Peter had, but still, he could sympathize with the plight of the sea creatures. The poor bastards were like Keating and Hansen, relatively innocent bystanders in Munroe's one-man war.

Can't believe I'm getting sentimental about a bunch of guppies, he thought with a frown. *I should get my head looked at.*

"We're getting close," he said aloud. "The tiger stripes are dead ahead."

"Are you going to tell me when to fire?" asked Peter nervously.

"It's not hard," Lowell told him. "If something gets in our way, blast it *out* of our way. Got it?"

"Sure," Peter mumbled. "Sounds great."

"Shouldn't be too hard for a guy with a high score in *Fallout: Mars*," Lowell pointed out.

They were only a hundred or so meters away from the plume, and Lowell could already feel how the water pressure had begun to fight the engines. The surface was miles away, but the ice was thinnest around the plumes. It would have been handy if he'd had just a little more information, but every time the scientists had tried to share their love of astrophysics with him, he'd actively tuned them out.

I should have listened more carefully when Dr. Hansen was explaining the mechanics of the plumes. Sorry, Fran.

Lowell had a sense of how fast he could push the ship under normal circumstances, but he wasn't sure how fast the geyser would carry them up. He was fairly sure that getting as close to the center of the stripes as possible would mean facing the thinnest, weakest portions of the ice. Obviously the geysers breached the ice at some point—but this ship was bigger than the pod, and Lowell had no way of knowing if it would fit through the fissures. The idea of being blown into a thick layer of ice at escape velocity made Lowell sick to his stomach. The good news was that if that happened, the ship would be crushed by the pressure almost instantly.

He didn't share his thoughts on this 'good news' with Peter. He had a feeling that the young scientist wouldn't think of it as an upside.

Instead, he turned to face Peter, meeting the kid's eye. "Are you ready?" he asked.

"Let's just get this over with," Peter muttered.

Lowell grinned. "That's the right attitude."

48

AS OF YESTERDAY MORNING, Peter Chang had never visited an alien moon, fired a gun, or seen a living animal that predated the dinosaurs. *I guess a person can get used to anything under the right conditions.*

Although even now, he wouldn't exactly say that he was 'used' to doing things that would most likely result in an immediate and horrifying death. It was more that he no longer had the emotional bandwidth to be worried about it.

He gripped the seat of his chair as Lowell accelerated. At some point, he could feel the engines' power yielding to the force of the pressure below the plume, forcing them upward. The sensation reminded him of being a little boy and getting on the Gravitron at the amusement park. His mouth had still tasted of cotton candy, and his father, who *never* took time off from work, had been electric with excitement beside him. The memory was vivid enough to send tears spilling over Peter's cheeks.

Every time he thought he'd made peace with his own death, he remembered something that made him want another chance at fixing his life.

All right, enough playing around, his father's voice told him. *Time to get serious.*

"Okay," he murmured.

Peter opened his eyes and, with a tremendous effort, lifted his hands to the controls. They were still gaining speed, and although it was impossible for Peter to measure distance at this depth with no point of reference, he had a feeling that he was going to need to be ready in case something got in their way.

Lowell was still messing with their navigation equipment, although Peter couldn't tell how effective it was. When he saw that Peter was watching him, he tipped his chin toward the screen.

"I'm trying to get us centered," he said. "The less debris you have to clear, the better."

"Got it," said Peter. His hand hovered over the target locking mechanism, poised in case anything interfered with the ship. His left hand rested on the refractor panel; his right hovered over the sonic cannon controls. There was no point in fiddling with the cannon settings. He'd fire whatever he could whenever he got the chance.

A hazy grey blur above came suddenly into view, and within seconds it filled the screen.

It's the ice, Peter realized. *We're moving even faster than I realized.*

Beside him, he could feel Lowell's whole body tense up. "Okay, I'll do my best to keep us in the open spaces between the ice. Get ready to fire."

"Are you sure that this is going to be more effective than the pressure of the plume?" he asked.

"You might have to shear parts of the ice to make the hole

bigger," Lowell told him. "The geyser should carry it out of our way."

After so many hours spent with only a night-vision visor, the filtered lighting come through the ice made it nearly impossible for Peter to see what he was looking at. Rather than risk an accidental collision, he began to fire at random, not bothering with the targeting system. Just as Lowell said, the refractor beam blasted debris out of the way.

"All right, all right!" Lowell said, pumping his arm triumphantly. "We're almost to the surface. Keep it up."

Even as his said it, Peter felt the ship slow down. "What's happening?" he demanded.

Lowell looked at the radar and groaned. "I think the pressure's failing. Whatever's happening down there on the sea floor is messing with the plume."

"No, no, no." Peter slammed his hand down on the sonic cannon's firing mechanism. "*I don't accept it.*" They were so close. "Give the engines everything. Even if one of them isn't enough to get us into the atmosphere, both of them together might be enough."

"I'll do my best, but I don't know..." Lowell began.

"We're going to give it everything we've got, dammit. Glass. Half. *Full.*"

Lowell laughed with genuine amusement. "Aye, aye, Captain!" he hooted.

Peter blasted one last chunk of ice out of their way, and a second later they emerged into the icy atmosphere, surrounded by mist that quickly formed into hailstones as it hit the low temperatures of the moon's surface.

"Come on, come on, come on," Lowell grunted, leaning hard on the controls.

Peter knew it should be trivial to break free of the weak

atmosphere, but he still expected the ship to peak like a roller-coaster at the top of its climb, and then deliver the stomach-turning weightlessness of a freefall back onto the doomed surface of a dying moon.

But he waited, and waited, and it never came. Instead, the ship jolted, and Peter heard an array of new equipment kick on. The siren from below was still wailing, but Lowell's shoulders had already begun to relax.

"We did it," he said, blinking stupidly at the controls. "Holy hell, Chang, we *did it*."

Peter began to giggle, and he held an unsteady hand up for a high-five. "We're alive."

Lowell slapped his gloved palm against Peter's and let out a weary sigh. "Nice going, kid. You're a pretty good partner. I'm impressed."

"Thanks." Peter grinned to himself and settled back in his chair with a satisfied little sigh. Then his gaze focused on the ships outside the glass. The one that Lowell had commandeered was bigger than the pod by a few orders of magnitude, but it was dwarfed by the enormous bulwarks that surrounded them. Each of them bore a different insignia, the brightly-colored emblem of a distinct international space force.

"What's going on?" Peter asked in a small voice.

Lowell looked around at the other ships, somehow managing to stay utterly calm. "Well, this is interesting," he said flatly. "Looks like we crashed a party."

49

THE ICE on the surface of Enceladus had begun to fracture and give way. Helena watched with interest as seawater welled up between the cracks; the pressure had begun to subside, so instead of bubbling free, water filled the cracks and instantly froze over into icy seams.

"No sign of Lowell and his pet scientist," Acosta observed.

Helena drummed her fingers on the control panel and grinned. "Not a peep."

"If we wait much longer, we could have a problem," Acosta said, glancing down at the readings. "The moon is essentially imploding, and the gravitational field is being disrupted."

"Meaning?"

"That we may find it hard to reach escape velocity if we stick around," Acosta said.

Helena considered this. She'd had plenty of experience with interstellar combat over the last few years, but she'd never quite worked out the math. She was going to have to take Acosta's word for it.

With a self-satisfied sigh, she gestured to Acosta. "Take us out of here." Then she switched channels and hailed the private connection to Munroe.

She'd never approved of the sort of bootlicking that went on with some of the younger recruits, and she certainly wasn't the type to run back like a dog to its master, wagging her tail and begging for a pat on the head. Helena usually didn't suffer from nerves, either, but when she hailed Munroe, she wasn't looking forward to telling him how much it had cost the team.

Munroe answered just as Acosta was laying on the throttle. "What have you got for me, Hellcat?"

Better rip off the Band-Aid right away and get it over with. "I'm down a ship, and it's just me and Acosta left, but we got them."

To her surprise, Munroe didn't sound angry. "You sure you got them?"

Helena nodded, forgetting for a moment that he couldn't see her. Being in the helmets all the time was like spending her days trapped in her own head, with no one but her thoughts for company. "I knocked out their engines, and we stayed behind to confirm that they didn't make it out. I don't know if you can see what's happening from up there, but the whole moon is going nova."

"I can," Munroe said, and the satisfaction in his voice made Helena smile. "It's beautiful, Hellcat."

"I take it that's what it's *supposed* to do, then," Helena said.

"If we're right about this, you're going to want to be here for it. Get off-world and head back to the ship."

"Already on the way."

Munroe nodded approvingly. "When you break atmo, we'll pick you up, and we can really get started." Munroe sighed. "I need somebody up here I can trust."

Helena never played the part of the good dog, but that didn't mean she was opposed to a little praise now and then. Besides, judging by the magnitude of the icy sea collapsing beneath her, things were about to get interesting.

50

AS HE TOOK in the array of ships before them, Peter was sure he looked like he was about to wet his spacesuit. Lowell didn't seem to notice.

"Looks like the gang's all here," Lowell said, gesturing irritably out of the window.

"The gang?" asked Peter weakly. "So these guys are all our allies, at least?"

Lowell hooked his thumb toward the side of the ship. "Yeah, right. Half of them would probably be happy to blow us out of the sky the second they spot our Space Corps emblem, and the other half would be thrilled to get in good with Munroe if they figured out that we're—" He paused. "Well, I guess that we're defectors."

Peter groaned. "Is it too much to ask that *one* thing go right today?"

"It's been going okay for us so far. We're not dead yet." Lowell reached over to pat Peter on the back. "And hey, we already got eaten by a shark-slash-dinosaur earlier, so are you really all that worried about the Germans?"

Germans? Peter scanned the ships in front of them, then spotted the distinctive German vessel. A few eggheads out of Cologne had gotten a patent on their energon wheel technology and leaned hard into the design. The main vessel was long and thin, and the round energon drive was contained in a circular frame at the front end of the ship. If anyone had asked, he would have said that the German ships looked like an obscene act mimed by a fifth-grader, but since the Germans had never asked his opinion, they'd ended up with a ship that was the laughingstock of the Corps. But the Germans, who had also patented a few innovative weapons that the Space Corps inventors were dying to get their hands on, didn't seem to mind the jokes.

"Yes," said Peter weakly. "I'm definitely still worried about the Germans. Is there a reason that nobody's fired on us yet?"

Lowell nodded. "Sure. Whoever fires first is going to start an international incident."

Peter thought back to their first encounter with the Chinese who'd fired on them on the ice of Enceladus. It didn't seem they were that worried about international incidents at the time. "So what are we going to do?"

It was a fair question, one that appeared to already have the cogs turning in Lowell's head. "I know next to nothing about the Indian fleet. Same for the Japanese. If I had to guess, the Germans will have already talked things over with Munroe—if we reach out to them, they'll hand us over."

"Reach out to them?" Peter asked. "Why would we do that?"

Lowell rolled his eyes. "And you're supposed to be the smart one, huh? Think about it for a second, Chang. We're in a little bitty ship bouncing around in a war zone with a busted engine and people who are actively trying to kill us. We can't take on every ship in the sky, and we don't have the juice to leave them all in the dust. Those are our two options, right? Fight or flight?"

"And neither of them is viable," Peter mumbled.

Lowell shook his head. "That's where you're wrong. There's a third choice. Remember that little lobster critter that used us to shadow hunt? That's what the smart ones do: team up with someone bigger and badder in the hopes of surviving."

"But you've just ruled out every ally we have," Peter pointed out. "I might not be up to date on current events, but even *I* know that our treaty with the Russians is on shaky ground, and the Tiān Zhuānjiā just tried to kill us."

Lowell licked his lip.

"Ooh." Peter shuddered. "I don't like that look."

"This is just what my face looks like," Lowell said.

Peter pressed his palms into his eye sockets and muttered incomprehensibly.

"Are you cursing me out?" Lowell asked, intrigued.

"In Akkadian," Peter confirmed. "Okay, walk me through it."

"The Chinese are the only known quantity here. They knew about the key. They also knew about Munroe, and they wanted to stop him."

"They already tried to kill us once," Peter pointed out again—rather astutely, he thought.

Lowell waved him away. "The Chinese aren't stupid. They'll have friends for this fight. Probably the Russians, who won't balk at taking on the Americans, so we'd have some firepower at our back if they decide to help us out."

Peter gawked. "You want to ask the Chinese to help us out? Why would they?"

"We have something they want."

Peter looked down at the stellar key, still clenched tight in his hands. "You mean this? But it's served its purpose, right? Besides—and I reiterate here—couldn't they just kill us for it like they tried last time?"

"Maybe, maybe not—but I'm not talking about the key." Lowell reached over to poke Peter in the middle of his forehead. "I'm talking about *you*. What we saw in that room down there? In that cavern on Enceladus? Nobody alive has seen that but you and me. I'm a meathead who thinks all that crazy writing looks like scribbles, but you? I bet that you could recreate that stuff from memory. Tell the Chinese all kinds of stuff, you know what I'm saying?"

A muscle jumped in Peter's jaw, and Lowell leaned closer.

"I'm saying that you're a valuable commodity, Chang. A bargaining chip. If the Chinese help us out, we go with them."

"That's a huge risk," Peter argued. "And I didn't get the impression that they like you very much. We don't have enough leverage to keep us both alive, and once they've got us onboard, they could kill you."

Lowell shrugged. "But one of us would make it out alive. Have you got a better plan?"

Peter stared at him, blinking rapidly. "Has anyone ever told you that you're a sociopath?"

"I work for the military," Lowell said. "Nobody's had to tell me. So what do you think? You want me to hail our contact with the enemy and see if we can get ourselves permanently marked as traitors?"

"You really know how to sell it," Peter sighed. "Yeah, all right, do it. But if it gets us killed, my last words are going to be, *I told you so.*"

"That's the right attitude," Lowell said, already reaching for the controls.

51

THREE WEEKS AGO, Peter had been a happy-go-lucky grad student who wanted to impress his boss and get the girl. Now, he felt almost as grizzled and jaded as Lowell.

Instead of relying on their helmets, Lowell pulled up the handshake channel on their main screen: Channel 444. Channel death-death-death. *Classy.*

"Does that strike you as ominous?" Peter asked. He wasn't superstitious, but his dad sometimes was, and Peter was pretty sure that the Tiān Zhuānjiā had taken that into account when they picked the channel.

"No more than anything else," Lowell said.

Bleak, thought Peter, *but accurate.*

It felt like the Chinese took forever to respond. Deep in the sea of Enceladus, Peter had felt trapped, hemmed in on every side by the water pressure and unseen creatures. Now, in the vacuum of space surrounded by potential enemies, he felt exposed.

The moment the thought crossed his mind, he knew exactly what Lowell would say if he had a direct channel into Peter's brain: *There's just no pleasing you.* The thought took the edge off, even if it didn't bode well that his inner voice now sounded like the crotchety Space Corpsman.

"What if they don't respond?" Peter asked.

Lowell crossed his arms and settled back in his chair, smiling crookedly at the screen. "Oh, they will. They're messing with us right now, you know? First, they're making sure that they look like they're just sitting around waiting for the call, and then they keep us on the hook. Most likely, they're monitoring the channel right now, seeing if they can make us squirm." He rolled his head to one side and met Peter's eye. "You squirming yet, Chang?"

"No, sir," Peter said.

"You want to play something to pass the time? Rock-paper-scissors? Solitaire?" He tipped his head back toward his shoulder. "Maybe we could play hacky sack with that magical key of yours..."

He was still grinning like a maniac when the screen flared to life.

"Hello, gentlemen," said He Ming. "General Wu would like me to tell you that this is an unexpected pleasure."

The stone-faced man sitting at her side inclined his head slightly, but his eyes were clearly fixed on Lowell. *That isn't how you look at an enemy soldier that you want to kill just for the hell of it,* Peter thought. *That's the look you give a man you want revenge on.* It disturbed him a little that he could tell the difference now.

It disturbed him more that they were going to try to cut a deal with this guy.

When they'd met on Enceladus, Peter hadn't been able to see He Ming's face—they'd only heard her voice through the helmets. Now, seeing her in person, there was no mistaking her. The woman's posture was as crisp and rigid as her speech. She sat beside the general, looking almost demure.

It's an act, Peter thought at once. *A show they put on when they're talking to the Space Corps—for any Westerner who buys into the stereotype.*

"Nice to talk to you again, Miss He," Lowell said. "Could you please ask the general not to shoot us full of holes until we talk?"

He Ming turned her head slightly and uttered a few quick words to the general, who nodded sharply.

"What has caused you to reach out to us?" she asked.

"We've got a bargain for you." Lowell reached over and squeezed Peter's shoulder. "My buddy here has some information you might be interested in."

He Ming translated this, and then listened intently to the general's response. "He would like to know what sort of information—and what exactly you plan to bargain for."

"We'd like some coverage. We're shopping this information around, seeing who'll bite." Lowell smiled, but it looked more as if he was baring his teeth. There was something wild in his expression, almost feral. "Insider intel that you can't get anywhere else."

He Ming nodded, but her eyes were flat and bored. "And in exchange?"

"Pick us up. We come to you, and we share what we know."

He Ming relayed this, but Peter could already see the truth in the general's expression. *He's not going to help us. He'd rather see Lowell burn than lift a finger to help us.*

Sure enough, the general shook his head and whispered something back. He Ming lifted her shoulders in a tiny shrug. "Unless you can be more specific, General Wu is not interested."

Lowell mirrored her little shrug. "Guess we'll try our luck with the Germans, then."

He was bluffing, and the problem was that He Ming knew it. The general knew it, too. Peter had no doubt that this was a tactic, but he could also tell that it wasn't working.

Before Lowell could open his mouth again, Peter reached out and laid a hand on Lowell's chest, shoving the man back into his seat.

"Miss He? I'd like to apologize for my friend's behavior. He's an idiot."

"Hey, now!" Lowell protested.

"I don't know where you're from, but my father was born in Yunnan. Do you know what he always said about women from China?"

He Ming didn't so much as blink.

"He said that everybody in the West underestimates them. If I had to guess, I'd say most of the Space Corps underestimates both of you. The general speaks English, right? At least enough to understand what we're saying without your help." Peter gestured to the screen, encompassing the pair of them. "This is mostly a tableau for the stupid Americans who can't be bothered to learn Mandarin."

A shadow of a smile appeared on He Ming's lips, or so it seemed to Peter. He patted Lowell's chest. "This particular stupid American thinks he's going to win macho points by being cryptic. So let me give it to you straight: we just came out of the Enceladean sea, where we saw some inscriptions left by aliens, and a bunch of creatures that looked a lot like extinct animals on Earth."

"Chang," Lowell muttered. "I think that's enough."

Undeterred, Peter turned and held up the stellar key to the screen. "We've also got this. Munroe told us it was a key, but I think it's more than that. I think it's a power source, and what's more, I think you need it to operate the weapon."

To some extent, he was shooting in the dark, but he had a hunch that everyone out here was. They were all more interested in keeping a potential weapon away from their enemies than understanding exactly what was going on. He saw the slight twitch in the general's face.

"You know the name Munroe, right?" Peter pressed.

This time, it was the general who answered. "Lieutenant Larry Munroe." It didn't take a linguist to detect the hatred in his voice.

"That guy wants us dead," Peter said. "Nothing would make him happier."

He Ming and General Wu glanced at one another. *I sure as hell hope that they hate him more than they hate Lowell— although I can't imagine that Munroe makes friends with foreign nationals. Then again, Lowell was about as blunt as a jackhammer.*

"Why reach out to us?" asked He Ming.

"Our engines are damaged," Peter said. "We're dead in the water. Or...you know." He waved around him at random. "In the ether, I guess?"

Lowell groaned and hid his face.

"If we pick you up, you will hand over everything you have?" He Ming asked.

"Only if you can guarantee that neither of us will be killed." Peter's gaze rested on the general. "I'm going to guess that you and Lowell have a history, but I want to know that we'll both walk away from this unharmed."

He Ming and the general looked at one another. Their body language wasn't hostile, exactly, but it was unyielding.

"It isn't enough," said He Ming at last. "I'd rather parlay with you than with him." She gestured to Lowell. "And certainly more than with Munroe, but our hands are tied."

That's a steaming sack of shit, Peter thought as he slumped back in his seat. *If you wanted to, you'd find a way.*

He had the uncomfortable feeling that the moment they dropped the call, the Chinese ship was going to fire on them—or pick them up anyway, and take what they wanted. Maybe he *had* miscalculated.

Lowell, however, sat forward. Taking Peter by the wrist, he moved his hand away. "What if we can get you something else, too?" he asked slowly.

He Ming tilted her head. "Such as?"

Lowell grabbed Peter by the shoulder and shook him, perhaps with a little more vigor than was really called for. "*This* American idiot has his heart in the right place—but the three of us? We know how politics work. If you fire on Munroe, the Tiān Zhuānjiā will come under scrutiny for breaking a treaty. If you wait too long, you might lose possession of the weapon. But what if someone else fired first?"

He Ming's demeanor didn't change, but her shoulders shifted ever so slightly. "You would start such a conflict in exchange for your own safety?"

"No," Lowell growled. "I'd do it to kill the biggest son of a bitch I've ever had the displeasure of meeting. Hell, I'd kill him for free—but if you play your cards right..." He pointed to General Wu. "You could avoid all of the tricky paperwork that comes with being the man who starts the war. And you could watch Munroe fry."

A cold fire had taken up residence in the general's eyes. "And Munroe dies?"

Lowell leaned forward slowly until his face was inches from the screen. "Munroe dies."

General Wu nodded once, then rose to his feet, walking out of the line of sight. For the first time, He Ming looked a little taken aback, but she quickly recovered. "Then we have an agreement. You initiate a firefight with the American forces, and we will take you into custody. I can't guarantee you immunity, but I can promise that we won't shoot you in the back."

"Or the front," Lowell added.

He Ming's mouth pulled up at the corners. "Or the front," she agreed. "Your move, Mr. Lowell."

She ended the call, leaving Lowell and Peter sitting there in silence.

52

"I DIDN'T KNOW that you were such a little diplomat," Lowell said as he got to his feet.

All of Peter's bravado seemed to have evaporated the moment they ended the call, but Lowell was still impressed. It took guts to make a bet like that. The kid had come a long way from the terrified scientist who'd cried after the shootout in the research station. "I figured it was worth a shot."

"Do you trust them to hold up their end?" Lowell asked.

Peter shook his head. "At this point, I'm not sure I trust anyone. Do you?"

"I trust them not to shoot us."

"Really? I thought you were more jaded than that."

Lowell chuckled. "Nah, they won't do us dirty. Not like that, anyway. They'll take us into custody, get their hands on whatever this weapon is, and then dangle us over the heads of the Pentagon —make the US look like the bad guys, then agree to extradite us. Everyone saves face, and we end up in prison on the moon to rot. If you're lucky, they'll forget about you. If you're unlucky, they'll pin the deaths of your archaeology buddies on you and sweep the rest of it under the rug."

Peter groaned. "I take it back. You're still just as jaded as —good Christ, Lowell, what are you doing?"

Lowell knelt next to Simms' body, unbuckling the man's chestplate. "What does it look like I'm doing? My suit's compromised, and when I shot Simms, I left his suit intact. I'm switching out before we do this. Come on, give me a hand."

Peter got shakily to his feet and crossed to where Lowell knelt. Gingerly, he helped Lowell lift Simms off the floor.

"I hate this," he muttered. "Just so you know."

"And *I* hate getting torn apart in the vacuum of space," Lowell said. "Help me get his arm out of his sleeve. Rigor mortis isn't making this any easier."

Peter's visage was ashen, but in the end, he got it together and helped Lowell pry the man out of his suit. It was almost enough to make Lowell forgive him for all that backtalk in front of the Tiān Zhuānjiā.

———

SIMMS' helmet was nowhere to be found, and Lowell didn't have time to go running around looking for it. Every moment they wasted just gave Munroe more time to question them.

"Can't we ask the Chinese to lend us one of their ships?" Peter asked.

Lowell shook his head. "That would negate the point of this little maneuver. We can't have it look like a Chinese crew fired the first shot—and you better believe that every one of these ships has livestream recording devices *and* a black box. It's all optics, Chang. We're stuck with this ship."

At least they weren't stuck in the pod anymore, with its

makeshift weapons and limited steering capabilities. They might be down an engine, but Lowell figured that their erratic movements would make them harder to hit once Munroe clocked them as a threat.

"I take it I'm on guns again?"

"Ding, ding, got it in one," said Lowell cheerfully.

"You're way too excited about this."

"This is the fun part." Lowell pulled his old helmet onto his head, then secured it in place. He felt sore all over, and he could tell that he and the ship were in similar shape: battered, bruised, a little worse for wear. The adrenaline helped with that, though.

Besides, pain kept him focused. It reminded him that he was still alive. "How are you doing, kid?"

Peter's laugh came out wild, and it cracked in the middle. "This is an insane plan."

"Wouldn't even call it a plan, really."

"Is that supposed to make me feel better?" Peter asked in disbelief.

Lowell shrugged. "Not really. Just wanted to put things in perspective for you. Are you ready?"

Peter pointed at his controls. "Refractor, sonic cannon ... wait, will that work in a vacuum?"

"The smart kids who made it say so," Lowell grunted. "It travels along a low density particle beam until it hits something."

Peter nodded. "Is there any part of the ship I should be trying to hit in particular?"

"Whatever you can get a sight on."

Peter took a deep breath and Lowell knew what was coming next. His voice got quieter. "We're going to get a lot of people killed, aren't we?"

We're going to get ourselves *killed most likely,* Lowell thought. He considered saying it to Peter, but that was foolish. "Nobody on that ship is naive. Nobody on *any* of these ships is naive. They know what they're getting into."

"But still..."

Lowell nodded. "But still." There was nothing else to say. Peter knew better than Lowell what was at stake.

Peter took another deep breath, then rested his hands on the controls. "Let's get this over with."

Before he fired up the engines, Lowell reached over to shake Peter's hand. "It's been a pleasure serving with you, soldier."

He couldn't see Peter's face, but he could hear the incredulous smile in his voice. "It's been something, anyway."

Lowell nodded, then turned back to the controls. "All righty, little buddy—let's go ruin this bastard's day."

53

LARRY MUNROE STARED out the window and watched as Enceladus collapsed inward. The scientists who'd spent their lives studying the moon would have been sorry to see it go, but they were long gone. If anything, they would become part of the moon's legacy—there was poetry in that, certainly. They had given their lives studying its unique atmosphere, never guessing that its value was far higher than that of mere scientific interest.

It wasn't just an interesting little galactic anomaly. It had a use. A *purpose*.

And after years of biding his time, Munroe was finally going to be able to take advantage of it.

All of the other space forces were circling the moon's frozen carcass like birds of prey, waiting to see what would emerge. Munroe suspected that most of them—aside from the Tiān Zhuān-jiā, maybe—had no idea what was about to happen. There was no way of knowing how much intel they had, and at this point, he didn't care. He'd do whatever he had to, while the rest of them sat on their laurels and worried about what the International Criminal Court would rain down on them if they broke the rules.

Once Munroe had the weapon, courts would be a moot point. There would be no need to worry over a slap on the wrist, not when he held the power.

He was reveling in this fantasy when he spotted a Space Corps vessel approaching. When he ran its ident, it came up as one of the two vessels he'd sent out with Hellcat. It seemed to be limping along, on a direct but wobbly course to intercept his own vessel.

Frowning, he hailed Hellcat. "How close are you?"

"We just broke atmo. Shall I send you my coordinates?"

Munroe stared at the incoming vessel. "Unless you're looking at me right now, it doesn't matter."

"Sir?" she asked in bewilderment.

"You told me that you lost the other ship. Is there any chance Simms made it off-world without you realizing it?"

He was pretty sure that he already knew the answer, and it wasn't like he was going to take a chance. Hellcat's silence only confirmed what he already suspected. "I don't see how," she said at last.

"I'm disappointed, Helena," he said. He knew full well that it pushed all of her buttons when he used her given name, which was exactly why he did it. "You had one job."

"Yes, sir," she said in clipped tones. "My mistake, sir. I don't see how he got off-world, especially since he didn't use the egress point—"

"Well, he clearly managed it," Munroe snapped. "I didn't ask for excuses, Hellcat. I asked for *results*."

"Yes, sir," she said.

He ended the call with no further explanation, then headed toward the bridge. He was done sending incompetents to deal with a problem that he should have dealt with himself a long time ago.

I should have known that he'd be trouble when he started asking questions on Mars. If I'd had any sense of how out of hand this would get, I would have laid him out in the dust with Keating and saved myself a whole hell of a lot of time and energy.

At least Munroe was capable of learning from his mistakes, and if this tedious showdown had taught him anything, it was that if he wanted something done right, he would have to do it himself. He couldn't think of a single act that would give him more pleasure than finally killing Carpenter Lowell.

If he was going to become the most powerful man in the universe, today seemed as good a time as any to wipe the slate clean and start fresh.

———

MAJOR GENERAL YEVGENIY ILIN answered on the third ping.

"Is it time already?" he asked cheerfully. "I've been looking forward to this for ages. Which one of us gets to do the honors, General? Perhaps we shall flip a coin?"

"Neither of us will be firing the first round," General Wu informed him. "We've made an agreement with a man named Lowell. Do you know him?"

Ilin shrugged and shook his head. "No. Who is he with? The Germans?"

"An American defector," Wu replied.

Ilin stared at the screen for a moment, and then began to laugh. "Incredible. So we can blame everything on the Americans, and we have the perfect cover in the meantime. I must say, that is a remarkable turn of events. However did you get so lucky?"

"We don't have much time," He Ming reminded the general.

Wu nodded. "Once the fight breaks out, chaos will soon follow. We need a plan, Major General. While everyone is distracted by the Americans, we must fight fire with fire."

"You want to incapacitate the rest of the fleets?" Ilin asked. "Very well: We'll take Germany, you take Japan, and then we work our way through the rest."

General Wu tilted his head to one side. "And then what, Ilin? When your fleet and mine are the last two left standing?"

Ilin paused, then folded his hands in front of him and leaned toward the camera. "I think we both know what happens then, General. It's a race to the moon, no holds barred—just like in the old days." He chuckled. "Funny to think that we'll be engaged in another space race, only much further from home this time. Tell me, General, because it seems to have slipped my mind—did my people win the first one, or did yours?"

General Wu didn't reply.

"Ah, yes, I remember, we did," Ilin said. "Maybe history will repeat itself. What do you think?"

Still, General Wu held his tongue.

"Oh, it's all in good fun, General. Shall we make a private deal, just the two of us? Neither of us fires on the other. We're good friends by now, aren't we? We're in no hurry to harm one another. We're not like the Americans, rabid dogs spoiling for a fight. Let the officials back on Earth decide what happens then."

He Ming watched General Wu out of the corner of her eye.

"This is a sensible suggestion," Wu said at last.

"Then we're agreed. Once the American fires, the real fun can begin." Ilin rubbed his palms together. "I can hardly wait."

He Ming stared at the screen for a long time, even after they ended the call. It seemed to her that Ilin was still on the screen.

The Americans were one thing, but she couldn't say with any certainty what the Russian's intentions were.

It was a strange thing, to place trust in your enemies and doubt your allies. It almost seemed to her that the world had turned upside down, as if gravity itself was inverted.

Except, now that she thought about it, all the gravity out here was artificial. Natural laws no longer applied.

"Do you think he will keep his promise?" she asked.

The general shrugged. "Will we?"

54

PETER WISHED that he knew more about the structure of spaceships. It would also have been helpful to have a deeper grasp of physics.

And munitions.

And campaign strategy.

And how the damn guns worked.

"Hey, calm down," said Lowell. "I can hear you hyperventilating into the mic. Take a deep breath and focus on the target. We'll be in range in about a minute."

He had no idea how Lowell managed to keep his hands and voice so steady, or how he could keep the ship moving steadily forward, as if nothing was wrong. Peter was shaking like crazy, and he was pretty sure that he was having a panic attack.

"Can't you go any faster?"

"Maybe, but they're more likely to notice that there's something wrong if I go zipping around like a lunatic. Just keep your fingers crossed that they think Simms is on the way back from his mission."

Peter twisted in his seat to look at the body lying face-down on the floor behind him in nothing but skivvies. "Right," he said. "Pretend we're Simms."

Didn't really end well for him, though, did it? he thought.

"Yup. Nice deep breaths and...*son of a—*"

Peter was thrown out of his seat as Lowell accelerated unexpectedly. Through the window, Peter saw a large object sail by. A moment later, the ship rocked again, and an awful noise came from below.

"What was that?" Peter asked.

"Remote-detonated missile," Lowell grunted, fighting the controls. "Looks like they figured out that we're not Simms. Okay, hold on—the jig's up and we're going in."

"I think that maybe you're mixing your meta*phors—!*" Peter was halfway to his chair, and he had to wrap his arms around the back to keep himself from falling again as the ship jolted forward.

"Stop worrying about my grammar and get back on duty!" Lowell snapped. "Unless you want to be turned into pâté."

Peter tumbled into the chair and slammed his palm down on the targeting mechanism. He wasn't really aiming, just hoping to fire something. The moment the target locked in, he fired the refractor. As satisfying as it had been to blast through the ice with it, the shower of sparks that accompanied the shot was even better.

"Do I have to worry about running out of juice?" Peter asked.

"Nope," Lowell assured him. "That's the beauty of these ship designs—no ammo and unlimited firepower."

It might be unlimited, but Peter could see that it was less than effective against the larger vessel. The original plan had been to get as close as possible before they started firing. Now he understood why. Each shot was about as effective as a mosquito bite—and their ship would be about as easy to crush as an irritating pest.

If they were going to stand a chance of surviving this, Peter was going to need to do more than fire at will.

Lowell banked the ship to one side in order to avoid another missile. This time, Peter could hear shrapnel peppering their hull. At least they both had working suits again—not that they'd provide much protection if the whole ship blew, but they were better than nothing.

"Any idea where those missiles are coming from?" Peter asked.

"Sure," Lowell said. "There's an array off the port beam."

"Can you take us closer?"

"To the firing mechanism?" Lowell asked.

"I want to try something," Peter said.

Lowell looked over at him, and Peter was just barely able to make out his expression through the visor. *The maniac is smiling.*

The ship dove forward recklessly. As they skirted close to the enormous hull of the Space Corps vessel, Peter kept firing. He didn't want Munroe to realize that they were up to something, and there was always the chance that he might get in a lucky hit along the way.

As the missile launcher came into view, Peter took a deep breath. The refractor hadn't done much damage so far, and he hadn't bothered with the sonic cannon. It hadn't been enough to incapacitate him, so he figured that it wouldn't do much against the metal plating. Besides, it was harder to aim.

But if he could pull this off, it might well be worth the risk.

The idea was that firing the sonic cannon at the perfect moment would send the missile careening back into Munroe's ship. There were plenty of games—like *Fallout: Mars*, which Peter had spent half his life playing—where deflecting an OP enemy's attacks was the more effective way of doing damage. It was time to put that gaming theory to the test.

"Get us in the launcher's sights, and then hold your position," Peter said.

Peter was ready for some pushback from Lowell. After all, if he missed this shot, their ship would be blown to smithereens. But Lowell just grunted and slid the ship into position.

A moment later, the launcher fired.

Peter wasn't a physicist, and he wasn't a rocket scientist. He was just a guy with a high score in a space-combat video game who'd learned sixteen unique button combinations in order to max out his damage.

One.

Two.

Three...

Lowell finally murmured, "Chang..."

Peter ignored him. If he mistimed the shot, even by a fraction of a second, they were done. If he fired too early, the cannon would miss. If he fired too late, it would—quite literally—blow up in his face.

Peter hit the button right in the sweet spot. He couldn't have timed it more perfectly if he'd been sitting at home in front of his gaming rig.

His aim, on the other hand, left a lot to be desired.

The missile was indeed thrown back, but instead of crashing into the American ship, it flew wide. Peter watched helplessly as it sail away into open space, thinking he'd missed his one chance.

Then the missile seemed to hesitate in space, its thrusters flaring uselessly, before it was yanked sideways—and was sucked up into the energon ring that powered the German vessel.

The explosion went off like a neutron star, and Peter had to lift his arm and squeeze his eyes shut to keep from being blinded. A few seconds later, a wave of what looked like sand pattered against the window: all that remained of the German ship.

For a few seconds, the only sounds in Peter's ears were the pounding of his own heart, and the ragged breathing that echoed through the mics.

"Was that your plan?" Lowell asked at last.

"Not exactly," he croaked when he finally found his voice.

Lowell whistled. "Let's just pretend that it was. Because that's one hell of a way to start a war."

And indeed, a moment later all hell broke loose.

55

CHANDRAN BHATT HAD JOINED the Indian Integrated Space Cell in 2051 as a lowly technician, and had slowly worked his way up the ranks. He knew full well that he'd never become a ranking officer, but early on he'd set his sights on becoming a starfighter pilot, and he'd finally managed to land his first assignment in 2060 aboard the IAF *Kovind*, pride of the Indian Forces' fleet. The climb had been long and slow, but he'd been sustained by his childhood dream of visiting other worlds. He'd imagined himself as an explorer.

Of course, the military had other plans.

Still, he got to travel. At the moment, he was looking down at Enceladus, marveling that he'd been chosen to be sent on a mission to one of the places he'd dreamed about as a child.

It looked different than he'd expected. Smaller. In fact, to Chandran's consternation, it seemed to be shrinking by the minute.

His artilleryman, Tuhin, sat in the canteen beside him, eating his packet of khichdi and pickle. Chandran preferred the shahi paneer. It tasted less chemical—it wasn't fine dining, of course, but if he had to subject himself to the Cell's rations, he could do worse.

"It's not as impressive as I thought," Tuhin said. "Like a sad little snowball. Where's the plume?"

"We've become jaded, haven't we, when looking on another world becomes a bore?" asked Chandran.

Tuhin shrugged, his spoon halfway to his mouth, when a burst of light from outside made both of them gasp in surprise. A moment later, the *Kovind*'s alarm sounded. Tuhin dropped his spoon into the half-finished pouch of khichdi without a second thought and lobbed it over his shoulder into the trash. Chandran did the same, and the two of them sprinted toward the hangar where their two-seater starfighter waited.

Chandran viewed his vessel with all the pride a parent might have had toward a beloved child. Most of the other pilots left the job of maintaining their ships to the mechanics, but Chandran had never been comfortable letting anyone else handle his ship. He'd seen first-hand how careless the mechanics could be. Most of them were good at their jobs, but why take the risk, knowing that it would be his neck on the line if anything went wrong?

Ratri was his pride and joy, and she'd served him well so far. Just before he pulled on his helmet and slid into the cockpit, he pressed his gloved fingers to his lips, then brushed his fingers across the side of the fighter.

"Have our orders come in yet?" he asked.

In the seat in front of him, Tuhin shook his head. "Not yet. If you ask me, none of them know what's going on, any more than we do."

All the pilots and their artillerymen were already boarded, and the bay doors had begun to open.

"Let's get out there," Chandran suggested. "Then when our orders come in, we'll be ready to go."

Tuhin didn't argue, so Chandran lifted off, steering them out of the bay and into space beyond. He was so focused on navigating that he didn't register what was wrong until Tuhin asked, "Where's the German ship?"

Chandran looked up. Sure enough, the German ship had disappeared entirely. They'd been staring it down for the last three hours, and now it had just...vanished.

"Where could they have gone?" he asked, puzzled. The energon drives were powerful, but he'd never seen one initiate a jump that fast.

"Engage evasive maneuvers," Tuhin suddenly barked. "Enemy fire at ten o'clock."

Chandran reacted instinctively, bringing the fighter around to bear. His mouth fell open as he realized that the Tiān Zhuānjiā battleship was firing on the Japanese fleet.

"They broke the treaty?" he asked softly.

"Focus, Bhatt. We've got another problem."

A green bolt shot past them, barely missing their engines; the fighter behind them wasn't so lucky. Instead of exploding, the ship behind them simply seemed to fall apart. Chandran watched in horror as its crew tumbled free, their suits melting away from their bodies even as he stared.

"What is *that?*"

"Chemical munitions," Tuhin said.

The words leapt to Chandran's mind: *The Russians.* They'd been working on them for years.

He wrenched his eyes away from the unfortunate crew and refocused on the ship that had fired on them. Sure enough, it bore the Russian insignia.

When I started in the Cell, we were allies, he thought. The idea of deploying a weapon like that, something that would melt flesh off the bone like *ghee* left in the sun on a hot day...it was reprehensible.

Still, he was a realist, and he had to face facts. Whether he respected it or not was immaterial—it was already happening.

It suddenly occurred to him where the German vessel had gone.

Tuhin, always the consummate professional, was already firing on the Russian ship. The *Ratri* was outfitted with light railguns. The disadvantage was that the fighter could only carry about twenty shots' worth of ammunition, but on the bright side, shields couldn't deflect it. The artillery, affectionately known as 'cockleburs,' was magnetized, which also meant that it was unlikely to miss. Once it struck the target, the prefragmented shells burst apart, often piercing an enemy hull. They were only slightly less efficient than the American missiles, and cost about a third as much to manufacture.

And Tuhin was a wizard with them.

In the early days, Chandran had kept an eye on his partner, trying to anticipate the artilleryman's movements and strategies. Over the years, they had practically learned to read one another's minds. Chandran no longer worried about where Tuhin planned to aim; his friend's strategy was consistent, and Chandran knew it by heart. As long as he lined up the shots, he could count on Tuhin to take them, and the man never missed.

"Orders are in," Tuhin said. "We're to incapacitate the Russian vessel, if we can. Take out its towers." His head lifted from the controls, and even though Chandran couldn't see his face from here, he knew that the man was counting off their targets. "I've got eyes on three of them."

"I'm running a roundabout," Chandran said. Without waiting for a response, he took the fighter in a wide arc, hooking them past the Russian ships' engines. Most of the other nations had moved away from manned spacecraft, opting for drones whenever possible. The Cell got a lot of flak for relying on their pilots, but as far as Chandran was concerned, there was no substitute. AI drones were too predictable, and even remote craft couldn't provide a full picture of the battlefield.

Some of the less experienced pilots took their artillerymen in for a direct hit, firing broadside at the Russian ship. They made themselves an easy target, and Chandran flinched as two more of the starfighters were disintegrated by Russian chemical munitions. These were men and women he'd served with, people he'd joked and laughed and eaten dinner with.

In the fourteen years that he'd served with the Cell, he'd seen a lot of people come and go. It had never gotten any easier for him.

A skilled pilot presented a moving target, which was exactly what Chandran did. Keeping them on a steady course meant that Tuhin could pick his targets without having to communicate them in advance. Chandran felt a thrill of satisfaction as Tuhin took out one of the chemical munitions towers; the cocklebur tore the weapon off the side of the Russian ship, then burst apart, shearing a hole in the hull. A moment later, he watched in satisfaction as the chemical residue began to eat a hole in the Russian armaments. They would have planned for this when they designed their ships, of course, but Chandran knew that even adequate safety measures didn't make a ship impervious to damage. A couple more holes like that, and the Russians would be in trouble.

"Shall we focus on their munitions towers?" he asked. If their firepower was stripped away, the rest of the fleet would stand a better chance.

Tuhin responded with a coordinate, and Chandran brought them around. He'd have had to break up their flight pattern either way—if you got *too* predictable, you made yourself easy to target. Sure enough, one of the Russians fired their chemical beam right in the spot where the *Ratri* would have been if they'd stayed the course.

They missed. The fighter was long gone, aiming for the next tower. It took two well-placed shots to knock the next tower free, but the resulting damage left the Russian ship in a rough position. Tuhin whooped with adrenaline, pumping one fist in the air.

Even Chandran smiled. He could see that there was only one tower left, and the Russian vessel looked like the carcass of a dying animal. Their engines were still good, but they only had one weapon left to fire with.

For now.

"Taking us in on tower three," Chandran said. "Hold your fire for evasive countermeasures."

Tuhin didn't need to be told twice.

By now, the Russian commanders must have worked out that the *Ratri* should be kept in their sights, which meant that they were going to have to be extremely careful on this last attack. Careful and *fast*.

Chandran brought them in for the final sweep. Instead of pointing the *Ratri* right at his target like a greenhorn would have done, he kept them on a steady patch flanking the tower, bringing them in close on an elongated arc.

"Hold," he said.

Tuhin made a quiet noise of understanding.

There was an optimal range for the cockleburs: close enough that the targeting system could be fairly accurate, and far enough back that the shrapnel didn't catch your own ship. Chandran had seen a lot of new recruits mistime their artillery attacks and pay the price.

The Russian artillerymen were clearly tracking them, and the tower swung around to keep them in its sights.

Chandran held his breath, waiting for the moment that they

were just shy of the perfect range. He saw the green ripple of the Russian equipment, the only warning that they were about to fire.

"On three," he cried, and immediately threw their own ship into a reverse course, swinging them backward in the equivalent of a three-point turn. The Russian munitions hit the spot where they would have been.

Three seconds later, Tuhin fired.

They were, technically speaking, too close to the blast. The *Ratri* was pointed right at the Russian vessel, and Chandran got a front-row seat to the tower's final moments. He wasn't sure if the tower itself was manned, or if it was operated by remote personnel. Given what they'd done to his fleet, Chandran didn't care.

"Nice shooting," he told Tuhin.

"Nice flying," his partner replied. "If they don't give you a commendation this time, I'm writing headquarters."

This had become a little joke between them, one without any heat. Tuhin had been decorated for his marksmanship twice now; Chandran had gotten a handshake and a form letter to congratulate his navigation abilities. A commendation would be nice, certainly, but that was never the point. Out here, all he really wanted was a team he could trust and a chance to see the universe.

"Shall we head back to regroup?" he asked. His satisfaction at their flying was short-lived when he looked back to find that nearly half of their fleet had been blown apart.

For what? What's the point of all this death? Chandran glanced toward the icy moon Enceladus, wondering if whatever was down there could really be worth it.

"I don't have further orders," Tuhin said. "That's protocol— we've disarmed the Russians, so until..."

He trailed off into silence.

"Tuhin?" Chandran asked.

Then he saw why their commanders hadn't issued their next round of orders.

The Tiān Zhuānjiā vessel had finished off the Japanese warship; while the fleet had been distracted with the Russians, they'd moved in alongside the main Cell carrier craft. Small dark dots streamed out from the side of the Chinese ship, drifting closer to the Cell craft.

"What are they?" Chandran asked.

"Drones," said Tuhin flatly.

Chandran sucked in a breath. He'd always thought pilots were irreplaceable due to their skill set, but he hadn't thought in terms of pure numbers. There weren't just dozens of drones, or hundreds of them.

There were thousands.

"I can take us in," Chandran said. Tuhin didn't respond. "Preparing for evasive countermeasures..."

"There's no point," Tuhin said. His voice was flat and empty. "There's no point in trying to fight them. We have, what, fifteen burs left? Maybe less? What do you think we're going to do against that?"

Tuhin had never been defeated before, not by enemy gunners, not by training modules, not by the odds. Chandran had never expected to hear the man sound so utterly destroyed by anything as he did now. They watched in silence as the drones detonated.

There were no sparks, no flames, no magnificent final act for the *Kovind*. Instead, it simply looked as if someone poked holes in the massive ship, deflating it bit by bit.

There are hundreds of crewmembers still aboard. Ground troops, mechanics, specialists... Watching a ship give way like that was enough to break Chandran's heart.

It couldn't have been worse if the Tiān Zhuānjiā had fired on him point-blank.

It was over in less than a minute. Outside, Chandran could see the rest of the fleet hovering in the void, not sure what their next course of action should be. They had no orders, and in the wake of numbers like that, there was nothing they could do but watch.

Their comm system thrummed to life, and without a word, Tuhin powered it on. A crisp voice spoke in accented Hindi with all the precision of a recording.

It's the Tiān Zhuānjiā, Chandran thought. He closed his eyes, preparing for the inevitable moment when the *Ratri* was blown to pieces.

"I am He Ming," said the voice. "*I speak on behalf of the People's Republic of China. As you know, we are now at war. You are stranded far from home in ships not built for long-distance travel; even if you had adequate fuel and supplies, you would likely die of old age before making it home.*"

Tuhin sighed. "Just get on with it already."

"*However, we are prepared to offer you a deal. We have a common enemy: the United States Space Corps.*"

"So what?" Tuhin muttered. "You want to make another alliance? We've seen how those end."

As far as Chandran knew, the Tiān Zhuānjiā couldn't hear them—which was probably for the best.

"*This is our offer—you have three choices. Those who fire on our ships will be instantly eliminated. Those who retreat will be left to face the void on their own. Any of you who choose to fire on the American vessel and survive will be brought aboard and be made prisoners of war. The choice is yours. Namaste.*"

The communication ended abruptly, leaving a static hum in Chandran's ears. For another moment, he sat there, frozen.

The other pilots knew the *Ratri*'s reputation. Whatever Chandran did, they'd most likely follow his lead.

"What do we do?" he asked.

Tuhin snorted. "Didn't leave us a lot of options, did they? We survive, Bhatt. That's what we've always done."

He was right, of course, but as Chandran looked out at the icy moon, he felt nothing but misgivings. If the Tiān Zhuānjiā wanted to get there so badly, it couldn't bode well that they were winning.

On the other hand, in his years in the service, Chandran had learned that one truth superseded all others out here: in the void, he became a man without a country. The only people he could rely on were the ones fighting at his side. Betraying the Cell was an ugly thing, but betraying Tuhin?

Never.

With shaking hands, Chandran brought the *Ratri* around to face the American vessel.

Eager to be told what to do, the others followed.

56

"WHAT IN THE hell is going on out there, Grady?" Munroe snapped.

The young private was clearly panicking. "I don't know, sir—it looks like the ship deflected our fire and...and took out the German ship?"

Munroe snarled, slamming his fist down on the controls. "Son of a *bitch.*"

Within seconds, the Chinese vessel opened fire on the Japanese spacecraft; by the time Munroe pinpointed Lowell's commandeered craft again, the Russians were firing on the Indian Integrated Space Cell fleet.

Looks like those bastards managed to push their chemical munitions through, Munroe thought, half-impressed in spite of himself.

He was similarly impressed with Lowell—somehow, not only had the man managed to trick Munroe into firing the first shot of the battle, but he had the American ship chasing their tail while everyone got down to brass tacks.

Death was too good for him. Munroe wanted to make him suffer. But time was tight, and Enceladus was a ticking time bomb now—in a pinch, dead would have to do.

"Pull up the ship's data," Munroe barked at Grady.

"Data, sir? What's the point?"

Munroe was at the end of his rope. "The point is that I'm going to break your neck with my bare hands if you don't learn to follow orders. Pull up the damn controls and then get out of my way."

For once in his life, Grady managed to do his job properly. When he was done, he stepped aside, letting Munroe get to work.

"For your information, Grady, I'm doing what I would have done if Hellcat had been honest with me in the first place—I'm jamming their weapons equipment." Back in the day, when men knew how to follow orders, this kind of backup system would never have been necessary. Traitors like Lowell were why the Corps had needed to retool their weapons.

He had to enter three layers of passcodes, then bend over the console to provide a retina scan, but when it was all said and done, the weapons on the little ship blinked offline.

"There," Munroe muttered, glaring at the radar. "Let's see how you like playing this game when you've got no firepower."

He sat back, feeling smug, then turned to Grady.

"I want Lowell's ship taken out first."

"And then the Chinese, sir?" asked Grady, clearly cautious about asking too many questions.

Munroe considered his answer, then shook his head. "No," he said, and his gaze turned toward the surface of Enceladus. "After that, we make a beeline for the target." He smiled at his own wit, even though Grady was probably too stupid to get the joke. "We've got bigger fish to fry."

57

THE GERMAN SHIP WAS OUT, the Japanese ship was a wreck, the Indian mothership was being swarmed by the Chinese, and Peter was still alive. Sure, he'd single-handedly started a war, but he'd kept them alive. Peter was feeling pretty cocky about the whole scenario—until the lights on his dash went out.

He didn't stop fiddling with the controls right away. Maybe there had been some sort of power blip? He jiggled the joystick furiously, praying that it would come back online. If they were going to stand any chance of defeating Munroe, they'd need firepower.

"No point," Lowell sighed. "They jammed our weapons systems." He pointed at the controls, where a bright red light was blinking furiously.

Peter groaned. "They can do that?"

"They can do whatever the hell they like," Lowell said drily. "He'd have killed our atmo if that was an option, but he'll just send a missile after us instead, and this time we're not going to be able to deflect it." He snorted. "Hey, Chang, wanna take bets on whether our good buddies over at the Tiān Zhuānjiā are going to stick their necks out for us? Maybe we should call for backup."

"No bet," said Peter wearily. "They'll probably be thrilled to hear that we're in trouble." The Chinese fleet may have been reluctant to fire the opening volley, but they'd probably have no such concerns when it came to *ending* the fight. After all, they had about a million drones in space right now, hellbent on dismantling the Indian vessel. Peter and Lowell had served their purpose as scapegoats. He Ming and General Wu wouldn't need them anymore.

Lowell might have convinced himself that they'd made an alliance, but the only thing Peter was prepared to count on was the fact that they'd eliminate Munroe if they got the chance.

Lowell checked their rear cameras. "Dammit," he grumbled. "Looks like we've got more company."

Peter turned his head to watch in silence as a fleet of small ships jetted toward them. They were all nearly identical, roughly the size of sleek sports cars with wings, although they sported a variety of decals and paintings on the side. The colorful little ships had more personality than the uniform vessels piloted by the Tiān Zhuānjiā and the Space Corps.

"And they are?" he asked.

"Looks like Cell fighters." Lowell let out a low growl. "Probably here to take out Munroe. Dammit, Chang, all I want is a cup of coffee and a ham bar. Is that too much to ask?" His controls, at least, were still working, but he just sat there, shaking his head.

Peter frowned and shifted away from him. "What are you thinking?"

"Who says I'm thinking?"

"We just started an international space battle, and now we're unarmed!"

"Hold on," Lowell barked, and the ship hummed to life. Peter's eyes had been focused on the Cell ships, and he hadn't noticed that Munroe had fired another missile at them. And this time, Peter had no counterfire available. He clung to his chair as Lowell executed a series of spins and turns that sent the missile flying past them. It clearly wasn't designed to target anything as small and maneuverable as their ship, but the missile began a slow arc in space as it turned lazily around to come at them again.

What's the range on something like that? Peter wondered. Most likely, it didn't matter. Their ship only had so much fuel, and they were too far away from the next closest outpost. Besides, they were *persona non grata* with the Space Corps already, and who else would even consider taking them in? The Germans? They were fugitives with a whole galaxy at their disposal, but no safe place to rest their heads.

"The missile's locked on our ship," Lowell said. There was a strange expression on his face. "Since this is a Space Corps ship, they have that data on us."

"You say that like it isn't a terrible thing."

Lowell turned to Peter, and he was smiling. "It's not terrible, it's just a unique circumstance. It means this missile can't be confused. It'll stay on this ship no matter what."

"And that's a good thing?"

Lowell abruptly changed course, putting the missile right on their tail. "Grab your spacesuit and head to the airlock. There *might* be a way to do this without getting killed in the process."

"But?"

Lowell's laugh was so low that at first Peter thought it was an engine malfunction. "But probably not."

58

LOWELL HADN'T FLOWN evasive maneuvers in a long time, but it was a bit like riding a bicycle. True, a bicycle only involved two pedals and one crankshaft, as opposed to a nuclear fusion reactor and a hundred individual buttons, but other than that it was pretty much the same.

Even so, there was only so long that Lowell could avoid the missile. Knowing that Chang was more or less out of harm's way made him feel a little better, at least.

"You got your helmet on right this time?" Lowell asked.

"Yeah," Peter said. He was already in position far below, prepared to bail out of the airlock at a moment's notice. "You're not going to ditch me, are you?"

"You could bail now, you know," he told Peter.

The kid laughed through the link. "Yeah, right. Just step out into the night by myself? No way. I'll wait."

"That's the spirit."

Lowell was closing fast on Munroe's ship, which was already

charting a gradual course toward the surface of Enceladus. The engines—a prime target on most of the other military transport vessels—were more heavily armored than on a standard ship, and they had an expulsion field around their weakest points. Free-floating debris was forced away from the apertures, and most artillery didn't stand a chance of getting close.

So we don't aim for the engines, Lowell thought. *We aim for the bridge.* If he plotted his course correctly, the smaller vessel would go right through the glass, wrecking the controls and compromising the ship's integrity, while the missile would finish what they'd started.

Outside, the stars were streaking by, and Enceladus had split open like a dropped egg. The whole damn universe was falling apart, but Lowell couldn't worry about that.

Eyes on the prize. Head in the game. All that shit that they'd told him in basic, when the guys got so tired that they were ready to drop. Chin up.

Semper fi.

The phrase made Lowell think of his father, and how his old man had put that promise of loyalty first, before everything. In a way, this was the mission that most tested Lowell's loyalty: not to his commanders, but to the ideals that he'd always kept close to his chest. Lowell had never really lost faith in the mission or in his people, only in the commander who had done the unforgivable and in the system that had kicked him to the curb when he tried to make things right.

"Almost there," he told Peter in his best impression of an airline flight attendant. "This is your captain speaking. Please keep your arms and legs inside the cockpit, and make sure that your seatbelt is fastened. We're on our final descent."

Munroe had taken everything from him: his reputation, his

career, his family, and his sense of self-worth. Time to return the favor.

Lowell flipped the controls over to autopilot and bolted belowdecks.

59

LARRY MUNROE LEANED EAGERLY over the dashboard as the ship charted a course for Enceladus. This mission had cost the Corps millions of dollars in damages and more than a handful of lives, but that was all just collateral. In the end, Munroe had won. The scales were back in balance.

He was already contemplating how he would celebrate. Luxuries were few and far between out here, but he had a half-bottle of good port in the safe under his bunk. A cigar would have been better, but smoking onboard was a major hazard; once a spark got into the electrical circuits, it could rage out of control. Safety first. Munroe could wait until he was back on Earth, in the Pentagon with the big boys, toasting his own success and smoking a hand-crafted cigar courtesy of the Space Corps.

No, not just his success. They'd be toasting his promotion. General Larry Munroe. That had a nice ring to it.

Only, what if he was thinking too small? Why should he jump just because the Pentagon gave orders? Operation Cascade was minutes away from going down in the books as a raging success, but only if Munroe agreed to play ball with high command. This was his weapon now. He could hold it over their heads. Ask anything they wanted. General Munroe? Screw that. How about President?

And why stop at the United States, now that he was thinking about it? He could be the man in charge of the galaxy. That sounded pretty sweet, didn't it? If he phrased it nicely, he might not even have to threaten anyone to make it happen. And if anyone *did* want to give him hell about firing that first rogue shot, intentional or not, he could always defect—he could bargain with the Tiān Zhuānjiā. China might be willing to deal with him. It would be the Cold War all over again, except that there would be no one to stand against him.

"Sir?" said Grady nervously. "There's something you need to see."

He pointed to the comm, where He Ming's placid face stared up at them. Munroe was tired of looking at her—if she'd been in the room, he would have happily shot her point-blank, just to spare himself the trouble of dealing with her again. She was so goddamn smug. Didn't she know who she was dealing with?

Well, they'd all figure it out soon enough.

"What can I do for you?" he sneered.

He Ming gestured behind her to the stone-faced general. "My commander would like to make you an offer. If you will refrain from firing on our ship, we will recall our drones."

"Hold my fire?" Munroe demanded, then burst into a fit of laughter. "No, I think we're past that, Miss He. We're not equals in this game. But I'll tell you what: once I get to the weapon, we can talk. Maybe we can come to some other mutually beneficial arrangement...after you acknowledge that I've won."

"Sir?" asked Grady from behind him. "We're not authorized to parlay."

Munroe's eyelid twitched. God, he hated that boy's whiny, pathetic voice. Couldn't he just man up and pull himself together?

"Let me make one thing very clear to both of you," Munroe said, gesturing to He Ming with one hand and Grady with the other. "My whole career has been leading to this moment. *You*" — he gestured to He Ming—"are not going to intimidate me into sharing my moment of triumph, and *you*"—he indicated Grady— "are not going to convince me to stand down. Do you know how hard I've worked to get here? What I've had to do?" Turning his eyes away from both of them, he looked down at the moon below. "We're finally here. This is my day, ladies and gentleman. This is where it ends."

A deep, self-satisfied voice echoed out of the comm, one that Munroe didn't recognize.

"You have no loyalty," said General Wu. "And no regard for rules."

"Rules are made so that lesser men can know their limits," Munroe said. "Men like..."

He pointed through the glass toward where Lowell's ship had been, and now saw that it was careening right toward him at full tilt. Munroe's mouth fell open.

"No," he murmured. "Today is *my* day."

"I agree," said General Wu. "And I'm honored to be here to witness it."

The next thing Larry Munroe knew, the world was on fire.

60

"WHAT IS THAT PILOT DOING?" asked Tuhin. "He's on a collision course with the ship. Are his controls malfunctioning?"

Chandran leaned forward, breathing hard. Adrenaline was the only thing keeping him upright at this point, but as he watched the little vessel jet toward its Space Corps mothership, something bloomed in his chest. He understood that pilot, even if he had never laid eyes on him in person.

"No," he said, "it's a suicide mission."

"Maybe we should consider a mission of our own," Tuhin said darkly.

Chandran knew that the artilleryman was thinking of their friends and allies who'd been on the *Kovind*, all of whom had died at the hands of the swarming drones. "You mean against the Chinese? No, my friend, not today. There's no point in killing them now. Then the Russians would win—they'd get the weapon we've all come to claim, by simple virtue of the fact that they're the only ones still standing. I don't intend to die just to let the Russians win."

"Then what?" Tuhin demanded, gesturing toward the Space Corps transport vessel in frustration. "They're armored. Our shots are useless. We're dying out here anyway. What's your plan?"

The smaller American ship stopped swerving through the sky, making a beeline for the bridge of the transport ship. Chandran saw something bright flash behind it; it appeared to have dropped a payload.

"We follow that ship," he said decisively. "We see what kind of damage it does—and then we'll finish what it starts."

61

LOWELL HAD NEVER FELT like such an old man before; he practically fell down the steps toward the port where Peter waited for him, then swayed on his feet.

There was no point in maintaining the atmosphere on the ship, so Lowell didn't waste time with safety protocols. He grabbed Peter firmly by one arm, reaching for the controls with his free hand, and pulled the level that would release the airlock.

When Lowell had come aboard, they'd been deep below the frozen sea. It had pressed down on him like a ten-ton weight, made all the more painful by the fact that his suit had been compromised. Now, a vacuum awaited them outside; it tore the hatch out of Lowell's hands before sucking both men into the void. It took all of Lowell's strength to hang on to Peter, who yelped at the pressure of the bigger man's grip, but he wasn't going to let go. If he did, they'd both be alone out here.

Lowell shoved his foot against the lip of the hatch as they spiraled out into the darkness, with enough momentum to get them out of the way of the missile. He could just make out its sleek form. Lowell was reminded suddenly of the shadow-hunting crustacean that had dogged them along the ocean floor. It was, in effect, hunting their ship.

There I go, anthropomorphizing the equipment, just like the scientists did in the research station. I'm turning into a softie at the end.

"Come on," he breathed. He *wanted* the missile to strike home, but not until the ship paved the way. It would be satisfying as hell to turn Munroe's last shot against him.

Unfortunately, the missile was gaining ground. Lowell's whole body tightened with anticipation as the two machines raced toward their ultimate goal.

To Lowell's dismay, the ship lost the race.

When the smaller ship and the missile collided a few seconds before they met the hull, Lowell almost let go of Peter's arm. He had nothing left: no weapons, no plans, no recourse. What was the point?

"Dammit," Peter gasped, apparently sharing Lowell's feeling on the matter. The impact had been enough to tear metal segments away from the hull and reveal some of the mechanical components beneath, but they weren't enough to take Munroe's whole ship out of commission.

Lowell gritted his teeth. After all that, Munroe was just going to get to walk? Maybe it was a sign that Lowell was in the wrong. Maybe the universe *wanted* Munroe to win. *It's just like during the court martial. Shit doesn't stick to that bastard. Munroe wins again.*

Lowell didn't quite understand what happened next. Maybe one of the Cell pilots had seen an opportunity, or maybe it was pure coincidence that he'd followed in the missile's wake. All Lowell knew was that one of the little two-man fighter ships fired a shot right into the shallow crater left by Lowell's efforts.

At first, it seemed like this shot had been as ineffective as Lowell's plan. Then there was an electrical spark from the ship's circuits, smothered almost instantly by the lack of oxygen. The inside of the ship burned bright for a moment as a blinding light—a fire, perhaps, or a chain reaction set off by the damage Lowell had done—flared to life.

And then, almost in slow-motion, the ship fell apart.

62

PETER LET OUT a whoop of excitement.

"He might still be alive," Lowell said. "If Munroe was wearing his suit, the Tiān Zhuānjiā will probably take him captive."

Even as he said it, the Chinese ship swept in, its drones picking over the carcass like so many small crabs feeding on the walls of the underwater tunnel. The Cell fighters dispersed, heading off toward the Chinese transport ship, which had bypassed the wreckage and was headed straight for Enceladus, with the Russian ship limping along in its wake.

I wonder what that's about, Lowell mused.

Peter pumped one arm victoriously, and Lowell realized that he was still holding the stellar key. As far as Lowell was concerned, they should have left it on board their ship before sending it off to Munroe with love. The key had started all of this, and it belonged in the void. Lowell wished fervently that he had never laid eyes on the thing.

"Yes!" Peter yelped. "Take that! Hahaha, oh my *God*, Lowell, we did it! That's for Jana and Amira and Connor, you bastard! That's for the scientists who died on your stupid mission!"

"Settle down," said Lowell, although he was smiling, too. *That's for Dr. Fran Hansen and Samuel Keating, for Lily and Anjali. That's for the people who outclassed you by a mile, and who died for your stupid mission.*

Still, it wasn't an ideal time to celebrate. They were floating freely through deep space, with no end in sight.

Time to call in the reinforcements.

Lowell reached up to his helmet and linked into channel 444. "Hey, Miss He. How did you like our fireworks show?"

It took a moment for the Chinese translator to answer, and when she did, her voice was perfectly neutral. "That was very impressive, Private Lowell. Your attention to detail is astonishing."

"Yeah, that's what I thought." Lowell stretched, wincing as his body complained. He'd been through the mill, and his mouth still tasted like old pennies. A little medical attention wouldn't go amiss. Nor would a nap.

Well, there would be plenty of time to lie around in captivity. He could sleep for a year if he wanted. At the moment, that sounded pretty damn fine.

"You mind giving us a ride?" he asked cockily. "I can send you our coordinates."

Someone else spoke in Mandarin—General Wu, probably. He Ming's voice was regretful when she replied.

"I'm sorry, Mr. Lowell, but the Tiān Zhuānjiā are under strict orders not to take political prisoners at this time. There is no clear protocol for prisoners taken in a deep-space war zone, and given the delicate nature of our work here, we have no wish to compromise the mission. I'm sure you understand."

Bastards.

Lowell sighed. If anything, he was disappointed in himself for expecting a different outcome. Peter and his optimism were rubbing off on him.

"I guess the fact that we had a deal doesn't matter to you. So much for all that *honor* your side likes to talk about, right, He?"

It was the only knife he had to twist, and it wasn't much.

"I'm afraid that the situation has changed. We're at war now."

"That was the whole damn point," said Lowell bitterly.

But he could hear the moment that channel 444 went dead, becoming nothing but white noise against background static.

Well, he thought. *Shit.*

He tuned back into the private channel that he shared with Peter. "They're not coming," he said. Better to tear the Band-Aid off quick, after all. "We're alone."

"I figured," Peter said, sounding resigned. It seemed Lowell was rubbing off on Peter, too. "It's easier this way, right? They get to keep their hands clean. Munroe's out of the picture, and they don't have to deal with any of the red tape."

Lowell said nothing. What was the point of killing Munroe if it meant that the weapon on Enceladus was going to fall into the hands of people who were equally immoral?

Maybe it didn't matter who won. Maybe they were all equally corrupt, and this was an exercise in utter futility. The Russians, the Tiān Zhuānjiā, the Cell—who cared? In the end, whoever held the power wasn't obligated to be decent.

At least Lowell wouldn't be around to see the fallout of his own failure. All he had to look forward to was a day or two of free-floating in deep space, followed by a slow death by dehydration.

Nah, Lowell thought, *I won't let it get that far. If it comes down to it, I'm taking the helmet off.*

I'm going out on my own terms, just like I always promised.

63

WATCHING his ship implode had been bad enough, but getting picked up by the Tiān Zhuānjiā was the final insult. As the Chinese militiamen flanked Munroe, he scowled around at them. They'd zip-tied his hands behind his back when they picked him up, and no matter how he flailed and thrashed, he couldn't get free.

"Go right to hell," he snarled after one of the men removed his helmet.

The man blinked at him impassively, then forced Munroe to his knees.

Ignorant bastard probably doesn't even speak English. How am I supposed to threaten him if he doesn't understand?

It was cold comfort to look over and find Grady beside him. If he'd been asked to predict the young man's behavior, Munroe would have anticipated that he'd blubber and cry, but to his surprise, the kid just knelt there, eyes unblinking and unfocused.

"Do you have a gun on you?" Munroe hissed. "Or a file?"

"No," Grady said, his expression still perfectly blank.

"Well, what good are you?" Munroe snarled, loud enough that

the other soldiers took notice. "Good God, Grady, you're the sorriest excuse for a second-in-command I've ever been cursed with in all my years of service."

Grady turned his head slightly, watching Munroe with those flat eyes. "Sir?" he said. "Stop embarrassing yourself."

Munroe gaped at him. A number of suitable punishments sprang to mind, but he was powerless to enact any of them. He yanked at his confines once more, and when they held, he bared his teeth at Grady.

Grady just looked away, unflappable.

Munroe was distracted by the arrival of the Chinese officers. They strode into the brig, looking back and forth between the two men. He Ming looked the same as ever, but there was a slight smile on General Wu's lips as he examined Munroe's vulnerable position.

"Greetings, Lieutenant," He Ming said, as if he was a guest rather than a prisoner.

"Oh, cut the crap," he snarled.

He Ming turned to Grady, nonplussed by Munroe's vitriol. "You are one of the two survivors we have pulled from the wreckage," she said. "I believe that the general has something to say to you."

The older man stepped forward, and Munroe writhed. *Look at me!* he wanted to scream. *I'm the one that you should be worried about, not him! I'm the one that matters!*

"I am prepared to make a deal with you," said the general in his quiet, steady voice. "We will keep you as a political prisoner, but only if you will agree to send a message to your commanding officers in Washington. We will edit this video together. It will be completely true. You will explain that Mr. Munroe betrayed your country—"

"*Lieutenant!*" Munroe howled.

"—and confirm that this battle was started by a traitor, at which point you will be sent home."

Grady considered this. "You want me to lie?"

"No," said the general. "Isn't this the truth?" At last, he turned to Munroe, the small smile still in place. "We have a recording of this man acting outside of his government's orders. If we establish that he was a traitor, then we can proceed accordingly."

Grady turned his head, examining Munroe with the same little smile that General Wu wore.

They're all conspiring against me, Munroe thought wildly. *They're all jealous—they know they can't face me one-on-one, so they've banded together to take me out!*

"I won't lie," Grady said firmly. "But I can see how telling the truth would benefit my country, and I'd be happy to do so."

"I'll bury you, Grady, just like I buried Lowell," Munroe spat. "Your career ends here, and once I'm cleared by an inquest, you'll wish you'd never been born. I will *wreck* you, Grady."

The general's smile never wavered as he took a step forward. He lifted a small gun and held it right to the middle of Munroe's forehead. "I think you will find that difficult, Mr. Munroe."

There was no time to argue, no time to complain—no time to contemplate that General Wu had staged this conversation so that Munroe's last thought would be the knowledge that his reputation would be dragged through the mud, or that the last thing he saw would be the same thing Dr. Samuel Keating had seen in his final moments on Mars.

He was dead before he hit the steel-plated deck.

64

MAJOR GENERAL YEVGENIY ILIN'S ship had seen better days, but he looked a hell of a lot better than the Space Corps vessel did, so that was something. Everyone else was gone except the Chinese fleet and their Cell POWs.

"You've settled everything nicely, General Wu," he said, leaning back in his seat. Below them, Enceladus looked shrunken and shriveled, like an old fruit left out to spoil. Its transformation from complex, biologically promising moon to lifeless rock was not yet complete, but even as Ilin watched, the ice on its surface was melting away to reveal its rocky core. Instead of a frozen tundra, Ilin was now presented with a matte grey face, little more than limestone.

"I'm glad that we've been able to come to an arrangement, Major General," said Wu. "Our alliance is invaluable to me. I hope that it will continue."

"Do you think that is possible, given what awaits us on the moon below?" Ilin asked.

He watched Wu carefully, wondering exactly how much the other man knew.

"It doesn't look like much," the general said. "But you and I both know that there's more beneath the surface, don't we? The galaxy is full of secrets, Ilin."

The Russian commander smiled. "How forthcoming has your government been with you, General Wu? Do you know what to expect down there?"

"I know very little about the mechanics," Wu replied. "But as for the weapon itself? I know it is the...what would you call it? The Holy Grail of weapons? And that whoever controls it will have enviable power over his fellows."

General Wu stared at him, and Ilin didn't look away. Instead, he waved one hand carelessly. "Well, you've seen to it that the Space Corps doesn't hold that power." He wasn't sure just how much the general knew, and he didn't want to reveal the extent of his own knowledge—or lack thereof. Like his uneasy ally, Ilin didn't know the mechanics of what awaited them when Enceladus finished sloughing off its skin, but he knew that its stone exterior was just one more layer that protected the *real* jewel within from prying eyes. Beneath the gleaming ice, beneath the unflattering pockmarked mantle, Enceladus had guarded a precious secret for centuries.

Ilin enjoyed games, and he knew from experience that sometimes winning a round wasn't the most important thing: what really mattered was making sure that his opponent didn't win, either.

"You've taken some prisoners from the Cell, I see. What about the Americans? I saw two of them floating away—will you be collecting them, too?"

General Wu looked away. His translator sat in silence, her hands folded in her lap, staring down at the moon.

"My son was shot down on Mars four years ago," the general said. "Lieutenant Munroe may have given the order, but our intelligence suggests that the American pilot was the one who pulled the trigger. I am not in any hurry to save his life, Major General. Let him try his luck in the darkness. At last, my son's spirit is at peace."

"Harsh," teased Ilin, "but well-deserved. I'm sorry for your loss, General."

The three of them sat in silence. Half of Ilin's mind was occupied with questions about the moon, and what exactly it would take to activate the weapon at its core.

The other half was wondering how long the alliance with the Tiān Zhuānjia would last.

No doubt I'll end up killing them in the end, Ilin mused. *And when I do, I shall have to time it just right.*

Then Enceladus would yield to him, granting not just the power to defeat his enemies, but the ability to unmake worlds at will.

65

"HOW LONG CAN these suits keep us going?" Peter asked.

He cradled the silvery orb between his hands. It was fitting, after all, that he had come full circle. He'd been drawn into this mess when he unearthed the tablet in Ur-An, which now felt like a lifetime ago. The tablet had led him to Enceladus. Now Enceladus was gone, and Peter was left with nothing but the other half of the artifact duo: the stellar key.

Lowell's grip on Peter's arm had never slackened. "Six months, or something like that. Of course, we'll be dead by then, so it won't really matter."

"If the right people find us, they'll have something to cremate." Peter let out a laugh that sounded more like a sob as it echoed back through his ears. "I think my dad would appreciate that I get a burial in space, at least. Maybe I'll end up as debris in the rings or something. Or we'll get sucked into Saturn's gravitational field." Peter looked up past Lowell, toward where the gas giant awaited them. "That would be something. I always wanted to visit another planet."

"You were already on Enceladus," Lowell pointed out.

Peter scoffed. "That's a *moon*. It doesn't count."

Lowell coughed, although it sounded as if he'd said, *Nerd.*

"What made you want to come out here?" Peter asked.

Lowell sighed wearily. "For real? You want to talk about this now?"

Peter gestured to the expanse around them. "Did you have something better to do?"

"I didn't *want* to come out here," Lowell said. "If it was up to me, I would still be on Earth."

Peter clutched the orb tighter. The gloves were just soft enough that he could feel its solid shape, but too thick for him to make out the details of the ridges and indentations carved into its face. It was beautiful, even out here, even after everything.

This would have made one heck of a dissertation, he thought. *Too bad I'll never get to find out what those carvings in the seabed were all about.*

"Aren't you going to ask me?" he said aloud.

Lowell groaned. "Ask you *what*, Chang?"

"What made me want to come out here?"

Peter could practically hear Lowell rolling his eyes. "I'm pretty sure the fact that Munroe held a gun to your head had something to do with it."

"Before that," Peter said. "When I was a kid."

"You probably wanted to meet aliens," Lowell said.

"Eventually, yeah, but more than that: I wanted to be part of something big." Peter clutched the orb to his chest. "I wanted to feel like I had a place in the universe...and barring that, I wanted to make a discovery that would change the world."

"Well, Merry Christmas, kid, you got your wish," Lowell deadpanned. Then Peter felt the other man's grip on his arm shift, and heard the cadence of Lowell's breathing increase as he twisted around. "Goddammit, *now* what?"

Peter turned to see what Lowell was looking at. Only moments ago, when he'd looked straight up, his field of vision had been dominated by the beige expanse of Saturn's surface. Now, a ship stood in their way.

"The Tiān Zhuānjiā?" Peter asked. Maybe He Ming and General Wu had changed their minds. This ship, however, looked nothing like the Chinese vessel that they had hailed earlier. It was silvery and sleek, shaped more like a disc than any of the bulky international transport vessels that they'd faced off against.

As Peter stared, a silvery-green beam of light emanated from the ship, aiming straight for them, surrounding them in a glowing column that seemed to pull them in.

"What's going on?" Lowell muttered.

"Alien abduction?" Peter suggested, then laughed. It was a giddy laugh. Maybe it was the lack of sleep, or the fact that he'd burned through every ounce of adrenaline in his body, but he couldn't muster the energy to be frightened. Instead, he felt punchy. They were going to die if they stayed out here. What was left to fear?

"If they *are* aliens, they'll probably want to probe you." Peter snickered again. Was he delirious? Was this even really happening?

The light drew them toward a circular opening in the belly of the ship, and Peter let himself go limp. Lowell didn't let go.

As they passed through the airlock, Peter squeezed his eyes closed, blinded by the green glow. *I'm dead,* he thought. *This isn't really happening. Maybe my suit got punctured and the oxygen's running out, or my organs are failing after the beating I took in the ocean. This is the kind of thing people talk about seeing at the moment of death—I must be hallucinating.*

Gravity kicked in all at once, and Peter collapsed onto a solid surface, the back of his head knocking around inside the helmet. He felt impossibly heavy.

Lowell tugged on his arm. "Get up, kid."

"I'm good," Peter said weakly. "I'm just going to lie here and become one with the floor."

"Chang," Lowell repeated, a newfound urgency in his voice. "*Get up.*"

Peter opened one eye. The room was a brilliant white, impossibly bright, reminiscent of the reflective surface of Enceladus. Peter wasn't sure how he'd gotten here at first, but when he sat up, he realized that seams ran through the floor. After they'd been pulled into the ship, a gate had shut behind them before the gravity kicked on.

It was hard to see, and Peter held up one arm to block the light through his helmet. Lowell's fingers were still closed around the other arm. He could feel the man's fist shaking.

Lowell was scared, but Peter was relaxed. Calm. A government conspiracy was one thing, but this was too surreal to accept. It was only after blinking several times that Peter saw the figures surrounding them. They were tall and willowy, and the suits they wore gleamed silvery-blue.

"Do you recognize the uniforms?" he whispered.

Lowell shook his head.

Without warning, Peter's mic crackled, and he tried to cover his ears out of habit before remembering that the mic was right against his head. Immediately, someone began to speak, but Peter couldn't place the language—it sounded like utter nonsense, to be honest. Peter knew enough about languages to recognize phonemes, but this sounded like nothing he'd ever heard. It was more like birdsong than speech: beautiful, but untranslatable. Peter listened in silence until it came to an end.

The voice died for a moment, then tried again, speaking in a completely different language this time, but still one that bore no relation to anything he'd ever studied.

"Hello?" Peter asked.

The voice paused. After a moment, it began again. The cadence was similar to the first two attempts, but again the phonemes made no sense.

"What's going on?" Lowell asked.

He sounded nervous, and Peter had only seen the soldier nervous a few times, mostly when he had no control over what was happening around him. Apparently the noises hadn't put him at ease, but nothing relaxed Peter more than an academic mystery.

"Hold on," Peter said slowly, "I think I understand."

"Understand?" Lowell echoed. "Are you making sense of this?"

"Maybe." Peter sucked in an excited breath, clutching the stellar key tight. "I don't know the words, but yeah, I think it's just another language."

He had a vivid memory of standing in the underwater cavern, his light held up to illuminate the wall, a Rosetta Stone of alien tongues laid out before him on breathtaking display. Some of them had barely looked like languages at all, just as these words didn't seem like anything that might be formed by a human tongue.

He might not have known all of them, but he knew one.

"Hello," he said in shaky Akkadian. "Can you...understand me?" He'd never really tried to *speak* dead languages so much as read them—there no point, because who could you speak them *to?*—but there were still a few communities that maintained a modern version of Akkadian, and Peter had been excited by the idea that a language could stick around for almost five thousand years. It had piqued his interest for a semester in his undergrad years. His pronunciation was probably abysmal, and his grammatical structures were iffy at best, but at least he knew the vocabulary.

"You speak Akkadian?" the voice asked. The tone of surprise was familiar, although Peter couldn't have said whether it was a woman speaking, or a man.

"A little," Peter said. "Badly."

"You are from Earth?"

Peter nodded.

"What are they saying?" Lowell demanded.

"Hold on." In Akkadian, Peter asked, "Why did you pick us up? Who are you?"

One of the nearby figures stepped closer, pointing at the silver object clutched in Peter's hand. "We have come for the stellar key. Is it yours?"

Peter hesitated. Laying claim to an object that had just destroyed a moon made him nervous, but he'd been raised on popular media. When someone asked him if he was powerful, he knew to say yes. "For now."

"Show me your face," the figure commanded. "I want to see who I'm dealing with. Rest assured, the atmosphere is compatible with your nervous system."

Obediently, Peter reached back to undo the latch of his helmet. Lowell protested, but Peter couldn't hear what he said; he was already taking the helmet off, and he was no longer mic'ed in with Lowell. He tucked his helmet under one arm and took a step toward the figure. Sure enough, he could breathe just fine, but his heart was pounding so hard it made his vision blur.

The figure before him cocked its head, then reached for its helmet as well.

A hundred wild possibilities occurred to Peter. He'd made a study of Akkadian art, and he half-expected that when the helmet came off, he would be facing a person who looked identical to the carvings and sculptures of Sargon, with high cheekbones and an elaborately curled beard.

But Peter was wrong. Instead of a human countenance, he found himself staring into a pair of large, nearly black eyes that dominated a teardrop-shaped face. The mouth was small, the nose barely a bump on an otherwise smooth skull.

"What the..." Lowell whispered from behind, his own helmet now removed.

"It's a Grey," Peter said, a smile breaking over his face. "They're all *Greys*. We're in an honest-to-God UFO, experiencing a real alien abduction."

He felt no anxiety at all. All his life, people had denied his belief that there was life on other worlds, *intelligent* life that had influenced the course of human history. And now, he was here, living proof that every theory he'd pored over in his late-night research dives was based, at least in part, on the truth.

All of his questions were finally going to be answered.

EPILOGUE

THE *CADMIUM III* hadn't quite finished the complete map of the Challenger Deep, but Captain Avery Mills was determined to see it through this time. The images that he had picked up so far were absolutely stunning: slopes and ridges, stone pinnacles, calcified outcroppings that mirrored the complexity of coral reefs—it wasn't enough just to know that he could go down there. Avery had to map every inch of it, and he was getting closer by the day.

Most other researchers had grown bored of the deeps. Why bother with exploring Earth's final frontier when they could aim for the stars? But Avery had been hooked ever since his first dive, and he'd come to think of himself as a cartographer. He'd seen things no other human had ever seen before. Some people craved the giddying altitude of Everest, but Avery was addicted to the pressure of the trench. The soft hum of the equipment around him, even the stale smell of recycled air, made him feel more alive than anything on the surface did. It wasn't natural for a man to survive down here, yet man had found a way, and Avery relished every moment of it.

"Are you coming up soon?" one of his crew asked over the radio.

"I've got a little energy left in me," Avery said. "Give me another half hour and I'll... *oh...*"

"What is it, sir?" asked the crewman nervously.

"Nothing bad," Avery assured him. "The headlights just caught something. It's..."

He fell silent as he wove the sub through the fissure in which he found himself. He'd seen a flash of some bright metal, silver as a fish scale but much larger than any creature Avery had spotted at this depth. Then he came around the corner, and he gasped.

It looked as if a portion of the sea floor had been coated in liquid silver. Among the dull volcanic stones, this section of the sea floor was an anomaly.

"Are you seeing this on the cameras?" he asked.

"Yes, sir," said the crewman, clearly puzzled. "What is it?"

Avery had no answer. The bright surface was marred with lines that looked almost like symbols inscribed into its surface—a visual trick, obviously, but that made it no less stunning.

Avery guided the sub over it, almost vibrating with excitement. This was probably how treasure-hunters felt, he reckoned, when they saw the first golden gleam of a doubloon in the sand.

"Take some stills," he instructed. "We'll have to report this. This is going to be big."

"I don't understand what it is," the crewman asked. "Shouldn't most mineral deposits tarnish at this depth?"

Avery wasn't listening. As he drifted down the side of the silvery patch, he saw that there was a divot in the side, just large enough for a man's fist.

Funny, he thought, *it almost looks intentional. Like something is meant to fit in there...*

———

FIND OUT
WHAT HAPPENS
NEXT!

Click here to read
CASCADE
(Saturn's Legacy Book 2)

GET FREE BOOKS!

Building a relationship with readers is my favorite thing about writing.

My regular newsletter, *The Reader Crew,* is the best way to stay up-to-date on new releases, special offers, and all kinds of cool stuff about science fiction past and present.

Just for joining the fun, I'll send you 3 free books.

Join The Reader Crew (it's free) today!

—Joshua James

ALSO BY JOSHUA JAMES

Lucky's Marines (Books 1-9)

Lucky's Mercs (Books 1-4)

The Lost Starship (Books 1-3)

Planet Hell

Gunn & Salvo (ongoing)

With Scott Bartlett:

Relentless Box Set: The Complete Fleet Ops Trilogy

With Sean D. King:

Honor in Exile (ongoing)

With Daniel Young:

Oblivion (Books 1-9)

Outcast Starship (Books 1-9)

Legacy of War (Books 1-3)

Heritage of War (ongoing)

Stars Dark (Books 1-8)

———

Click here to read
CASCADE
(Saturn's Legacy Book 2)

.

Printed in Great Britain
by Amazon

37806174R00195